MARRY ME AT

Dawn

MARRY ME AT

Dawn

A Romano Family romance

Lucinda Whitney

Lange House Press

Edited by Michele Holmes and Julie Carpenter
Cover design © 2019 Lange House Press
Layout and Formatting by LJP Creative
Published by Lange House Press

First Printing October 2019

ISBN 13: 978-1-944137-45-8
ISBN 10: 1-944137-45-9

A família que nós escolhemos tem mais significado.

It's the family we choose that means the most.

Romano Family

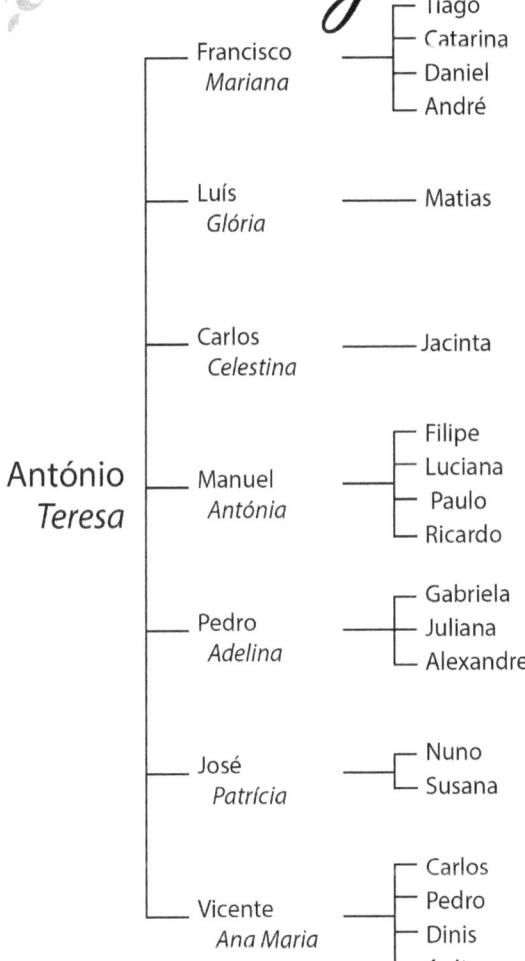

António
Teresa

- Francisco
  Mariana
  - Tiago
  - Catarina
  - Daniel
  - André

- Luís
  Glória
  - Matias

- Carlos
  Celestina
  - Jacinta

- Manuel
  Antónia
  - Filipe
  - Luciana
  - Paulo
  - Ricardo

- Pedro
  Adelina
  - Gabriela
  - Juliana
  - Alexandre

- José
  Patrícia
  - Nuno
  - Susana

- Vicente
  Ana Maria
  - Carlos
  - Pedro
  - Dinis
  - Anita

CHAPTER ONE

𝒢abriela Romano stretched her legs on the chaise lounge and relaxed her body against the cushioned back.

In the past two weeks, she'd taught herself how to calm her body, soothe her mind, and ignore her heart. Not through yoga or meditation. Not through therapy or reading self-help books. Not even with the help and support of her family and friends.

She hadn't told anyone what had truly happened. As she didn't have a husband, a fiancé, or even a boy-friend to worry about her physical health and mental well-being, there had been no one to accompany her, no one to offer explanations to.

One moment she'd been at home reading a book before going to bed and the next she was on her way to the hospital, the ambulance screeching and speeding as she writhed in the most excruciating pain she'd ever experienced. When she woke up from surgery, an emergency hysterectomy, she couldn't even remember dialing the emergency number.

Gabriela had arrived at the Hydrangea Manor five days earlier, the unassuming name not doing justice to the five-star resort. It was exclusive and small, a private paradise to recover and recharge both body and mind. Gratitude filled her again that her cousin Filipe had arranged for her stay, for as long as she needed, as he'd assured her repeatedly. Her body was mending, every day a little better. As for her mind and heart—it was better to not spend time thinking about them.

The view from the patio spread unfettered before her, the blue of the sea blending with the blue of the sky in the not-so-far distance.

This was the place where all the colors of nature lived in riotous harmony. In late May, the small island of Faial, in the Archipelago of the Azores, was nothing but flowers and trees in bloom, contrasting against the black of serpentine roads and verdant hills so bright.

Everywhere she looked, hydrangeas abounded. Mostly blue, in different shades, each outdoing its neighbor, some pink and even light green. In round bushes and linear hedges of varied heights. With mild temperatures and a peaceful sea on the horizon, could it be any more of a perfect day? If only she could absorb the weather and the setting to get over her depressing thoughts.

After spending the last three days of her stay in her suite—mostly sleeping, sometimes crying—Gabriela had finally emerged from her lethargy yesterday. She'd opened her eyes to the beauty of the place and couldn't get enough of the surroundings and view. For the briefest moment, she even forgot about the circumstances that had sent her here.

Had she even thanked Filipe and his wife Celeste? She hoped she had. They had offered to have her come stay with them, to take care of her, and help her recover. Their house was large and located by the beach, and it would have been a great place to spend some time.

But they were still in the newlywed-bliss phase of their relationship and being around a happily married couple was not what she needed to mend her broken heart.

So they had put her on an airplane in Lisbon, someone had picked her up at the small regional airport of Horta and driven her to the manor. Her every need was filled and she didn't have to worry about cleaning, cooking, or laundry and wardrobe—the highly efficient, discreet staff provided everything. It wasn't even required of her to interact with anyone, if she so wished.

She'd made a small effort on the first day after arriving, not knowing what to expect from the resort, or how she was supposed to behave. When was the last time she'd gone on vacation? Never. Her career in advertising had taken so much of her time for so long, she could hardly remember what her life had been before that. Other than a few weekends with her family and extended family, she hadn't gone anywhere.

Yesterday she'd traded the comfort and shelter of her suite for the common area at the manor, an elegant lounging room with floor-to-ceiling glass windows overlooking the southern view to the ocean. Despite her plans to be more social, Gabriela hadn't encountered many other guests, and the few she'd seen had mostly kept to themselves, like the middle-aged German couple. Out on the south patio, away from the building, a young couple with a baby had been oblivious to anything else around them, keeping their attention on the precious little one bundled inside the pram. The father hovered awkwardly and the mother smiled serenely and, although he looked familiar, Gabriela couldn't quite place him.

What would it be like, to be married and have a baby, a family of her own? A husband and child to love?

Her heart hiccupped at the memory of that young family and she breathed in deeply. She hadn't actually seen the baby, not from her chair positioned by the French doors. Her imagination had been enough to fill in what her eyes had missed, and she couldn't decide what was worse—wanting a baby that wasn't hers, or imagining one she'd never have.

It would never happen. What man would want to marry her when she couldn't have children?

After the couple continued on their walk, Gabriela returned to her suite, not wanting to risk another glimpse of them and their happiness.

But today she felt restless from so much inactivity and in the mood to explore, willing to face whatever—and whoever—she might encounter in the lounge and on the grounds. She was now three weeks post-surgery. The doctors had told her to take it easy for six weeks, and she intended to follow their directions; ending up in the hospital for being careless with her recovery was the last thing she wanted. Even though her life had taken a 180° turn, some things were hard to let go of, and, after leading such a busy professional life, there was only so much sitting around she could put up with.

After a fortifying breath, she swung her legs to the side and straightened her back. On the small tabletop near the chair, a glass bottle of spring water and her sunglasses sat beside each other, along with a book about the island's history from the resort's small media room. For a moment, she looked around for her smart phone and then remembered she'd turned it off when she'd arrived at the Hydrangea Manor.

Part of the holistic approach at the resort included depending less on phones and tablets, and for such, the Internet available to the guests was turned on for only two hours a day, one in the morning and one in the evening. It suited Gabriela just fine. She'd told her immediate family she was on vacation and would talk to them when she returned to Porto. Other than

Filipe and Celeste, nobody knew she was recovering from surgery, and even they believed it was from an emergency appendectomy, not a hysterectomy. Only her doctor in Lisbon had that information and she intended to keep it that way.

She didn't dare tell her parents. As much as she loved her mother, Adelina Romano was the smothering type and she'd try to get the truth out of Gabriela.

Gabriela glanced at her wristwatch. Dinner was still an hour away, which gave her plenty of time for a walk around the gardens and grounds. Each suite had a private outdoor area and access to the whole property as well. When she'd arrived, her lack of curiosity toward the resort and the island hadn't prodded any explorations, but the feeling to discover more had been steadily growing. Maybe she'd find a way to visit Horta, the small capital of the island, by the end of the week. For now, exploring the property on foot was enough to satisfy her interest.

As she rounded the western side of the resort, a stone brick footpath led her to a small copse of flowering trees. A tall gate swung open from a partially hidden fence and, beyond it, the vegetation thickened in purposeful patterns of native plants on both sides of the path. Gabriela walked through it, the sound of babbling water growing louder until she came to an alcove fountain flanked by benches.

She slowed down. The calmness in the air infused her, lending a measure of the peace and serenity she so desperately craved. She slid into the nearest bench, tipped her face to the dappled sun, and closed her eyes, taking a deep breath. What she would give to stay in this paradise, away from the realities of life, from the weights and chains that dragged her new existence. Escape was what she needed.

The sound of a mewling animal broke the air. Maybe a cat, though she hadn't seen any around. When the cry came louder a few seconds later, Gabriela rose from the bench and followed the sound, arriving at another brick patio situated at the back of a large house. In the center, a man paced back and forth with a young baby crying lustily.

Gabriela stopped and watched them. It was the man from the day before, holding the angriest baby she'd ever seen. The child looked to be about two to three months, red faced and with her back arched, as her father tried to calm her down with a bottle. He hadn't noticed Gabriela yet, but it would have been hard to, with all the noise and flailing.

Something twisted inside Gabriela's chest at the baby's distress. It didn't help that the child's father looked almost as strained. Where was the mother? As the father offered the bottle full of formula again, the baby threw her little head back, startling the man. His other hand flew to support her better and the bottle fell to the ground. The crying intensified and the man said something under his breath, his discomfort obvious.

Against her better judgment, Gabriela raised her voice, hoping he could hear her, wondering if she'd come to regret getting involved. "Do you need a hand?"

The man looked at her, momentarily speechless and surprised.

Gabriela stepped forward and picked up the bottle, then handed it to him, but he didn't take it.

The baby continued crying, quite inconsolable.

"How did you get in here?" he finally said in English.

He was American. That explained his height. Gabriela repeated her question in his language.

He frowned as he looked at her, then his expression relaxed. "I've seen you before. You're related to Filipe Romano, aren't you?" He kept the baby firmly in his arms and talked loudly over the noise.

At his words, she remembered where she'd seen him before. "Yes, I am. I saw you at his wedding last year. I'm Gabriela, one of Filipe's cousins." She gestured behind her back. "And the gate was open."

"Right. I stopped by to congratulate him, but couldn't stay for the ceremony." He glanced at his daughter and frowned again. "I'm sorry. I don't know what's wrong with her. It's quite impossible to keep talking like this."

She held up the bottle again.

"I'll have to go wash it." He looked between the baby and the bottle full of milk, then turned his attention back to Gabriela. "I'm Damian, by the way."

"And your baby?"

His expression blanked. "My baby?"

Gabriela gave him a small smile. "What's your baby's name?"

"Uh, Claire," he replied with a hint of uncertainty. "This is Claire. She's not very happy today."

"Poor thing," Gabriela said, her heart squeezing again. "Is your wife not around?"

Damian's expression furrowed in confusion. "My wife?"

"I saw you three taking a walk yesterday."

Little Claire wailed again.

"You know what," Damian said abruptly, "I'm going to take your offer."

Before she knew what was happening, he passed the baby to her and took the bottle from her hands, then turned in the direction of the house.

Gabriela stilled for a brief moment, then raised the baby to her shoulder and supported the small body against hers, cuddling her against the crook of her neck, patting Claire's back in slow circles. Gabriela inhaled the baby's sweet scent, wishing she could commit it to memory and remember this moment forever.

Immediately, Claire calmed down. After a minute, she let out a burp, the rumbling volume taking Gabriela by surprise.

Damian stopped at the French doors and looked back.

"That was her, not me," Gabriela said.

"How is someone so small able to burp like a grown man?"

Gabriela shrugged lightly, not knowing what to say.

He motioned to the house. "Come in, please. I'm going to wash this."

She followed slowly, afraid to jostle Claire into crying again.

Once inside, a large room with a soaring ceiling took her by surprise. A kitchen and dining area took half of the space and an informal living room the other half. The predominant style was casual, comfortable, with an understated elegance peeking through in small bursts.

Damian stood at the sink, rinsing the outside of the bottle. He looked over his shoulder. "How did you get her to stop crying?"

"It wasn't me. I think the burp did it." She eased Claire away from her shoulder. Although she wasn't crying, the baby gnawed fiercely on her fist. "Maybe she'll take that bottle now."

Damian approached and handed her the bottle. When Gabriela brought the silicone nipple to Claire's mouth, the baby eagerly took it as Gabriela and Damian watched.

Elation followed quickly by despair collided within Gabriela. What was she doing, feeding a baby, holding this infant in her arms as if she had some right to be here or even did this on a regular basis? This was the last thing she should be doing right now.

I was beginning to think she would never stop crying," Damian said quietly. He indicated a stuffed chair and Gabriela took it gingerly, perching at the edge.

"How long was she crying for?"

"It feels like all day, but it was probably only an hour," he said in a quiet voice, so different from the man she'd seen just a few minutes before outside.

Gabriela turned to look at Damian. She now remembered her impression of him when she'd seen him talking to Filipe. Back then he'd been impeccably dressed in a dark blue suit, the color enhancing his eyes, his dark blond hair styled to perfection.

Just like then, a prick of attraction flicked inside her. Today, he wore jeans and a simple T-shirt. His hair stuck in all directions, and a light scruff covered his face, as if he hadn't been able to shave that morning. Despite the more casual look, he was still as attractive as before, and he was probably one of those people who always looked good in whatever he wore.

He took a seat across from her on the sofa and scrubbed his face wearily, then leaned against the sidearm as if contemplating a short nap.

Little Claire finished her bottle with a sigh and Gabriela returned her attention to the baby. She scolded herself for having such thoughts about a married man, and one who was a father as well. What was wrong with her? She could only think it was the bizarre situation she found herself in, so unlike the normal days at home.

After burping the baby again, she moved her from her shoulder to holding her in her arms. Now serene and satisfied, baby Claire drifted off to sleep.

11

Gabriela didn't dare move. The sweetness of the moment grew and expanded until she felt a warmth where Claire's little body snuggled against hers. As the warmth turned wet, Gabriela gasped.

Damian roused from his chair. "What happened? What's wrong with the baby?"

"I think her diaper leaked," Gabriela replied.

Damian shortened the distance between him and the chair where Gabriela sat with baby Claire. "What do you mean, her diaper leaked?"

Gabriela kept the same tranquil demeanor she'd had since taking Claire in her arms. It must be some kind of magic, the way the baby had gone from crying mad to relaxing calm when she took her. Though he'd just met Gabriela, he was already contemplating how hard it would be to convince her to stay on as a full-time nanny.

She shifted the baby, who still slept. Between their bodies, a large wet stain covered Gabriela's shirt and the back of the baby's clothes.

"We can't let her sleep wet like this," Gabriela said.

Probably not, but the temptation was there. Claire was likely to wake up and start crying again, and he couldn't entertain the idea of it going on for hours as before. He'd go insane.

When he didn't immediately reply, Gabriela stood. "Where's the nursery?"

Damian took a deep breath, hoping it didn't come out as a sigh. "This way."

He led her down the hallway toward the guest suite where he had set up a crib, a changing pad on top of the dresser, and a gliding chair, all conveniently within reach of the queen-size bed. On the opposite corner, a large box of diapers and another of baby wipes lay on the floor with open flaps, as if he hadn't been able to find a better place to stash them.

He hadn't yet, despite the bedroom's large square footage.

In truth, he'd never planned for a baby, let alone one he hadn't fathered. But that didn't matter to the state of New York since it was his name on Claire's birth certificate. How that had come to happen, he had yet to find out.

Gabriela paused at the door. "You have the nursery in your bedroom?"

"No, this is the guest suite."

She frowned at him.

"It's temporary." As was the baby, he hoped.

He stood awkwardly in the doorway, remembering the last time he'd changed Claire's diaper which hadn't gone so well. He had no desire for a repeat, particularly in front of Gabriela.

He gestured to the dresser. "The supplies are right there."

"She needs a change of clothes and a cotton blanket."

"Her clothes are in the second drawer."

Gabriela hesitated. "Would—would you like me to change her?"

"Sure." Yes, please. He probably appeared over eager. "She seems to like you."

Gabriela crossed the room.

"What about you?"

She shrugged at him then quickly returned her attention to the baby as she set her down on the changing mattress.

Damian gestured at the dresser. "Her clothes are in the second drawer."

He watched from the wall, expecting the baby to start wailing at any minute but, even though Claire woke up, she didn't cry. With gentle movements and a soft voice, Gabriela changed Claire's diaper, wiped her clean, and dressed her in dry clothes.

"I should probably put her in the crib before your wife returns," Gabriela said, looking between the crib and the door.

"If you mean the woman you saw with me yesterday, that wasn't my wife," Damian said, keeping his voice down. "That was the nanny, and we had to fire her shortly after." What a mess that had turned out to be. "I'm not married," he added, wanting to clarify his status to Gabriela, even if there wasn't a reason to do it.

He moved to the closet and rifled through the contents until he found the shirt that was part of the lounge clothes outfit the resort provided for guests. He dropped it on the chair. "If you want to change, here's something clean and dry."

Just then, a voice reached them from the other side of the house. "Damian, I'm back."

Gabriela and Claire startled and Damian winced at the loud volume. "That's Luke. Excuse me."

He found his friend in the kitchen, helping himself to something from the fridge, already out of his suit jacket, with a loosened tie, and his shirt sleeves pulled back. A carry-on suitcase stood by the door.

"Did you forget there's a baby in the house?" Damian asked.

Luke flinched. "Dang. Did I wake her?"

They both held still for a moment and, at the lack of crying, their relief was palpable.

Luke tossed a can at Damian then popped the tab of his diet soda and took a swig. "Did she actually fall asleep by herself?"

Damian took a seat on the sectional and put his feet up, holding the can in one hand. "Gabriela's got her."

Luke stilled. "Gabriela? I'm gone for a day and you hired an Azorean nanny?"

"She's from the continent, and she's not a nanny."

Luke's eyes widened. "You gave the baby to a stranger?"

"Well, no." Damian took a sip. "She's not exactly a stranger. I met her last year."

Luke came around the kitchen counter and sat opposite Damian. "If you met her last year, how come I never heard you talk about her?"

"You know I meet a lot of people when I'm traveling," Damian replied, his tone sounding more defensive than he'd intended.

If he admitted to Luke how well he remembered seeing Gabriela at her cousin's wedding, he'd be forced to confess how he'd thought about her for days after.

Something inside him had taken notice of her the very instant their eyes met back then, as if she were someone who could become important to him. With the impending ceremony and his own rush to return to his chartered plane, he didn't even have the time to ask Filipe to introduce him, but despite the brevity of the moment, the feeling had remained with him. In the end, it was better that way. The rules of his self-imposed celibacy existed for a reason.

Somehow, fate had brought them together again and Damian hadn't had the time to think what it might mean.

"What's her full name?"

"Gabriela Romano. She's Filipe Romano's cousin and I met her at his wedding last year."

Luke got quiet.

"I know what you're thinking, and I don't want you to do a background check on her."

"Maybe I won't need to, but let me be the judge of that," Luke said.

Aside from being his oldest friend, Luke was also Damian's lawyer. Corporate for the Vaughn Family Movie Channel had a team of lawyers for any kind of matter, but Damian liked knowing Luke had his back at all times.

Luke chuckled. "You're so distracted. You're thinking of her, aren't you?"

"I'm not distracted."

"Are you going to tell me how she got here?"

"She said the gate was open."

"That's not good," Luke said.

"No, it's not," Damian agreed. "I'll have to talk to security and find out how that happened. That reminds me, I need to go lock it again. I'll be right back." He stood and dropped the soda can in the recycling bin, then made his way out the double doors and into the courtyard.

With everything going on, Damian hadn't had the time to process Gabriela's appearance. Privacy was a delicate issue for him, especially now with a baby under his responsibility. Until he was ready to come public with the news, he did not want anything to jeopardize his image, and knowing anyone could have entered his courtyard left him feeling vulnerable and exposed.

When he returned, Luke was gone. Knowing his friend's unrepentant curiosity, Damian walked down the hallway to the guest suite. Luke stood by the door looking in. Damian joined him.

Gabriela had changed into the top he'd given her earlier and bundled the baby in a thin cotton blanket. She rocked steadily in the gliding chair and hummed quietly to Claire, who slept in her arms with a serene expression. This was the most content Damian had seen the baby since he'd gotten her from social services last week.

"They look so at ease with each other," Luke whispered.

Gabriela looked at them and raised a finger to her lips to shush them. Not wanting to wake Claire, Damian left and Luke followed.

Once back in the living room, Damian walked over to the glass doors and Luke took a seat on the sofa.

"If I didn't know better, I'd say that was a mom with her baby," Luke said.

"Am I imagining the connection between them?"

Luke shook his head. "If you are, then I am too."

"It can't be because Gabriela is a woman," Damian said, trying to make sense of how the baby had taken to her so quickly.

"The nanny was a woman and Claire wasn't comfortable with her."

"I thought Claire was cranky from the plane ride and time difference." He turned back to face Luke. "By the way, how did it go in New York?"

"You have nothing to worry about. Miss Melanie Bay is well aware of the legal repercussions that will be brought upon her if anything personal or professional regarding you and your family, present and future, is ever made public."

"Good," Damian replied, relieved to have that behind him.

Gabriela entered the room and Damian stood.

"I put Claire in the crib. She's fed and changed." The corners of her mouth stretched in a smile. "She should sleep for a while."

He could only hope. "I don't know what to say except thank you."

Luke rose from his spot. "Hi, I'm Luke Blackbourne." He took a step towards Gabriela and extended his hand. "It's a pleasure to meet you."

She took it. "Thank you, Luke. I'm Gabriela Romano. Are you Claire's other dad?"

Luke burst out laughing. Too bad he was out of reach for Damian to punch him in his arm.

Gabriela's cheeks reddened. "I'm sorry. Did I say something wrong?"

Damian stepped forward to block her view of Luke. "No, you didn't say anything wrong. Luke is my lawyer and we've been friends since our early days at Yale. We're not domestic partners, and he's not Claire's dad." Neither was he, but that story was too long and complicated to tell a woman he'd just met.

"I made assumptions again. I do apologize for that." She gestured at her clothes. "Thank you for the shirt. I'll return it once it's washed." In her hand, she carried the top she'd been wearing earlier, rolled up.

"Don't worry about it," Damian said. "You can return it to the laundry service."

For a moment, they watched each other. Maybe baby Claire wasn't the only one who felt a connection to Gabriela, as crazy as that sounded.

She moved toward the double glass doors and raised her hand. "I'll be going then."

Damian followed her. "I'll need to lock the gate again after you leave."

The silence between them hung awkwardly as they walked through the courtyard. Gabriela met his eyes a couple of times, with a tranquil kind of smile almost enough to erase the uneasiness. He had questions he wanted to ask her but, by the time he figured how to approach the subject, they'd arrived at the gate.

He unlocked it and opened it wide for her. "Thanks again for coming to mine and Claire's rescue."

She shook her head and looked away. "If only you knew." She looked at him and touched her fingers to the back of his hand briefly. "I should be the one thanking you." Then she passed by him and left.

Damian stood watching her until she turned the corner toward the manor.

Why should she thank him? What did she mean by that?

CHAPTER TWO

Gabriela returned to her suite, picked up a book, and forced herself to read. But too many thoughts coursed through her mind about the unexpected meeting.

She had always scoffed at the idea of love at first sight but here she was, completely in love with a two-month old baby girl named Claire. It was more than first sight—it was love at first touch, at first scent, at first everything. How was she to resume life as she'd known it without this little person being a part of it?

The truth was, she hadn't realized until now how sweet and soft babies were, having passed on the chance to hold one.

For a long time, her career had been the center of her life. First in college, then with work, and training, and getting ahead. This focus on her profession hadn't even raised the worry to slow down, to make the time for a relationship that might lead to marriage and family, under the wrong assumption she would have the time for it later.

But later had come and the possibility had been taken away from her.

And here she was, holding precious Claire, wishing the baby was hers.

How had she fallen into this trap?

Hadn't the therapist at the hospital said to embrace the thing she feared the most? At the time, Gabriela had felt insulted at the suggestion—where was she going to find a baby to hold, even if she would ever be ready to some day? And how would that help her past the pain of her loss?

Ever since her surgery, she'd been avoiding pregnant women, new moms and babies—the three groups of people she both feared and envied the most. In fact, she'd consciously planned to evade any kind of situation that would bring her in contact with mothers and babies.

Spending two hours with baby Claire had all but proved her wrong and the therapist right.

When the ringing of a phone interrupted her thoughts, Gabriela startled. She turned to the sound and found a land line cordless phone sitting on the far desk. She hadn't even noticed the phone before, but the ringing went on incessantly until she answered it.

A familiar voice greeted her from the other end. "Gabriela, how are you?"

"Juliana," Gabriela said, surprise tinting her voice. "How did you find me?" She slid the French doors open and sat outside.

Juliana was her sister, younger by five years. They also had a brother, Alexandre, four years younger than Juliana.

"Mom has been trying to call you and she got worried when you didn't return her call."

"I haven't used my phone since I got here," Gabriela said. "I think the battery ran out. I'll charge it tonight and call mom tomorrow, I promise."

"You do that. She just wants to hear from you and know you're okay."

"So, Filipe told you I was here?"

"He must have heard we wanted to get in contact with you, but I don't know who told him. He sent me a text with the name of the resort where you're staying and I looked it up."

Gabriela suppressed an eye roll. She should have known her family would go looking for her. Although it was nice to know she was missed, it also rankled her how nosy they could be at times.

"Tell mom and everyone else I'm fine," Gabriela told Juliana. "Just enjoying some well-earned time off." That was the truth, even if not the whole truth.

"How much longer are you staying there?"

Gabriela took a deep breath. "I haven't decided yet. Right now, I'm not in a hurry to get back."

"Is the firm okay with that?" Juliana asked.

The firm was the second-most successful advertising company in Lisbon where Gabriela worked as a senior specialist.

"Yes, of course. I earned this vacation."

"That's a nice perk," Juliana said.

Gabriela didn't correct her. Let her think the company paid for her stay at the Hydrangea Manor instead of Filipe. Some secrets were hers to keep.

A knock sounded at the door to the suite.

Gabriela walked toward it and opened it to a waiter pushing the dinner cart.

"I have to go, Juliana. Tell mom I'll call her tomorrow."

Juliana said good-bye and they hung up.

Gabriela thanked the waiter and replaced the phone to its cradle on the desk. She ate her dinner out on the patio off her suite, the view to the sea and the light salty breeze adding a subtle note to her evening. The southern orientation didn't have a direct view of the sunset, but the colors and light reached the property obliquely, piercing through a line of low-hanging clouds that soon dissipated into the approaching night.

Sleep was a flighty affair that night. She dreamed of Damian pushing a crying Claire in the pram and she followed behind them, unable to catch up. It unsettled her, and she woke up in the early morning, before sunrise, in a sweat and tangled in the sheets.

After spending too long thinking about the questionable meaning of her dream, she changed into yoga pants, a T-shirt, and a light hooded jacket and went for a walk.

The beach was not accessible from the back of the resort's property but sometime soon she would find out how to get to the closest one. For now, she contented herself with a walk around the perimeter of the property. In the early hour, she was the only one around, thankfully. She was not in the mood to see or talk to anyone and didn't want to appear rude.

When the sun rose, the glorious beauty of it took her breath away. Long fingers of warm color stretched from the east side of the small island bathing everything in light in their wake. The hydrangeas and flowering trees came to life and Gabriela stood watching, hands in her pockets.

Was this what she had to resign herself to, with only sunrise and sunset marking her days? As much as she liked her job, it was not enough to see her through the rest of her life. She wanted more. Needed more.

All the dreams she'd had and the plans she'd made after graduating university—find a good job in her field, marry, have children—she'd achieved only one out of three.

Damian came to her mind. If a man could have a baby without a wife, why couldn't she have one without a husband?

Sure, her grandparents would be shocked, maybe even her parents, but, as much as she loved her family, this was her life, not theirs. If she couldn't have a baby the old-fashioned way, she could adopt, couldn't she?

She doubled back and returned the way she'd come, her mind too full of new dreams and hopes she didn't dare say aloud yet.

Instead of returning to her suite, she entered the manor house and approached the dining room. The floor host seated her by the panoramic window and she ordered a latte and whole wheat toast for breakfast, along with an orange juice and a pastel de nata, the egg custard tarts she absolutely loved.

When her tray arrived, Gabriela tucked into it with energy. Walking had opened her appetite and food always tasted better when she didn't have to prepare it herself.

"Do you mind if I join you?"

Gabriela looked up to find Damian regarding her. How had she not noticed his green eyes before?

Her heart raced for a quick moment and she fought the urge to settle a hand over her chest.

On closer inspection, deep dark circles shadowed those gorgeous green eyes of his. It was safe to guess he hadn't had much sleep.

She'd been so focused on Claire the day before. Now that he was by himself, Gabriela had more time to pay attention to the man and not just the dad with an adorable baby.

"Yes, of course." She motioned to the chair opposite hers. "How's Claire? Did you find a new nanny?"

Before replying, Damian signaled the waiter and asked for a macchiato and a croissant with fresh, uncured cheese.

"Unfortunately, no, I haven't found a nanny yet. Luke is watching Claire so I can have a break to take care of a few things that need my attention this morning."

"Did you get any sleep?" she asked.

"A little. I'm beginning to understand why they tell new parents to sleep when the baby does."

His breakfast arrived and he took a long sip from his cup, then smiled. "The morning doesn't feel right until I have a good cup of coffee."

Gabriela nodded. "I feel the same way when I'm working. Here, I don't need as much caffeine." Though she could use a pick-me-up to get her going when the days dragged on.

"How are you enjoying your stay?"

Gabriela finished chewing and put down her knife and fork, searching for the right words.

"Don't feel obligated to tell me the place is amazing," Damian said, a hint of teasing in his voice. "I already know it's excellent, but not everybody feels at peace here at the resort."

"I am enjoying my stay," she replied. "My life in Lisbon is all about work. When I go to Porto, I'm surrounded by family." She gestured around her and out the window. "Here, I've had the time to think about me, as hard as that may be at times."

Before Damian replied with something serious that she wasn't ready to discuss, Gabriela continued. "How does an American end up building an exclusive resort in a tiny island in the Atlantic anyway?"

He regarded her for a moment, probably wondering at the change in her tone. Then his expression relaxed. "Have you heard of the volcanic eruption here in Faial between 1957 and 1958?"

Gabriela nodded. "I found this little book in the media library about the history of the island and I read about it. I hadn't heard of it before."

"Then you must have read about President Eisenhower signing the Azorean Refugee Act in 1958, which allowed the immigration of many victims. My maternal grandparents were among those who settled in New York."

"So, you're one fourth Portuguese?" That was surprising to find out. His physical features didn't give away that part of his ancestry, what with his height, green eyes and light brown hair.

"I am indeed," Damian replied. "My dad's side of the family are from England, almost all the way back to the Mayflower." He finished his croissant and fresh cheese, then drank the rest of his coffee. "A few years ago, I had the chance to visit this island and the place where my grandparents had lived. They never wished to come back. Too many memories, I guess. After their fatal car accident, we lost direct ties to the island."

Gabriela finished her breakfast and pushed her plate away. "When did you decide to build this place?"

Damian's phone pinged and he shifted to retrieve it from his pocket. "Sorry. It's probably Luke asking me to come change a dirty diaper. He hates those." He smiled at her.

Gabriela returned the smile, all the while resisting the urge to offer her help. For sure he would find her strange.

"Dang it," he said after reading the text. "I need to go back."

"Is everything all right?"

"Everything's fine. Luke just needs to go. I'll have to finish what I started another day." He stood. "Thanks for let—"

Gabriela pushed back her chair and shot to her feet, catching the cloth napkin in her hand before it fell to the floor. "Can I come see Claire? Please?"

For a moment, Damian didn't say anything. She cringed inside, waiting for his expression to change from friendly to alarmed. As much as she wished, it was too late to take the words back. She twisted the corner of the napkin.

But the change didn't come. His posture relaxed and the corner of his mouth rose in a soft smile. "Sure. Come along. I'm sure she'd love to see you."

Gabriela placed the wrinkled napkin on the table and followed after him, the bloom of hope in her chest growing wider with each step.

As much as she wanted to see Claire, why had she asked him? She was only setting herself up for more heartache in the long run.

When Damian and Gabriela entered the house, a cranky Claire could be heard from her swing in the living room. She wasn't crying fully yet, but it was coming soon. He was beginning to learn her moods in the short time since he'd picked her up from Child and Family Services in New York.

Luke stood from the sofa, the baby swing only a few feet away. "Sorry, man," he said. "Did you have time to finish everything?"

"No, but that's fine. I'll do it some other day."

Gabriela walked past Damian and knelt in front of Claire. "Hi, sweet girl. How are you?"

Claire stopped fussing and her eyes went wide.

Gabriela reached her hand to release Claire from the swing but then looked over her shoulder at Damian. "May I?"

"Yes, of course," he told her.

The moment Gabriela stood with Claire in her arms, the baby smiled as he hadn't seen her smile yet. Gabriela smiled back and cooed at the baby.

There was that connection he'd seen the day before. Luke exchanged a pointed look with Damian, and Damian nodded at him.

Gabriela moved to the sofa and sat with Claire cradled in the crook of her arm, the two absorbed in each other as if they spent every day together.

"I'll try and come back later today," Luke said as he prepared to leave.

"I might have some time if she takes a nap," Damian said. He eyed his laptop sitting on the dining table. He'd have to wait before he went back to the work he'd started earlier.

"Text me later and let me know then." Luke held a hand up. "Nice seeing you again, Gabriela."

"I'll watch Claire," Gabriela said.

Damian and Luke paused.

"Excuse me?" Damian asked.

She looked up from interacting with Claire and faced Damian. "I can watch Claire while you go finish your work, or whatever it is you need to do."

"I appreciate the offer but you didn't come to Faial to babysit."

"That's true, but you have things to do and I'm not busy right now. I really don't mind."

Damian looked at her, not knowing what to say in response. Luke hadn't left yet, watching them both as if waiting for their reactions.

Gabriela rose from the sofa and approached them, holding Claire upright with a firm hand on the baby's neck and back.

She tipped her head toward the laptop on the table. "Do you have an office? You can take your computer there and I'll stay here with Claire."

Did he trust her? He'd known her for less than twenty-four hours but the trust was there, even if he hadn't considered it until now.

"I have a desk in my bedroom."

Gabriela's shoulders relaxed. "Then go. Claire and I will be fine, won't we, baby?" She cooed at Claire again and was rewarded with a toothless smile.

Claire would not miss him. If she could talk, she'd be the first one to say so.

"If you're sure," he insisted.

"I am. I wouldn't have offered if I weren't."

Damian relented. His concern stemmed from imposing too much on Gabriela, who'd come to the Hydrangea Manor to relax and enjoy her time there. And now she was babysitting the daughter who wasn't his.

He moved to the kitchen and showed her where he kept the formula and bottles. "Help yourself to anything you want or call the concièrge and they'll deliver it. I'll be done in an hour."

"Take your time," Gabriela said. "Claire and I are not in a hurry."

"Don't hesitate to knock on the door if something happens."

"If I need to, I will," she replied.

He thanked her but she already had her attention back on the baby, cooing and talking in Portuguese.

Damian grabbed his laptop and cords, and Luke walked with him to the front door.

"Am I crazy for accepting Gabriela's help?"

Luke shrugged. "Hey, you left Claire with me and I have no experience."

"That's different. I've known you for over a decade."

"I don't think you have anything to worry about, but I'll look her up anyway."

Before Damian could reply to that, Luke got in behind the wheel, started his car and left.

Damian walked to his bedroom and closed the door, hoping it would provide him with the quiet he needed to work with minimal interruptions.

But, as he set up the laptop, his mind wandered to Gabriela. She intrigued him.

He remembered well the first time he saw her at Filipe's wedding, holding onto the little boy's hand. She'd worn a pale blue dress that made her brown eyes and hair a deep rich color and, even though she wasn't the most beautiful woman he'd ever met, she had a certain quality about her that had grabbed his attention. He remembered thinking she was someone he wished he could know and the thought had surprised him.

Meeting Gabriela here at Hydrangea Manor had been completely unexpected. Faial was a vacation spot, especially in the summer months, but the manor was not the usual hotel people booked. Which meant she'd come for a specific reason.

Damian stood from the desk and shook Gabriela from his mind. After grabbing a cold water bottle, he worked for the next while, answering emails, reading pitches for movies, and making phone calls to New York.

A rap sounded at the door and Luke peeked in. "How's the work going?"

Damian waved him in as he typed. "Almost done here. And you?"

Luke carried a brown envelope in his hand. "Did as much as I can from here. Did you grab lunch yet?"

"Is that the time already?" Damian saved his work and closed the laptop. "I didn't realize I've been at it for over two hours."

"Sounds like you had a productive morning," Luke said, sitting down on the leather chair by the window.

Damian passed a hand through his hair. "Had a bit of a problem focusing at first."

"Too many worries?" Luke said.

"Something like that," Damian conceded. He wasn't ready to tell his friend he'd spent too much time thinking of Gabriela.

Damian stood and stretched the kinks out of his shoulders, then took the matching chair.

"Are you ready to talk about Claire and her mother?" Luke asked.

Damian nodded. "What have you found out?"

"I haven't been able to find anything about what Elsie Barr did in the last year. What do you remember about her?"

"She dated Paul Rogers on and off from her sophomore year until the end of her senior year. She was quiet and seemed level-headed but I didn't know her very well. I remember Paul mentioning she had plans to attend Princeton after high school, but I can't even remember the degree. I lost contact with Paul after he went to Stanford."

Luke removed a page from the envelope and set it in front of Damian. "She did go to Princeton for a year. Then she transferred to a local college from which she graduated with a law degree. About a year ago, she resigned from her job at a prestigious firm in New Jersey."

"That would have been when she got pregnant with Claire, right?"

Luke nodded. "I believe so, yes. With your permission, I'd like to hire a private investigator to fill in the gap between her leaving her employment and Claire's birth. We know Elsie Barr passed away from cancer when Claire was five-weeks old, but we don't have anything else to go on."

"What about her family?"

"She had no family. Her parents are gone and we couldn't find grandparents, siblings, cousins, Nothing," Luke said.

"And Paul Rogers? He might know something."

"Yes, he might. I'll add him to the list."

Damian rubbed his chin. "This is such a bizarre situation. How does a woman I haven't seen nor had any contact with since high school name me as the father of her newborn baby? Why did she do it? Where's the real father?"

"It doesn't make much sense, I know, but we'll get the answers."

"Go ahead and hire the investigator, the sooner the better." Damian let out a deep breath. "I assume until we find out the birth father's identity that I'm Claire's legal father?"

"Legally and de facto, yes. There's no way to contest it until we know more."

"Which means I need to plan my return to New York very carefully. I don't want the news about Claire to leak before I'm ready to announce it." Even with expertly crafted words and strategic timing, the news of his sudden fatherhood had the potential to explode into social media and generate the wrong kind of publicity.

Luke reached for the envelope, retrieved another piece of paper, and held on to it for a moment. "I have an idea."

"Judging from your expression, I'm not going to like it," Damian said, suddenly wary of his friend.

"Probably not." Luke placed the paper on the coffee table and slid it in Damian's direction. "This is about Gabriela Romano."

Damian slid it back. "I'd rather not read this." Why did he feel disloyal to Gabriela if he read the information?

Luke took the paper back. "It's fine. I'll tell you the highlights. Gabriela Romano is thirty-two years old. She lives and works in Lisbon as an advertising senior specialist. Her parents and siblings live in Porto, as do some of her relatives. You already know Filipe and the rest of the Romanos are a large, close-knit family." Luke looked at the sheet before continuing. "I couldn't find out any recent relationships, but she's never been married and doesn't have any children. She's very dedicated to her career and, until now, she's never taken a vacation other than long weekends with her family. She did spend three days in the hospital last month but I couldn't find out the reason for it."

Damian held a palm up. "We don't need to know. I feel like we're invading her privacy without any valid motives. I doubt she'll want to be Claire's nanny." As great as that would be, for him and Claire, Gabriela was a career woman and wouldn't be interested in his offer. "Besides, if she had health problems recently, she's probably at the manor to recover. Thanks for the idea, but it won't work."

"Hiring Gabriela as a nanny wasn't my idea," Luke said, his tone measured and his words slow.

"If not as a nanny, then what?"

"As a wife, Damian. You ask her to marry you."

Damian shook his head and rubbed the back of his neck. "I must be more tired than I thought. Did you say ask Gabriela to marry me? Are you crazy? I don't need a wife. I need a nanny. Someone I can trust and if Claire likes her, even better."

"Stop and listen to yourself, man." Luke gestured in the direction of the living room, where they'd last seen Gabriela this morning. "That's her. She's the woman you need. Claire likes her. She likes Claire and you obviously trust her or you'd never have let her in yesterday, let alone leave her alone with Claire."

He was right, of course. Damian had always prided himself in his rock-solid instincts. He could read a person upon meeting them for the first time and had seldom made business decisions that steered him wrong. How could this be the same?

"But why marriage?" He held back from cringing at the thought. "That's so final. Why can't I ask her to be Claire's new nanny instead and make an offer that might tempt her?" Or at least, think about it.

"Because a nanny is only an employee. She's there for the baby, not for you. You need someone at your side who's at the same level as you, not only emotionally and mentally but also legally. A wife will give you the protection you need to keep your image above reproach, especially now with a baby in your care. Not to mention, she'll help your transition into the role of a father go much easier, and that includes how the public views you. There's always speculation about a single man with a baby. But it's different for a married man. If your goal is to protect your image, then having Gabriela at your side as your wife is the perfect solution."

"You always make the best arguments, don't you?" Damian turned back and faced Luke. "You know how I feel about marriage." The weariness in his voice almost turned into a sigh.

"I also know you're not your father."

No. That he wasn't.

Walter Vaughn and his philandering ways had nearly destroyed the family-oriented movie company started by his own father. He'd eroded the public trust and sullied the company's image until their professional reputation had nearly been done away with. By the time Damian was old enough to take over the company and savvy enough to know what he was doing, he'd had to start over with only his grandfather's name and a handful of employees who had as much interest in succeeding as he did.

That had been twelve years ago. Damian had been able to reverse the damage inflicted by his father, and not without personal and family costs.

But in the years following his official take-over, the scattered feelings and thoughts he'd had in his late teens became more of a personal mantra, something he'd reoriented his life by—everything his father had done, Damian would do the opposite. Just as his father had married and then repeatedly cheated on his wife, Damian would remain single. If he ever did marry—and that would be much later in life—it would only be after a long period of courtship, when he was absolutely certain he'd found the one woman with whom he wanted to spend the rest of his life.

All that had changed two weeks ago when he'd received news about a baby girl whose birth certificate had his name as the father.

That was one meeting that hadn't gone the way he'd planned. The plan had been to not accept the baby. Luke had gone with him to the office of Child and Family Services, and Damian had been shocked and angry to be there, ready to prove his innocence by submitting to a DNA test and contest his paternity.

But upon meeting the infant, he'd felt something unexpected and he'd remembered a service project he'd been involved with in his high school junior year, putting together care packages for foster children.

Those stories had an impact on him, an impression that hadn't left. At that moment, looking at Claire's little face, he'd gone with his gut instead, knowing he couldn't leave this baby in the care of the state.

Luke hadn't been happy with Damian's change of heart back then, and here he was now, presenting a wild idea.

"So, you're telling me I should propose a marriage of convenience to Gabriela."

"It doesn't have to be as cold as you make it sound. Marriages of convenience are not a thing of the past." Luke leaned forward in his chair, his expression sincere. "I know of couples who've done it for various reasons. It's like a business transaction benefiting both parties, with expectations and the marriage terms all spelled out in the contract."

Damian rubbed his chin. "A contract? She'll think I'm crazy if I tell her all that."

"You won't know unless you ask."

"Why am I even considering this? I can't ask her to marry me."

He couldn't, could he?

CHAPTER THREE

Gabriela checked her reflection in the mirror one more time. Dark skinny jeans, a T-shirt and a light cardigan would have to do. She hadn't brought much else to wear, and hadn't anticipated the need for her favorite summer dress, the peach one in a midi length.

Quite unexpectedly, Damian had called the suite's phone just before dinner time yesterday and had asked her to go on a drive with him and Claire this morning. At first, she wasn't sure of what to say, but between her curiosity and her wish to spend time with the baby again, she'd accepted the invitation.

And here she was, second-guessing her outfit as if she was going out on a date. It wasn't a date. It was an outing with a man she'd known for two days and his adorable baby girl she couldn't stop thinking about. To be honest with herself, she'd thought about the baby's father more times than she ought to.

He wasn't the kind of man she'd thought him to be at first. The way he interacted with Claire was endearing to watch and, despite his lack of experience, he tried hard. Other men would have hired another nanny by now but Gabriela got the impression that Damian wanted to find the perfect person for the job.

This trip was turning out to be completely different from what Gabriela had imagined—lots of quiet moments, meditation, not having to do anything. She'd had plenty of those between bouts of crying and feeling sorry for herself.

Then she'd met Damian and Claire and she'd nearly forgotten her health problems or how much they'd changed her life.

Gabriela slipped on her crossbody purse, a small one that fit a pack of facial tissues, a tube of chapstick, her key and her phone. She'd charged it overnight, just in case the chance arose for pictures.

Taking the path Damian had shown her yesterday, she walked around the manor until she arrived at his house, then knocked on a side door near the garage.

"Come in. It's open," he said from inside.

Gabriela pushed the door open and found him in the hallway, holding Claire in his left arm and feeding her a bottle with his right hand.

Was there anything more attractive than a man holding his baby in such an adorable way? Once again, she wondered why Claire's mother was not around.

"Hey, Gabriela. Come this way," Damian said.

She followed behind him. The thought came into her mind that everything she wished for was right in front of her—a caring man and a baby. A family.

But they weren't hers and she would do well to remember that.

"Can I help with anything?" she asked Damian.

"Just need to grab a couple of diapers and some wipes. Do you want to finish feeding Claire?"

"Yes, of course."

She walked over to him and raised her arms to take the baby. For a moment, his wiry arms tangled with hers as they moved Claire between the two of them.

Gabriela's cheeks heated. She took the bottle and turned away from Damian, hoping he hadn't seen her blush.

The way her body—and mind—reacted to his presence and nearness kept escalating every time she met with him. It wasn't good.

He returned with two diapers and a pack of travel wipes. "We'll go when Claire's ready," he said. "I'll get the car seat."

Gabriela held Claire next to her shoulder and patted her back. "Don't forget her diaper bag."

Damian stopped and turned back. "That might be in her bedroom."

He probably didn't go out much with her, if he couldn't remember where the diaper bag was.

When Claire was done with her feeding, Gabriela changed her diaper and made sure the baby was ready for the car ride.

Damian returned a few minutes later, holding the car seat in one hand and a brown bag with pink accents in the other. "It's a bit more pink than I remember," he said.

Gabriela held Claire in the crook of her arm and took the car seat from Damian. "Is the bag all packed?" She gently settled the baby and strapped her in.

At the lack of response from Damian, she turned around to look at him.

He met her eyes. "I packed the diapers and wipes."

"What about the rest?"

"What rest?"

"What did you have in it before?"

By now, he looked perplexed. "I'm not sure. The bag came with her."

That was a strange thing to say. "We're going to need more than a couple of diapers and wipes," Gabriela said. "Stay here with Claire and keep her company, please. I'll finish packing the bag."

Damian watched her but didn't comment.

When Gabriela was done, she showed him the bag. "In addition to the wipes and diapers you had, I put in a few more diapers and some ointment, just in case, a change of clothes, a cotton blanket and, of course, formula, water. Bottles, and two pacifiers."

"How do you know so much about babies?" he asked her.

The question took Gabriela by surprise and she stammered, not wanting to tell him the truth.

"You're not hiding out at the resort as a break from your five children or anything, are you? I mean—it wouldn't be the first time a mother has needed to escape for a while." He continued.

She shook her head. "I come from a big family. I guess I just pay attention."

Her answer seemed to satisfy him for now as he picked up the car seat with Claire in it and walked to the garage. Gabriela shouldered the bag and followed.

A few minutes later, they were on the road, the windows rolled down a little and a gentle breeze sweetening the spring air that filled the car. The sky shone blue and bright and bushes of hydrangeas alongside the two-lane highway rivaled in color and brilliance. Every so often, white houses with red roof tiles dotted the sides of the landscape as reminders that people did inhabit these hills right alongside the sheep.

"I think Claire fell asleep," Damian said.

Gabriela peeked in the back and found the baby sleeping soundly in her car seat. "Yes, she did." She couldn't help but smile as she watched the beautiful little face.

Until the baby woke, Gabriela could focus on the amazing scenery.

Damian glanced at her. "How much have you seen of the island?"

"Other than the view just before landing, not much. I've been at the manor the whole time." Until recently, she hadn't felt like sightseeing.

"So, you haven't had the chance to visit Horta yet?"

"No, not yet."

"We'll set you up before you leave," he replied. "Today we're taking this road around the island, then we'll stop at one of the promontory parks to check the view before returning. At least, that's the plan." He tipped his head towards the back seat. "Let's hope she cooperates."

Along the way, Damian pointed at landmarks and points of interest, filling in with tidbits of local history.

"How often do you stay here in Faial?"

"At least once a year, sometimes twice," he replied easily. "When I need to get away from all the crazy in my life, I come here."

"Does it work?"

He nodded slowly. "Better than I always expect. By the time I return home, I'm ready to face whatever it was life threw at me."

If Gabriela hadn't looked at him just then, she would have missed his wistful sigh and the vulnerability in his eyes. This was a side of Damian she hadn't seen before, but the honesty and frankness there were too genuine to dismiss.

Damian followed the hydrangea-lined roads with hedges separating lush fields where black-and-white cows grazed. The landscape was like a colorful children's book, each stretch like flipping a surprising page until the next one appeared.

Just as he pulled over into a small parking lot, Claire started fussing. "Perfect timing," he said. "This is the Faial Botanical Garden. I thought we could visit before going back home."

Gabriela got in the back seat, unbuckled the baby and held her. "Let me find a restroom and change her diaper first."

Damian handed her the diaper bag. "I'll wait by the entrance."

Claire was definitely happy to be out of the car seat. By the time Gabriela was done changing her, the baby was ready for a bottle.

A few minutes later, Damian had found them a bench in the shade overlooking a small pond and Gabriela fed Claire, who was calm and content. It was the kind of contentment and calmness that marked a moment into a strong memory, one Gabriela wished to fix in time and never forget.

How had she gone from a post-surgery recovery last week to a morning spent in the company of a baby and her father today? The more time she spent with them, the harder it would be to say goodbye.

As Claire finished her feeding, Damian anticipated Gabriela and took the empty bottle from her hand. Their fingers grazed and the skin on her hand tingled. Her cheeks heated, her whole body strumming and hyper-sensitive to the man beside her.

"Thank you," she said, looking away from him and propping up Claire until the baby burped. Then she switched the baby around and settled her on her lap.

Was it all in her head, this tension between them, her awareness of him?

After Damian made a few random comments on the plants around them, he lapsed into silence. They turned their attention to a middle-aged couple and two teenagers who came into view on the other side of the pond, but Gabriela wished to ease the mood between them, even if it was all in her mind.

"I'm sorry to interrupt," said an older lady. "We're American too. We heard you speak English earlier." She smiled and gestured to her husband whose hand she held. "We're not in the habit of accosting people, but we just wanted to tell you what you a beautiful family you have."

Damian stood and shook their hands. "Thank you. We certainly appreciate it."

Gabriela smiled only, not knowing what to say and taken by surprise at the compliment. But more surprising was Damian's reply and his natural tone.

The couple went on their way and Damian sat back down, a big smile still on his face. He reached for Claire and held her.

"It doesn't upset you that people think we're a family?"

He moved Claire to the other leg, ending up closer to Gabriela. Their arms brushed and her skin broke into goose bumps. All day she'd been reacting to his physical proximity, feeling the pull of attraction as she hadn't felt it in such a long time.

"No. Does it upset you?" He turned to look at her. "It would take longer to explain and then they'd feel awkward for assuming. It's easier this way. Do you think it's wrong?"

She shook her head. "I guess it's harmless." To them, maybe, but not to her.

Before he could ask her any more questions, Gabriela stood and retrieved her phone from her purse. "Do you mind if I take a picture of you and Claire?"

He smiled and held up Claire until her little head was at the same level with his. Gabriela took the picture and then turned the phone around to show him how it turned out.

"Sit with us and I'll take a selfie," Damian said, holding out his free hand for her phone.

"Why don't I take that picture for you two instead?" said a man in Portuguese.

It was the father from the family with the two teenagers she and Damian had seen across the pond earlier.

"Sure. Thank you," Gabriela said as she handed the phone to the man.

His wife approached and stood by his side. "You two are too far apart. Sit a little closer." She motioned the gesture.

Damian hesitated for a moment, then he moved Claire to sit on his lap in front of them both, and brought his free arm around Gabriela's shoulders.

There went her heart, somersaulting in her chest. Damian was embracing her with a natural ease he faked much too well. He was solid, warm, and smelled divine.

The guy took the photo and the wife leaned in to see. "It turned out great. Your baby is so adorable."

The man handed back the phone and Gabriela stood to take it. "Thank you."

"You're welcome. Enjoy your little one." He turned to look at his kids. "They grow up too fast."

As the couple left, Damian rose. "That was nice of them."

"I thought you didn't speak Portuguese."

He shrugged. "Technically I can speak it, but I don't like to because my accent is terrible."

"You understood everything that couple said to us."

"Understanding is a lot easier than speaking," Damian said. "Sorry. I wasn't trying to hide it."

"I'm not mad, just surprised."

"Any chance I can have a copy of that photo?"

"Yes, of course."

Damian recited his phone number and she sent him copies of the pictures using the free wi-fi at the garden.

The walking tour of the grounds didn't take as long as she'd expected but, as they made their way back to the front, Claire's patience had run out and she was ready to return.

When Damian parked in the driveway of his home, Gabriela released the car seat from the base and set it down on the pavement. In just a few seconds, she had Claire in her arms.

Damian unlocked the door and let her pass first. "She doesn't like the car seat too much, does she?"

"She prefers to be held. I can't blame her," Gabriela replied. "A warm, firm embrace is always better than the hard plastic of the car seat."

"I'm sure it is. She loves it when you hold her."

Again, her cheeks heated. "I'll change her and feed her before I go," Gabriela said, on the way to Claire's room. "Would you prepare—"

"On it," came the prompt reply.

Once settled on the gliding chair, with a ready baby in her arms, Gabriela took her time feeding Claire, and when the little one fell asleep, she placed her in the crib and lingered for a moment, watching her—the perfect rosy cheeks, the long eyelashes fanning the delicate skin, the little fingers relaxed into a gentle curl.

The scraping of a shoe on the floor alerted her to Damian's presence. How long had he been there?

After a moment, he walked to the kitchen and Gabriela followed him.

"Thank you for inviting me to come with you and Claire."

"You're welcome. I'm glad you came. Will you stay for lunch? I called the manor and had it delivered." He gestured at the table where a meal was already laid out.

Despite his easy words, he talked too fast and appeared distracted, avoiding her gaze.

"What's wrong?" she finally asked him. "I don't know you well, but you look—"

"You're very perceptive, Gabriela." He pulled out the chair for her. "There's something I'd like to talk to you about."

She waited until he sat down across from her. "Is this about Claire?" Was Damian about to ask her to be Claire's nanny? And if so, how crazy was it that she would consider it and had imagined such a scenario already? She could ask for a leave of absence from the firm.

"Some of it is about Claire, but probably not in the way you're thinking."

"What then?" Dread rose within her. Perhaps he was about to tell her something drastically different—the opposite of her ridiculous fantasy about leaving her corporate job and living happily ever after in paradise while working as a nanny. She voiced her fear. "I've overstepped attempting to be helpful. I've invaded your privacy and—"

He caught her hand in his across the table. "I wouldn't have invited you today if I felt like that."

"Oh." She stared at their connected hands, the warmth of his touch already radiating up her arm.

"You're leaving soon. Is that it? Time to get back to the real world?" She was going to cry if she wasn't careful.

He shook his head. "No. Gabriela. I'm not going anywhere for the time being." He paused, and this time she waited, out of guesses, and on the edge of her own seat, as nervous as she'd accused him of being a few minutes ago.

Damian looked straight at her. "What would you say—if I asked you to marry me?"

Damian watched Gabriela's reaction.

Her jaw dropped. Then she closed her mouth and gave him a tight smile, her eyebrows knit together in a light frown. "I'm sorry. Could you repeat that? I don't think I heard you right."

He couldn't blame her, could he?

"I know this sounds crazy." He took a breath, then raised his hands in a conciliatory gesture. "I don't know how to say this any other way, sorry. I'd like you to marry me."

She leaned away from the table. "I thought you were going to ask me to be Claire's nanny."

"It did cross my mind at one point, but that's not quite what I need."

"You need a wife so you ask me?" She stood and took a step back. "Damian, we don't know each other. We met three days ago."

This was not going well. Was it too late to take it back?

Damian pulled away from the table and approached Gabriela. "Will you give me the chance to explain? Please?"

She said something in Portuguese that he didn't get, then faced him. "Part of me is saying I should leave because this is beyond insane, but I'm curious, Damian, and I want to hear this explanation."

He held back a smile. This wasn't the best time for it and Gabriela wouldn't appreciate it, but he liked this gumption of hers which showed a side of her personality he had not yet seen.

"Will you take a seat?" He gestured at the uphol-stered chair, affording her the chance to sit by herself, as he took the sofa. "Have you heard of The Vaughn Family Movie Channel?"

Gabriela raised an eyebrow. "Of course. Who hasn't? What does this have to do—wait." She paused and frowned. "Are you that Vaughn?"

"It was my grandfather, Sebastian Vaughn. He bought a movie theater in 1956 and, within a few years, he went from showing movies to making them. The com-pany grew on the reputation of clean, family-friendly movies, something anyone could watch, and he kept that image at all costs. Unfortunately, my father didn't. He was a liar, he cheated on my mother repeatedly, and he didn't care that his actions affected the company."

At the confusion in her expression, Damian changed his narrative. "I'm only telling you this so you can understand how important it is for me to keep my image clean. Like my grandfather, I believe that what I do in my private and social life has a direct effect on the company. I try to live above reproach and I expect the same from anyone that works at Vaughn's."

Gabriela nodded, her attention still on him.

"Three weeks ago, I received a summons to appear at the main office of Child and Family Services in New York City. Luke went with me as my lawyer. When we arrived, I was told I had a daughter and that

I was now responsible for her because her mother had passed away from cancer."

Gabriela gasped. "You didn't know you had a daughter? Why did the mother keep this from you?"

"I'm not Claire's father, Gabriela," he said, in his most even tone. It was important to him that she understood this from the beginning.

"If you're not the father, why did they say you are?"

"Because her birth certificate has my name on it as the father."

Gabriela sighed. "This is so confusing."

"Believe me, I know. Luke and I are still trying to figure out how this happened."

"So, you never met this woman and you don't know who she was?"

"Well, I did know her in high school. She dated a friend of mine, but she and I were never more than friendly acquaintances. We don't know much more than this, but we're hoping to find out soon."

"We?"

"Luke hired a private investigator for me, to discover what she was doing in the past year."

Gabriela looked out the window for a moment and he could almost see her trying to puzzle out the problem.

She turned back to him. "And you're positive you're not Claire's father?"

"We graduated from high school fifteen years ago and I never saw or talked to her again. Of course I'm not the father. Besides, I'm celibate."

Again, her eyebrow rose. "Celibate like a priest?"

Damian smiled. "If you mean no sex like a priest, yes. And I'm not what you assumed when you met Luke."

Gabriela's cheeks reddened and, for that brief moment, he wished he could read her mind to know what had caused that blush.

"I'm guessing you need a wife to make you respectable?"

He nodded. "That's the main reason. I came to Faial immediately after getting Claire. I needed to think and regroup, but I can't run the business from here. I have to return to New York. If I come back with a wife and a baby, the public opinion will be more lenient. There might be some speculation about the baby but the fallout will be much lighter with a wife beside me and, hopefully, it'll not have negative repercussions on the company."

Gabriela rose and walked to the French doors, her back to him. For a long minute, she stood there, an arm across her middle and her hand holding her chin.

What else could he say that would make a difference?

He walked over to her. "I know this is a lot to take in, but please know that I'm being honest with you." There was nothing he could hide from her, not with marriage to consider, even if it was a marriage of convenience.

She shook her head. "You don't know me," she said at last.

"I know you're kind, generous with your time, and you love Claire."

At his words, she looked over her shoulder. "I love Claire?"

Maybe she wasn't ready to admit that, as obvious as it was. Damian shrugged lightly.

Luke came in just then and looked between him and Gabriela, taking stock of the situation as he usually did when he entered a room. "I see you asked her."

Gabriela turned to Damian, her expression a mix of surprise and consternation. "He knows?"

"I told you Luke's my lawyer, and my very good friend. If you decide to say yes, he will draw up a contract for us."

"What contract?" Gabriela asked.

"The contract that spells out the marriage terms," Damian replied. "Whatever we agree to will be put in writing. I don't want any room for surprises or misunderstandings."

Luke sat down at the table and uncovered the chicken salad that had been delivered earlier. He retrieved an extra plate from the cupboard then gestured for Damian and Gabriela to join him at the table.

Gabriela took a seat across from Luke and Damian sat on the chair across from her. He didn't want to crowd her or leave her feeling intimidated, but being able to see her expression, her eyes, was important to him.

"If I consider this, and I mean *if* with capital letters, I'd have to quit my job in Lisbon and leave my apartment."

Luke took her plate and served her a portion, then did the same for Damian and himself.

"That'll be taken care of in the contract," Luke said. "A monthly salary for the duration of the marriage, plus a sum when the divorce is final. As for the apartment, if you want to keep the same one, the monthly mortgage would be paid, or you could put it up for sale and buy another one when you return to Lisbon. That's for you to choose."

"Those are quite the terms," Gabriela said, her voice even.

Damian watched her, trying to gauge her mood. She hadn't left like he thought she would, which was a good sign. Maybe she was open to the idea.

"There are more details we can go over later. And let's not forget the prenuptial agreement," Luke added.

Damian scrubbed the back of his neck. He had indeed forgotten about the prenup. "It's only to protect the company, Gabriela. It was drafted years ago."

"I understand. How long would this marriage that you're proposing last?"

Luke finished chewing before replying. "At least six months. We need time for the investigation and for the DNA test."

"A paternity test?" Gabriela asked.

"That was the plan, to take the test and prove that Damian is not the father," Luke said. "But that's not how things went." He looked at Damian sideways.

"When I met Claire, I didn't want her to become a ward of the state once the test proved I'm not her father," Damian told Gabriela. "So, I didn't contest it. This way we have more time for the investigator to discover who her real father is." Besides, if this man doesn't appear to be a good person, I cannot in good conscience simply turn Claire to him."

Gabriela's eyes softened and her expression was one of approval, much to his relief. "I'm afraid six months is not long enough. My family will be suspicious. They'll know it's not a real marriage, especially with a quick divorce."

A wave of dread surged in Damian's chest. "What about a year?" he rushed to say. "And instead of divorcing, we can just quietly go our separate ways."

Luke sent him a warning look, but Damian ignored it. "We'll make sure the papers detail everything, including the financial support and the time line."

Gabriela bit her lip. "So, we'd stay married and live apart after one year? What if—" she paused. "What if the situation changes?"

"If something changes, we can quickly draft a divorce then," Damian replied.

"What about Claire?" Gabriela asked.

Damian frowned. "Claire?"

"Babies form strong bonds in their first year of life. Claire will get attached, as she should for her normal development. Separation would bring serious concerns, and not only for her."

Her implication was clear that she too would suffer from a separation. "I've thought of that, but I still think this is better than the alternative of her being in foster care. I promise we'll do everything we can to find her real father and resolve the issue quickly."

"And if he isn't someone who should be raising a child? What if he is unfit? For all we know, he is, and that's why her mother named you as the father."

"I don't know," Damian responded honestly. "It's a possibility. I realize this is crazy—or maybe I'm the crazy one for asking you to do such a thing. But I'm trying to do right by this baby girl. For whatever reason, fate placed her in my hands, and I feel responsible for her. That you've somehow landed here too, seems nothing short of a miracle. When you appeared in my yard the other day—as if out of thin air—and took Claire in your arms and calmed her…" He shrugged. "This sounds crazy too, but you seemed heaven set. To me, to Claire, in that very moment we needed you."

Luke raised an eyebrow in silent applause as he leaned back in his chair, but Damian hadn't been acting. He'd meant every word. He'd thought Gabriela a Godsend that day. He'd think her even more so, if she'd only give this absurd idea a chance.

She didn't immediately say anything, but seemed to ponder his words.

"A year then," she said at last.

"A year," Damian repeated, with far more confidence than he had.

The idea of being married for a year was something he had to get used to. If Gabriela accepted, Luke would push for the wedding to take place as soon as possible, and Damian was still coming to terms with this plan.

Gabriela placed her utensils on the brim of the plate. She'd picked around her food but had barely eaten any of it.

"I'm sorry but I can't give you a reply right now. There's too much to think about."

Was it his impression or did her mouth tremble?

She turned her face to the side then rose. "I'm leaving. Can I call you tomorrow morning?"

Damian stood from his chair "Yes, of course. Can I walk you back to the manor?"

She held a hand up, ready to stop him. "Thank you, but no. I—" she paused.

"You need to be by yourself," Damian finished for her.

She nodded. "Thank you."

Luke had left the table as well and he approached Gabriela with a folder. "Here, take this with you. It's a draft version of the contract, a very rough one. Subject to changes by both parties, obviously."

She took it from him, a hint of reluctance in her eyes. "I'll be in touch."

After she left, Luke returned to his plate and resumed eating.

"How can you eat after what just happened?" Damian asked.

"Hey, I'm hungry," Luke replied, taking another bite.

Damian sat down, his elbows on the table and his head down. "I scared her. I could see it in her eyes. What was I thinking to ask a woman I've known for three days to marry me?" He should have waited.

"We don't have enough time to take it slow. You know that," Luke said.

He was right, and it didn't make the wait for Gabriela's reply any easier.

The rest of the day passed slowly. Damian's concentration was gone, and he spent his time tending to Claire. Luke had given him a list of prospective nannies, but Damian hadn't looked at it. He wouldn't think about hiring a new nanny until he found out Gabriela's reply.

What was she doing right now? Packing, getting ready to leave? Writing a reply that would let him know what she thought of him and his proposal?

Despite his nervous state, Damian fell asleep faster than he had in days. Claire woke up once and, after being changed and fed, went back to sleep without any resistance.

In the early morning, before the sunlight arose, Damian woke with a startle and sat up in bed. He listened for Claire in the next bedroom but silence enveloped the house at this hour.

Then he remembered—the marriage, the contract. Gabriela.

Would she agree to his proposal?

If someone had asked him two days ago about getting married, Damian would have replied with a solid, emphatic no, never. But here he was, unable to go back to sleep, thinking of Gabriela and knowing nothing but a yes from her would satisfy him.

If he were honest with himself, he wouldn't feel the same way with any other woman. That was the truth. Not only did he need a wife, but the wife he wanted was Gabriela.

He slid out of bed, washed his face with cold water, and pulled on a hoodie and sweat pants. Maybe going for a walk would clear his head until he heard from her. She'd said she'd call him this morning, but probably not at five thirty.

In the guest bedroom, Claire slept as an angel, her jammies a little tight around the middle. She'd grown already, and no longer comfortably fit the few clothes that had come with her. Damian made sure the baby monitor app was on and working before leaving the room.

In the other bedroom, Luke slept like he didn't have any worries, which Damian knew wasn't true.

He locked the door behind him with a soft click and set out toward the hills on the other side of the road. While crossing to the hiking path, a familiar silhouette caught his attention and his heart tripped at the sight of Gabriela. Immediately he adjusted his way to meet with her, but hesitation followed and he paused. What if she didn't want to see him this early? Or see him at all?

In the end, she saved him from his indecision and raised her hand in greeting. Relief filled him and Damian walked to her.

"I couldn't sleep," she said softly.

"Neither could I." Damian slid his hands into his pants pockets, dousing his need to be closer to Gabriela and take her hand.

This attraction he felt for her—the way it grew each time they met—why did it set his heart racing and his fingers aching to touch her?

He wasn't used to this burning energy. It set him out of sorts and unsure of himself.

The hiking path was well-used and wide enough for the two of them to walk beside each other.

"Did Claire wake you up?"

"No, she slept soundly when I left." He retrieved his phone from his pocket and held it up for her. "The baby monitor app will let me know if she wakes up."

"Look at you," she said in a teasing voice, "rocking the parenting gig."

Damian chuckled. "If by rocking you mean faking till I make it, then yes, I'm rocking it."

"Did you find a nanny yet?"

"Well, huh—" He scratched behind his ear. "It depends on—I'm waiting to see before I make a decision."

"Oh," she replied. "Yes, that makes sense."

They found a bench in a clearing and took a seat, just as the first rays of sun burst from the east and splashed over the side of the hill. Only the sound of their breaths and the breeze filled the air. With the view of the ocean past the manor and grounds, right now and right here made the most perfect moment and place.

Only him and Gabriela.

How long they sat there watching the sunrise, he couldn't tell.

After a while, Gabriela tucked her hair behind her ear. "I didn't expect to see you this early when I left this morning."

"I didn't expect to see you either. We can just pretend we didn't, if that's easier."

"The easy way is not always the best way, is it?"

"I suppose not." He didn't know what else to say. What did she mean with that?

"I came to the island looking for a change of scenery and pace, and I got much more change than I anticipated."

Damian looked at her with a raised eyebrow. "Is that good?"

She closed her eyes and nodded. "Yes."

When he didn't say anything, she turned to look at him. "My answer is yes."

His eyes widened as understanding dawned on him. "You mean—"

"I mean yes, I'll marry you, Damian Vaughn."

Relief surged through him, then contentment flooded his heart.

He extended his hand to her and she took it. The corners of his mouth lifted in a wide grin and Gabriela gave him a reserved smile.

"Come on," she said. "Let's go wake up Luke and show him the notes I made on the contract. I do have one condition we need to talk about."

As far as he was concerned, anything she wanted.

CHAPTER FOUR

*D*amian sat on the upholstered chair with Claire on his lap. Gabriela had changed and fed her and the baby was content for now.

Across from them, at the dining table, Luke and Gabriela went over the prenuptial agreement.

There were two words he never thought he'd see together in the same sentence. Was this marriage really happening? He'd never imagined himself married, let alone taking such a business approach to it. Yet, somehow, it felt right. Maybe the magnitude of what he and Gabriela were about to do would catch up with him later but, for the moment, Damian couldn't think of any impediments, any reasons to hold back.

Or maybe he'd lost his common sense and rational reasoning and was unable to see the disaster they so calmly planned.

After Gabriela read and signed the prenuptial agreement, Luke brought out the marriage contract.

67

He marked the notes as he read aloud what Gabriela had written on the margins of the paper for Damian's approval. "To summarize, you both agree to enter into a marriage for the term of one year, at which point you will separate into different households. This situation will continue until you both agree to a friendly, uncontested divorce." He went on with the financial terms.

"What about Claire?" Gabriela asked.

"What about her?" Luke asked.

Gabriela turned to face Damian. "I'd like her to come with me when we separate."

"Damian is not Claire's real father," Luke said.

"He is on paper," Gabriela insisted.

"But—" Luke started.

Damian shook his head and Luke stopped.

"You can keep Claire when we separate," Damian said. "Until we find what her situation is."

Gabriela took a breath. "Actually, I'd like to legally adopt Claire. People are going to assume she's mine anyway."

"Adopt Claire?" Luke asked with surprise in his face.

"Is this the condition you mentioned earlier?" Damian asked.

"Yes, I want my name on her birth certificate. Isn't that what happens with adoption? The birth certificate can be amended to have the adoptive parent's name?"

Luke nodded slowly. "That's true."

Damian found himself agreeing to Gabriela's

condition. "In that case, we can have the adoption petitioned as soon as the marriage is filed."

Gabriela's shoulders relaxed. "Thank you."

Luke stood. "I need a word with you, Damian. Will you excuse us, Gabriela?"

"Of course." She approached Damian and took Claire in her arms, then walked out of the living room area.

As soon as she left, Luke spread the papers out on the table. "Do you understand what you're agreeing to?"

"Absolutely," Damian replied.

Luke went on as if Damian hadn't said anything. "You're agreeing to marrying a woman you just met, to be her legal husband for at least a year, but maybe longer, to support her and the baby financially, and to make her the legal mother of this baby who doesn't belong to you."

"I know, Luke. I'm not going into this blind."

"What happens when we find out who Claire's real father is?"

"What if we don't find him? Or maybe we find him but he's unfit to be a parent?"

"We don't know that," Luke said.

"All I know is that Elsie Barr must have had a good reason to put my name down on the birth certificate." It only made sense to Damian that she had.

"I'm sure she did, but we don't know what it is. Gabriela gets to adopt Claire in the event that her real father is not found, or he's not suitable."

When Damian didn't reply, Luke let out a long sigh. "I'm trying to protect your interests, man. As your lawyer and as your friend.

"And I appreciate it. I really do." Damian quickly went over all the conditions, all the terms, in his mind. "I'm sure of this."

"Okay. That's all I need." Luke shuffled the papers back together.

"I'm glad I have you to look out for my interests, but Gabriela doesn't have anyone."

"We'll do the same for her. Don't worry," Luke said. "By the way, I suggest the marriage takes place as soon as possible."

"I agree. What do we need to do?"

"I'll talk to a buddy of mine to confirm, but I'm pretty sure we'll need your US documents translated into Portuguese and hers into English. Then we go to Lisbon and you get married there, and immediately after we go to the US Embassy to have the marriage certificate authenticated."

"Don't forget the adoption papers."

"We'll get started on those when we're back in New York."

"Let's get on it." With that much paperwork involved, Damian didn't want to waste any time.

They walked down the hallway to the guest bedroom where they found Gabriela playing with Claire laying down on the bed.

Luke raised the papers in his hand. "I'll get these ready for signatures, Gabriela."

She held Claire's hand and waved. "Thanks, Luke."

Luke hesitated at the threshold. "A piece of advice for you two."

Gabriela raised her head and Damian turned to his friend.

"If you have any hope of getting people to believe you two married for love, I suggest you get comfortable with each other."

"What do you mean?" Damian asked.

"What do people in love do?" Luke didn't wait for a reply. "They're physically close to each other. They hold hands, they kiss, they hug each other. That sort of stuff."

Gabriela immediately blushed and looked back at Claire, who smiled and cooed.

Damian patted Luke's shoulder. "Thanks for the suggestion, but we'll figure it out by ourselves."

Luke chuckled as he left, most likely too pleased with himself for his idea.

"Well, that was awkward," Gabriela said with a hint of a smile.

Damian entered the bedroom and sat down on the edge of the bed. "Yeah, but he's got a point. Society has certain expectations of a couple in love. If we act like we don't know each other, people will be suspicious of our motives."

"How do we get comfortable with each other?" she asked.

With a light finger, she gently stroked Claire's forehead and temples in concentric circles. The baby's eye lids grew heavy with each caress.

"Spend time together? Hold hands?" This conversation made him feel like he was back in high school.

"Is that it?"

He frowned. "What else?"

"I didn't want to bring this up in front of Luke after his suggestion." She added air quotes to the last word. "Even though I'm marrying you to help with Claire, you aren't expecting anything else as a perk, are you?"

"What kind of perk?"

"You know. Benefits," she replied.

At his lack of response, she added, "Sexual benefits, Damian."

A wave of heat swept up his neck and he brushed the spot, hoping she couldn't tell. "Oh. That."

"Maybe we should have a paragraph about physical expectations in the contract."

Damian got his phone out. "I'll send Luke a text and ask him to add a no-benefits clause."

"You don't mind then?"

He looked up. "Why would I? I'd never force you to do anything."

"I wouldn't force you either."

"Good. We're on the same page."

Damian put his phone back in his pocket. He'd talk to Luke instead. If he texted, Luke would end up asking too many questions.

"It's okay that you're not attracted to me. It doesn't offend me." She kept her eyes lowered, as if too focused on stroking the baby.

"When did I say I'm not attracted to you?"

The implication of his words brought a blush to her cheeks.

Maybe he'd been a bit too honest, but she might as well know lack of attraction was not a problem.

He was the first one to break the silence. "She's asleep," he said of Claire.

Gabriela's expression softened, as it usually did when she looked at the baby. "It's her nap time."

Damian rose from the bed. "Do you want to move her to the crib?"

"Not yet. I'll stay with her for a little bit."

He handed her a light blanket and she covered Claire. "I'll be there in a few minutes."

When Gabriela hadn't come back ten minutes later, Damian peeked in the bedroom. She'd pulled one of the pillows under her head and had fallen asleep next to Claire. He watched them for a moment.

How had his life changed so much in less than a month? He, who'd never planned to get married and have children, now had a daughter and soon a wife? He wasn't ready for this; he knew that. What if he messed up? Or if he turned out like his father? His shoulders slumped at the thought.

It wasn't too late to call everything off. He could file to have a paternity test done to prove he wasn't Claire's father. She'd be handed over to the state's custody. Gabriela would return to Lisbon. They could each go their separate ways before they linked their lives legally and effectually.

But even as he went through each scenario in his mind, he quickly dismissed them.

Until he knew Elsie Barr's reasons for making him Claire's legal father, he'd do his duty by the baby.

And he was marrying Gabriela Romano.

Damian walked back to the living room and powered on his laptop, planning to keep his mind busy with company work instead of hypothetical situations that raised his blood pressure.

A half hour later, Gabriela padded in from the hallway and sat down on the upholstered chair near the table.

"I'm sorry I fell asleep," she said, stifling a yawn.

Her hair looked rumpled and she had a wrinkle from the pillowcase on the side of her cheek. She looked adorable and younger than her thirty-two years of age.

"Don't apologize. Naps are healthy."

She passed a careless hand through her hair. "I put Claire in the crib and she only stirred a little. Maybe she'll sleep for another hour."

Damian closed the lid on the laptop, and grabbed his phone. "We need to discuss a few things and I'm going to take some notes."

She sat up straight. "Are we trading information then? Maybe I should write it down too."

"What information?"

"Our ages, birthdays, family members, work history." She shrugged. "Things people know about each other when they're about to get married."

"That's not a bad idea, actually." Damian opened a new document and typed what Gabriela had said. "I'll make a form and add it to a Google Drive. Then we both can add to it and access it when we need to know a detail."

She frowned. "A shared document? Isn't that a bit much?"

"It's pretty easy to set up and maintain. Remind me to show you later." He made a note to himself as well. "The first thing we need to talk about is the wedding. How many days do you need to plan a small wedding?"

"What about an elopement?"

Damian looked up from his note-taking. "You don't want a wedding?"

"The more I think about it, the less it makes sense to plan a wedding, however small. First, our time is limited. Second, I can't have my family attend."

"Why not?"

"Because they'll know we're hiding something. And I'm not talking about my parents and siblings only. My cousins, my aunts and uncles, my grandparents. Everybody will want to come and if we don't invite all of them, they'll be deeply offended. You didn't stay for Filipe's wedding last year, or you'd know what I mean."

"I had a glimpse." A very brief one, but he remembered lots of people. "Are you sure you don't want to invite your immediate family?"

Gabriela shook her head. "I'd rather we have a quick ceremony at the civil registry office. It'll be easier to ask for their forgiveness after this is done than have to explain why we're doing it."

"Shouldn't you at least call your parents and let them know before the news goes public?"

"I'll think about it." She didn't look convinced.

Damian put down the phone and relaxed against the back of the sofa. "You cousin is going to kill me when he finds out."

"You mean Filipe? Matias might react more. He's the oldest of the Romano cousins and takes his role as protector very seriously."

"Then I'll have two of your cousins after me," he teased. "But seriously, I think it's great that you have a family that cares." He missed that at times, if missing what he'd never had was possible.

"You don't have any brothers or sisters?" Gabriela asked.

"None. My mom separated from my dad after she discovered his infidelity. They divorced when I was ten years old." By then, he hadn't been surprised. He and mom had been living with his Vaughn grandparents for a few years.

"No cousins either?"

He shook his head. "Dad is an only child. Mom had an older brother but he died when he was five."

"Oh, that's sad."

"It's just me and mom and Grandma Vaughn. Grandpa died when I was twenty. Dad lives in San Francisco." It was the kind of arrangement that suited everyone.

"I can't even imagine having such a small family.

My dad is son number five out of seven sons and there are eighteen of us first cousins."

"That is a big family." What would that be like, to have so many people in his immediate and extended family?

"What kind of living arrangements will we have? You live in New York, right?"

"Yes, I live in New York." Damian squirmed, anticipating her reaction to the next bit of news. "And I'm afraid we'll have to share a bed."

LISBON, PORTUGAL
TWO DAYS LATER

Gabriela held Claire upright in her arms as they stood by the double doors looking out. The city shone bright in the late afternoon sun, the buildings and red-tiled roofs cascading down to the river in a parade of colors with the water as background. This was her city in a new way, from a hotel she'd never before visited, lending a perspective she'd never imagined.

They had arrived at the hotel from Faial just before lunch, and after changing, feeding and putting down for a nap a cranky Claire—who definitely didn't like flying—Gabriela ate a quick meal alone in their suite. Damian and Luke had left to procure the licenses and put the finishing touches on the rest of the paperwork.

77

Two bedrooms comprised the large suite, one to the left with a queen bed and large ensuite bathroom, and another to the right with a single bed and a crib, and smaller bathroom. In the center, a living room with a dining area occupied the center, along with French doors to a wide balcony. Despite Damian's suggestion she should take the master bedroom, Gabriela insisted on taking the single bed to stay close to Claire. Luke had a bedroom down the hall on the same floor.

From any room, the twelfth-floor suite commanded a striking view of Lisbon and Gabriela drank it in. How long would it be before she'd return? So much could change in one year.

So much had changed in less than a week.

"What do you see, little Claire? Such a big world, isn't it," she said to the baby in Portuguese.

Gabriela had taken to talking in her native language when no one else was around her and Claire, then reverting to English in Damian and Luke's presence. This beautiful blue-eyed baby would soon legally be hers and, at times, Gabriela could hardly believe the turn her life had taken. Did she even deserve this gift?

She knew Luke still had reservations about her request to adopt Claire, but Damian hadn't even asked her why. If he wondered about her motives, he'd kept it to himself. What if he asked?

How could Gabriela begin to explain her most heartfelt wish within her grasp? How could she tell of the sorrow and depression she'd felt after her surgery, and the hope Damian had unwittingly given her with his unexpected proposal?

Accepting a contractual marriage offer from a near-stranger was not a sign of desperation but rather a sound investment, a partnership to benefit them both. As complicated and far-fetching Damian's reasons were, Gabriela's were more self-serving than his—he wanted to keep his image intact for the benefit of his company, while she would be paid handsomely for a year and become a mother.

After extending his proposal, he'd asked her to think about it, and she had, of course, but being presented with the opportunity she most craved in life hadn't taken too much thinking.

Being the oldest in her family, and the oldest girl among her cousins, came with expectations. She had thought of marriage and children, but when the chances didn't come, she'd thrown herself into her career, pretending she had plans for neither, watching her younger cousins find love, get married, and have their own babies.

She'd been telling herself her time would come, that her dream of a husband and children would still happen, but then this medical disaster had swept all that hope way—the excruciating pain, the hemorrhage, the doctors telling her she had a tumor in her ovaries that needed immediate surgery.

All the dreams gone.

Damian had said she was like a miracle to him and Claire, but he was as much heaven sent for her. He'd brought back the dream of having a husband and child.

Gabriela had accepted him and his proposal, even as she had the impression he'd expected a different answer.

There had to be much worse things than being married to Damian Vaughn for a year. He was attractive, kind, and intelligent. As long as she kept her cool mind and sensible reasoning, she had nothing to lose.

Except her heart.

She had to guard it at all costs. It would be far too easy to fall in love with the handsome American.

A knock sounded at the door, immediately followed by the click of the electronic lock.

Gabriela turned and walked over as Damian entered the suite.

"Hey, look who's up. How is she feeling after her nap?" he asked.

"Much better, thank goodness."

He wore dark gray trousers and a striped button shirt in a matching color. The tie was already loosened and the sleeves pulled back to the elbows, as if he'd run out of patience before the end of the day. Well-dressed men, while enjoyable to look at, didn't usually stir pangs of attraction in her chest. But this one certainly did. Was it her heart giving her mind permission to enjoy the view, knowing she'd soon have a legal claim to the man?

How was that for hypocrisy? They'd added a no-sexual-benefits clause to their marriage contract at her suggestion and here she was, ogling Damian with clear intent. He'd only be hers on paper—nothing more. She'd do well to remember that often.

She crossed the room and sat down on an upholstered chair, propping Claire on her lap, as a makeshift distraction to dissipate any lingering discomfort between them.

"How was your day?" she asked.

Damian sat at the end of the sofa. "Very productive. What do you think of tomorrow at three PM for the appointment?"

"Which appointment?"

He rubbed the back of his neck. "The signing of the marriage certificate at the civil registry office."

"Oh," she said. That appointment.

"Luke says we should be in and out in less than fifteen minutes and then we go to the American Embassy. I figured after lunch would give time for Claire to eat and nap, and reduce the chance of crankiness. What do you think?"

"I think it's a great idea." A surge of worry ramped up inside her. What would she wear? Not a wedding dress, obviously, but she still wanted to look nice. "Can I ask what you plan to wear tomorrow?"

He lifted an eyebrow. "My dark blue suit is the nicest I brought. Will that be okay with you?"

"I'll need to make a trip to my apartment tonight and pack some clothes." If the light blue dress she'd worn to Filipe's wedding still fit her, it would have to work. She didn't have time to go shopping to find something nicer.

"Do you want some help? I can ask Luke to watch Claire."

"No, I'll be okay. Actually, I want to go as late as possible so I can avoid seeing my neighbors." Some of them would still peek through the peepholes, but at least she wouldn't have to interact with them.

"I'll have Luke drive you then," he said. "How did it go with your boss?"

She winced and shook her head. "Not pretty. He wanted me to come in to sign papers, but I called HR and they said it's not necessary." After sending an email to her boss resigning her position, he'd tried to call her repeatedly. Thank goodness for caller ID and call screening. "He has a hard time accepting no." As much as she hadn't wanted to leave the company like this, who knew what she would be doing a year from now?

It surprised how relieved she was, how she didn't feel more upset about leaving a career she'd dedicated so many years to build. That alone should tell her how unfulfilled she'd been.

"What about your family? Did you talk to any of them?"

"I talked to my mom and dad yesterday, but I didn't tell them I was coming back to Lisbon." She hadn't decided when to tell them she'd married after the fact. Maybe showing them their first grandchild would ease the announcement of her elopement. "Did you tell your mother?"

Damian chuckled. "No. And since she's staying in Millbrook at the moment, she won't even realize I'm turning my home office into a nursery."

He lived in a brownstone building in Manhattan. As he'd told Gabriela, his mother occupied half of the second floor and he had the third to himself, soon to be shared with her and Claire. Three adults and a baby under the same roof—how would that turn out?

Damian reached into his pocket and retrieved a small velvet box then scooted closer. "I should have done this in Faial, right after you accepted my offer, but I wasn't able to buy one there, and I apologize for that."

He opened the box. It was a ring. He had an engagement ring for her.

All at once, her heartbeat sped up and her temperature climbed. "This is a surprise," she finally managed to say. "I didn't expect it."

He shrugged and looked at the ring before looking at her again. "Well, we are engaged, soon to be married. It's tradition, and I don't want people speculating why I didn't give you one."

He wasn't doing it for her. Of course not. They had an image to keep up, a role to play. With Damian, everything was done by the book, as she was learning.

Gabriela held on to Claire with both hands. "It's really big, Damian. A simpler ring would have been enough."

"Somehow, I knew that about you and that's why I chose a round solitaire." He took the ring out of the box. "But I had to at least get a three-carat stone or my mom and grandmother will be wondering why I skimped."

After a brief hesitation, he reached for her left hand and Gabriela adjusted Claire on her lap, then extended her fingers to him.

He slipped it slowly down her finger, his skin leaving a trail of goosebumps that trotted up her hand and arm.

Goodness. She was definitely feeling extra sensitive today.

"It's a little loose," he said, still holding on to her hand. "We can have it adjusted after tomorrow. And if you don't like it, we can exchange it for something else."

"No, no," she hurried on to say. "Of course I like it. It's beautiful." From what little she knew about diamonds, she could recognize the high quality.

"It just needs to fit a little better."

"I never thought—" She paused, afraid she'd say too much and let the anxiety spill all her hopes and dreams. It was all happening according to plan, and all too fast. Instead of talking, she swallowed a wave of emotion and composed herself.

Damian shifted back. "Gabriela, if you're having second thoughts, it's not too late to cancel everything."

He'd misinterpreted her hesitation. Of course she wanted this. All of this. It frightened her how much she wanted to marry this man and be a mother to his baby.

Would he change his mind if he knew her secret, the real reason why she was marrying him?

"No second thoughts," she said. "I just wanted to thank you."

"I'm the one who should thank you." He smiled and moved toward her again. "Can I give you a hug?"

She nodded and lifted an arm, the other still firmly around Claire's middle. Damian approached and set his arms around her, awkwardly and stiffly at first, as if he didn't know how to go about it. Before he had the chance to pull away, Gabriela reached her free arm behind his back, removing the remaining distance.

At the same time his breathing relaxed, his embrace tightened around her and his face settled in the space by her neck and shoulder, turning the gesture from uncomfortable to intimate.

With her face resting on his chest, Gabriela closed her eyes and inhaled. He smelled so good. And he was warm and solid and real. She trembled and Damian pressed closer to her.

Her poor heart danced in her chest, filled with a warmth that was new, consuming, and terrifying.

A sound of protest rose from in between them, just in time to remind Gabriela of how much was at stake if she lost her heart.

She moved back. "Oh, little Claire, I'm sorry." She held up the baby against her shoulder, giving her more breathing room.

Damian chuckled and stood. "Someone doesn't like sandwich hugs. Or maybe it's just my hugs she doesn't like."

Not Gabriela.

It had taken only one hug from him to know she could easily be hopelessly addicted to having his arms around her.

CHAPTER FIVE

$\mathcal{A}$fter a busy morning of shopping, mostly for Claire, Gabriela fed the baby and put her down for a nap.

As traffic in Lisbon was always an unknown variant, Damian had asked her to be ready at two-thirty so they could arrive on time.

This was happening. Today was the day.

In just a few hours, she'd be married to Damian Vaughn.

The flutters in her stomach—those weren't pre-wedding jitters but rather the fear of messing up everything, especially her marriage. Could she last a year married to him? Could she survive after that year was over and they parted ways?

Gabriela was a Romano and the Romano family had a long line of happily married couples—her grandparents, her parents, and five of her cousins had found love, the forever kind that rallied through bad times and thrived in the good. She and Damian hadn't even kissed.

And here she was, with a contract marriage, a modern-day marriage of convenience where the word love had not been uttered a single time by either of them.

A knock sounded at the door and she rushed to open it before Claire woke.

It was one of the hotel pages delivering the flowers she'd ordered earlier from a local florist. A corsage of white, cream and pale pink roses with a matching boutonniere for Damian and a delicate headband for Claire. As Gabriela would be holding the baby, she'd opted for a corsage instead of a bouquet so her hands would be free.

An indulgence, but just because she wasn't marrying for love didn't mean she couldn't have flowers on her wedding day.

Her light blue dress hung behind the bedroom door. She'd sent it to the hotel's laundry service for a rush cleaning and they'd already returned it. It fit a little looser than last year, but nothing a good-quality padded bra couldn't fix.

At a children's boutique in downtown Lisbon, Gabriela had found a tiny, light blue dress with pintucks and piping in dark blue, which would coordinate with hers and Damian's outfits.

Was she going too far with the little details? They might not matter for a ceremony that would not last more than ten minutes. Nonetheless, Gabriela wanted photos to mark the event. One day, her memory might fail her and those photographs would be everything she had of the one time she got married.

After a quick shower, she styled her hair in loose waves with a borrowed curling iron from the hotel. Lately, she mostly wore her hair in a pony tail or a low bun, lacking the energy and interest to do more with it. But today was different and she wanted to look her best.

Her makeup skills were out of practice after so many days not going out, and she opted for a clean, fresh look instead of something more dramatic. She finished, putting on a pair of sweats and a T-shirt just as Claire woke up. Gabriela started the usual routine of changing, feeding, and burping the baby. After dressing herself and Claire, she placed the baby in the car seat and tucked a large bib around her that pretty much covered the entire blue dress. Claire sometimes spit up a little during car rides and Gabriela didn't want any stains on the beautiful outfit.

By the time Damian knocked at the door a few minutes earlier than he'd said, she was ready.

She opened the door and smiled. "Hi, Damian."

"Hey, Gabriela. I came a little earlier to help with Claire."

How could a simple tailored suit look so good on him? The dark blue contrasted with the crisp white shirt and the silver silk tie. "You look great. That's a good color on you."

"Thank you." He did a once over on her. "Is that the same dress you wore to Filipe's wedding?"

He'd seen her the one time and he remembered?

Gabriela winced. "I'm sorry. I didn't have the time to find anything else. When you said you'd be wearing your dark blue suit, I thought this dress would go well next to it." He still hadn't said anything. "I only wore it the one time."

"I love that dress on you," he finally said, a soft smile pulling at the corner of his lips.

Her posture relaxed at his words and she returned his, despite the tell-tale hot cheeks letting her know she'd blushed again.

"Hang on. I got us all something." She retrieved the flowers from the small fridge under the sideboard. "I won't put Claire's headband on her until we get there."

She approached with the three clear boxes and placed them on the table. "I hope you don't mind. I got us matching flowers," she said. "May I?" She removed the boutonniere and the pin.

Damian watched her with a curious expression. "I'm glad you thought about it. It didn't even cross my mind."

She stepped closer to him, but even in her heels, she couldn't get the right angle to pin the flowers to his lapel. "Do you mind taking a seat here?" She motioned to the closest chair. "I want to make it sure I get it right."

Damian took the chair and sat up straight, his head tilted slightly to the right. Gabriela held his left lapel with one hand while she placed the boutonniere and the pin next to the fabric.

When her hand brushed the front of his shirt, it trembled and she fumbled with the pin. "Sorry. It's not as easy as it looks."

Being in such close proximity to Damian didn't help either. The hug they'd shared the day before kept coming to her mind—like yesterday, the heat of his body, his scent. He wore the best after-shave, or cologne, or whatever it was. Tantalizing.

When he looked her way and locked his eyes on her, a flare of attraction zinged between them. If he would place his hands on her waist and bring her closer, she could bend down and kiss him—

Gabriela straightened the flowers and smoothed his lapel. "There. All done." She added a wobbly smile to her words, the image of that imaginary kiss still strong in her mind.

What was wrong with her? Cheeks flaming, hands shaking, skin prickling—all for this man. How was she going to stay away from him and keep her part of the contract for a whole year?

She turned away, intent of pinning on her own corsage, but before she'd even opened the box, Damian stood in front of her and took it from her hands.

"My turn." His voice didn't sound quite right. Gabriela didn't even trust hers to mutter a thanks, but stood stiffly as he leaned forward and began the first of several attempts to get the flowers on straight.

"You're right. This isn't easy."

She shook her head in agreement. "No, it isn't."

Nothing about this contractual marriage would be. She was in for twelve heart-pounding and ultimately heart-wrenching months. Surely she'd lost her mind. Or was losing it this very moment, the closer Damian's face came to hers.

His expression was adorable—some mix of frustrated concentration and… She couldn't quite put her finger on it. His breathing was deep and purposed, as if he was struggling to control it. Her own was barely coming, catching every other second as she inhaled his cologne.

As soon as he was done pinning it, the corsage drooped, and they both laughed at it, relieving the tension that had built between them just moments prior.

"After all that work," Damian said. "It looks very lopsided."

She chuckled again. "Don't worry about it. I appreciate your efforts." It comforted her to know that she could laugh with this man who didn't take himself too seriously in such a situation. If they could laugh together through the next year, she might just survive.

Claire had yet to utter a peep and Gabriela checked on her. "Let's get going before Claire decides she's had too much of the car seat."

He came beside her and gripped the handle of the car seat. "I'll take her. Luke should be waiting for us at the garage."

Gabriela grabbed the diaper bag, her purse, and

Claire's flowers, then followed behind him, clicking the door shut.

Hopefully, he hadn't noticed the way she flustered around him. She'd have no words to explain that.

Luke waited for them by a large black Mercedes SUV with heavily tinted windows. He opened the door for Gabriela while Damian installed Claire's car seat.

"You look beautiful, Gabriela," Luke said. "Ready for this?"

"Thanks, Luke," she replied. "Let's hope so."

The Portuguese driver had obvious experience and delivered them to the front of the Civil Registrar's building where they exited and quickly entered through the main doors. Luke guided them to the right office and, before entering, Damian handed him the car seat.

"Give me a minute, please," Gabriela said.

She retrieved Claire's headband, slipped it on her little head as quickly as possible, and removed the bib.

Both men looked at the baby.

"How appropriate," Luke said. "She matches both of you."

Damian looked between Claire and Gabriela, his expression unreadable. Why did she second-guess every decision she made, wondering if she had his approval? Would he tell her if he didn't like it?

Before she could spend any more time thinking about it, Damian took her free hand and tugged at it.

"Have you changed your mind?" he asked, his gaze unwavering.

She returned the direct look. "No. Have you?"

"No." His lips twitched with a small smile and he laced his fingers through hers, then gave her hand a squeeze. "Let's get married."

Whatever Damian had expected when he'd taken to Luke's suggestion of asking Gabriela to marry him, this was not it.

Not the knot in his stomach, not the beautiful woman beside him.

Certainly not the swirl of emotion and uncertainty while the confident assurance confirmed he was doing the best thing he could positively do.

The contradictions astounded him.

After talking to his Portuguese solicitor friend, Luke stood to the side, with Claire sleeping in the car seat at his feet and the diaper bag on the floor, and the biggest smile on his face, as if he were the matchmaker instead of the counseling attorney.

Luke had secured a small private room where they could have the ceremony without the curious eyes of accidental onlookers and the occasional paparazzi. And as the officiator knew English, even if with an accent, he'd be speaking in both languages, much to Damian's relief. As good as his Portuguese was, getting married was much too important to lose anything in translation.

The officiator started by requesting Damian's and Gabriela's identifications and making note of them.

"Welcome," the man said. He extended his hand and shook theirs in turn before continuing. "My name is Manuel dos Santos. We are gathered today to bring about the union of Damian Walter Vaughn and Gabriela Adelina da Silva Romano. Serving as witnesses, we have Pedro Manuel Oliveira Carvalho and Luke Daniel Blackbourne. If anyone present knows of any impediment to this union, please declare it now."

Damian's chest tightened. At his side, Gabriela remained calm, still holding his hand as if it were something she did every day. He glanced at her and she smiled at him, radiating confidence and poise.

The officiator looked around and waited for a full moment and, when no one intervened to stop them, he went on with explaining the rights and duties of the groom and bride according to the published civil code.

"Please face each other," the officiator said.

Damian turned to Gabriela and reached for both her hands. Her brown eyes calmed him and he relaxed his shoulders, then gave his whole attention to the proceedings.

"Damian, do you accept Gabriela as your wife? Please repeat, it is of my own free will that I marry Gabriela Adelina da Silva Romano."

His own free will. The simple, emphatic words touched Damian more deeply than he'd expected.

"It is of my own free will that I marry Gabriela Adelina da Silva Romano."

"Gabriela, do you accept Damian as your husband?"

Gabriela smiled at him, her gaze warm and firm. "It is of my own free will that I marry Damian Walter Vaughn," she stated clearly.

The man nodded with an air of satisfaction. "In the name of the law and of the Portuguese Republic, I declare Damian Walter Vaughn and Gabriela Adelina da Silva Romano united in marriage."

Gabriela and Damian both exhaled at the same time and they chuckled.

The officiator gestured at Damian. "Go on, kiss your new wife."

Damian quickly moved his hands to Gabriela's upper arms and leaned in her direction, planting his lips on hers as briefly as he could.

"Kind of shy, are we?" The officiator gave Damian a curious look then peeked over the front of the desk at baby Claire, his brows raised. "Or at least in public. Come now, Mr. Vaughn, you can do better than that. You're married now. It's perfectly acceptable to kiss your wife. I daresay she will expect it of you often. Now try again."

Beside them Luke coughed into his hand in a poor attempt at trying to contain a laugh.

Feeling sheepish at such a scolding, Damian met Gabriela's gaze. Her face was pink with embarrassment, but she didn't look away and instead tilted her face up bravely, in invitation, her brown eyes hopeful.

Well, then.

This time Damian approached Gabriela with intent. He wrapped his arms around her back, anchoring her to him, and she brought hers around his neck with no hesitation. Their lips met with purpose and softness, their mouths fitting together at the right angle and depth and, for a split second, he forgot where he was. Her skin, her taste, her scent.

He could do this all day.

But not here, not now. When Gabriela moved a fraction to inhale, his hands slid away from her back. She wavered on her feet, as if momentarily unstable. Damian gripped her elbow and leaned in to whisper in her ear. "You okay?"

She nodded, looking dazed and a bit unsure. When his hand founds hers, she clung on to his fingers.

Maybe the kiss had affected her as much as it had him. He wouldn't be forgetting it any time soon.

"Fast learner," the officiator muttered.

Gabriela blushed and nodded, as she tucked her hair behind her ear.

"Before we proceed to the signatures, you may exchange weddings bands and vows at this moment."

Gabriela's eyes widened, mimicking his.

Maybe Luke should have given them the heads up about the vows.

Luke stepped up, holding Claire in his arms—when had he picked her up from the car seat?—and passed the wedding bands Damian had bought yesterday to each one of them.

After a moment of mental scrambling, Damian opted for simplicity and sincerity. "Gabriela, I promise to respect you, appreciate you, and always be the friend you need through our journey together."

Not love. He couldn't promise her that. But friendship and respect he could.

After his words, he slid the band on top of her engagement ring, then rubbed the skin on her finger.

She took a deep breath. "I promise to listen to you, support you, and be the friend you deserve through our journey together."

She certainly recovered quickly. To anyone who didn't know better, it sounded like they'd written their vows together and with intent.

There they stood afterwards, watching each other, holding each other's hands, their new gold bands glinting in the ambient light.

They'd done it. They were married.

"Those were beautiful vows," the officiator said, smiling. "Love is not enough without respect, appreciation, and true friendship. I have no doubt you two will be successful in your marriage. Congratulations."

All too quickly, they signed the paperwork, then posed for pictures as a new couple with Luke's friend holding up a phone in front of them. After a few moments, Luke handed Claire to Gabriela and stood beside Damian for more photos, followed by a final group one where the officiator and Luke's friend joined in, taken by a young clerk Damian had failed to notice before.

Relief and concern warred inside Damian as the fleeting panic of momentary doubt swelled unchecked. But as Gabriela slipped her free hand into his, all his worries abated, replacing his confusing feelings with a calm assurance.

Luke herded them back into the posh SUV and they made their way to the American Embassy, where they signed more paperwork and posed for pictures again.

And just like that, Damian had a family, not only a daughter but also a wife. They depended on him and he was responsible for them.

As they stepped out into the hallway, Luke clasped Damian's hand and brought him in for a hug. "Congratulations, Mr. and Mrs. Vaughn," he said enthusiastically. "I'm happy for you, man."

Damian raised an eyebrow at Luke's words. What did he mean? Had he forgotten this was not a regular marriage? Damian and Gabriela were not in love.

Luke approached Gabriela and kissed her on the cheeks in the Portuguese fashion. "Welcome to the family, Gabriela."

"Thanks, Luke," she said, still holding Claire in her arms.

When they arrived back at the hotel, the driver parked in the underground garage, near the elevator. Luke didn't enter with them.

"You guys go on ahead," he said. "I'm going to make sure we got everything in place to start the adoption. Go rest, take care of that cutie, and be ready at eight tonight."

"What's going on at eight?" Damian asked.

"I made reservations for you two at one of the roof's private patios here at the hotel. Dinner for two. I'll be back to watch the cutie."

Typical Luke, always with a surprise up his sleeve.

"That's so nice of you, Luke," Gabriela said. "Thank you."

"Luke, why did you—" Damian started.

"Don't even thank me. It's my gift for the newly-married couple."

"We don't need—"

Luke leaned in his direction and lowered his voice. "Yes, you do, Damian. You and Gabriela need to talk and spend time alone as a couple. Now don't argue."

He wouldn't. Maybe Luke was right. What did Damian know? Too bad nobody today had handed him the manual for Marriages of Convenience in the Twenty-First Century. He truly had no clue what he was doing.

Once in their suite, Gabriela took the diaper bag from him. "I'm going to change Claire and feed her."

"Anything I can help with?"

"I got it, thanks.

She walked over to the bedroom, talking to the baby in Portuguese with a smile in her voice.

"Gabriela," he called.

She stopped and turned around.

Thank you for marrying me.

Thank you for being a mother to Claire.

Damian walked over, rested a hand on her shoulder, and leaned in to kiss her on the cheek. "Thank you, Gabriela." He stepped back.

She hesitated briefly, then smiled. As she opened her mouth to say something, Claire started crying and Gabriela quickly ducked into the room with an apologetic expression.

He removed his suit coat and draped it over the back of a chair. Then his tie came off, and his cuff links. Next he called his secretary in Manhattan and asked for updates on the redecoration to turn his home office into a nursery and in his bedroom to accommodate an extra person. She assured him all would be ready before he returned.

In two days time, they'd be flying to New York. He and Gabriela and Claire, with Luke accompanying them. After two weeks in Faial and three days in Lisbon, it was time to return to regular life. One thing was sure—it would never be the same as before, with all the recent changes.

He'd be sharing his bedroom with Gabriela and Claire's nursery was right next door. Was it normal to be nervous about it? He'd always had his bedroom to himself, the privilege of an only child. He'd be sharing the bed as well. Husbands and wives slept together, after all. What with his mother and the household staff living in the brownstone as well, it would be impossible to make other arrangements without them noticing. That was something he didn't want to have to explain to anyone.

101

His phone rang and he reached for it, looking at the screen for the caller's name.

It was mom.

Damian suppressed a groan. She'd always had the most uncanny timing but if he didn't take the call now, she'd keep trying until he did.

He swiped to answer. "Mom. How are you?"

"Damian, I haven't heard from you in a while. Are you still in Faial?"

"I'm in Lisbon at the moment."

"For how much longer? When are you returning?"

"The day after tomorrow. I should be home right after lunch."

"Wonderful. I'm returning the same day in the early evening. Will you have dinner with me or do you have plans?"

"Nothing planned. I'll be home that night." And all the nights after for a long time. He was a family man now.

"Excellent. I'll call Mrs. Harrison and ask her to make your favorite."

Lobster rolls. "Sounds great. Thank you." He paused to gather courage. "Listen, mom. I have a surprise. Actually, two surprises."

"Ooh, surprises," she said excitedly. "Will I like them?"

Damian chuckled lightly, hoping she wouldn't catch his uneasy tone. "Well, I can't return them, so I hope you will."

"I can't wait to see those surprises."

Would she feel the same when she found out what the surprises were?

After another minute of mom trying to guess, they said good bye and hung up.

Damian blew out a breath, relieved the phone call was over. He loved his mom, but her extrovert personality was too much for him at times.

How was she going to react to the news? The last time she saw him he was single; now he returned with a wife and baby.

Luke knocked at the door of the hotel suite at seven forty wearing a pair of sweat pants and old T-shirt.

Damian let him inside. "Dressed for the job, I see."

"Bring it on, little Claire, I'm ready," Luke said in an overly dramatic tone.

"She's actually asleep, so pipe it down."

Gabriela joined them. "If she wakes up, I left a list of what-to-do instructions." She and Luke spent a few minutes discussing the baby's habits.

Luke folded the paper and slipped it into his pocket. "I'll follow the instructions. Don't worry. You guys better get going so you don't lose your reservation."

When Damian and Gabriela arrived at the rooftop terrace, the sun still hovered above the horizon. The colors bounced off the buildings and roof tiles, casting an orange shade in the air.

After taking his name, the hostess guided them to a private alcove decorated with twinkling lights and potted lemon trees in the corners. The table was set for two and soft piano sounds emanated from hidden speakers.

He held the chair for Gabriela as she sat down.

"This is so nice," she said looking around the space.

Damian went around the table and took the seat across from her. "It really is. I've stayed in this hotel before, but didn't know they had these alcoves here."

After they ordered the appetizers and entrées, a waiter brought a bottle of champagne and filled their flutes. "For your celebration, sir."

Damian thanked him then wrapped his fingers on the stem. "It's been quite the day, Gabriela. I'm not eloquent and I never know what to say in situations like this. I mean, not that I've been married before." He chuckled lightly, unable to shake the nerves.

Gabriela smiled at him and rubbed an absent finger on the base of the glass. "I don't know about that. I think you did really well with your vows. Quick thinking on your part."

"You did too," he said.

"I just followed your lead."

He met her eyes. "I want you to know I meant what I said."

"So did I, Damian," she said softly. "The officiator is right. We won't make it through this marriage without respect and friendship, along with appreciation, support, and good listening skills. I hope we can both remember that."

Her genuine expression and sincere voice touched him and his heart pounded with an unnamed feeling.

Despite the evening breeze, his temperature rose.

"I can't promise I know what I'm doing, but I promise I'll always do my best. To us." He raised his glass.

Gabriela met him in the middle and touched her flute to his with a clear clink. "To us," she repeated.

After they took a sip of the champagne, Damian set down his glass and reached for her hand. The shape and weight of her fingers were becoming familiar to him and he liked the feeling of them. She gave his hand a squeeze and then they resumed their meal.

As the evening slowly turned darker, the strings of lights overhead brightened their alcove while still keeping the intimate setting and relaxed atmosphere. They talked about their time at the island and of Claire and, eventually, the subject of families came up.

"My mother called today but I didn't tell her I got married," Damian said.

Gabriela leaned toward him. "It sounds like you understand why I didn't want to tell my family."

"Yeah, I do. I'm sorry for pushing you. This is not a subject you can just drop on them."

She looked at her plate and played with the fork. "I have a feeling my family won't react too well."

"We can't blame them, can we? You're leaving everything you know—your apartment, your job, your city." He paused. "Your family and your country." Despite already knowing this, saying it out loud in a list brought the reality of what Gabriela was leaving behind much more in focus for him. She was giving up everything for him and Claire.

She raised an eyebrow, a small smile tugging at her lips. "I hadn't thought of it that way, but you're right."

"How does it make you feel?"

"I would be lying if I said I'm not nervous at all the new and unknown things I'll have to face. But I'm also excited and looking forward to it."

So was he.

After their plates were cleared, a different waiter approached with two plates of dessert. "With the compliments of the house."

"Ooh, such a pretty cake," Gabriela said. "What kind is it?"

"Wedding cake, ma'am."

Gabriela looked up from the cake to Damian and grinned. "They gave us wedding cake."

"So they did." He smiled as well, and archived the information for later, how a simple slice of cake made her happy. "Let's take a picture before the cake is gone." He swiped at the screen and got the camera ready, then asked the waiter to do it for them.

Damian moved his chair closer to Gabriela and, after sitting down, wrapped an arm around her shoulders. She leaned closer to him and grabbed his free hand in hers. For a moment, the urge to kiss her reared up unexpectedly. He wouldn't, of course, but nonetheless struggled with the decision until the waiter had finished taking their picture.

Despite his plans to the contrary, he was attracted to Gabriela.

How was he going to live with her and keep the truth to himself?

CHAPTER SIX

After an exhausting flight from Lisbon to New York with a very unhappy Claire, Gabriela exited the town car onto the sidewalk of a street with a row of identical brownish red brick buildings.

Luke had parted with them at the airport, promising to come by tomorrow. To give them time to settle in, he'd said. He probably meant to give them privacy and time for her to meet Damian's mother. Despite his assurance she had nothing to fear, she did have some apprehension about it.

Gabriela put those thoughts aside for now. Damian had told her his mother wouldn't arrive until later today, and that was fine by her. The time to decompress and rest would be welcome. She shouldered the diaper bag and her purse while Damian came around to grab the car seat with Claire.

109

"She's finally asleep," he said with a soft expression.

Gabriela peeked at the sleeping baby under the canopy. "Now that I need her awake to change and feed."

"She might wake up when we move inside," Damian said. He turned to the building and gestured with his free hand. "This is it. Home, sweet home. Welcome home, Gabriela." He cocked his head to the side with a playful expression. "I know it's tradition for the groom to carry the bride over the threshold—"

Gabriela shook her head. "I don't think so. Just carry the baby and you'll be fine."

He chuckled. "As long as the record shows I offered."

"The record shows I'm not interested in anything until I take a shower."

Damian had already moved toward the stairs leading to the large, ornate front door.

"What about the luggage?" she asked, climbing the stairs behind him.

"James will bring it up to our bedroom."

Sure enough, the driver had returned to the car and was now pulling it in to the garage at the street level.

Before Damian had the chance to unlock the door, it opened from inside and an older woman appeared with a smile.

"Mr. Vaughn," she said, "so good to have you back. Welcome, sir."

"Thank you, Mrs. Harrison. It's good to be back."

"And your brought friends with you," Mrs. Harrison said, looking between the car seat in Damian's hand and Gabriela, her expression pleasant but also curious.

Damian waited until Gabriela joined him at the door, then touched the hollow of her back with his free hand and they entered together through the wide door.

As unassuming as the exterior had been, she was not prepared for the grandeur inside. The foyer opened up to a curved staircase that disappeared into the second floor. Marble floors and polished walnut reflected the bouncing light from a massive crystal chandelier, and the effect both elegant and impressive. Gabriela caught herself with her mouth open, and she closed it just in time.

"This is my new family, Mrs. Harrison," Damian announced with a wide grin. "My wife Gabriela and my daughter Claire."

From his attitude and expression, he played the role of newly-married family man with surprising conviction. Gabriela could learn a thing or two from his enthusiasm.

Despite the obvious shock, Mrs. Harrison recovered quickly. "How wonderful. Congratulations to all, Mr. Vaughn."

"Thank you. Gabriela, this is Mrs. Harrison, our housekeeper. She runs this house and we couldn't do without her."

"Pleased to meet you," Gabriela said, hoping that was appropriate.

"You as well, Mrs. Vaughn."

That would take some getting used to, being addressed as Mrs. Vaughn.

Damian gently set the car seat on the floor. "Mrs. Harrison, will you send us a light meal in about thirty minutes?"

"Yes, of course," Mrs. Harrison replied. "Let me go see if everything's ready upstairs."

After she left, Gabriela tipped her head up to admire the chandelier and the ceiling medallion. "Why didn't you tell me your brownstone is actually an urban mansion, Damian? I figured you had some money, but this house—"

"Is not really mine. My Vaughn grandparents passed it to my dad, and my mother got it in the divorce. It'll be mine one day since I'm her sole beneficiary. At first I stayed so she wouldn't be alone, and then I got used to it. I never had a reason to get my own place until now." He paused to watch her. "I know I didn't say it before, but if living here doesn't work out, I'll get a new place just for us."

"Let's give it a chance first. I just got here." She looked around again. "And this place looks so big," she said with a hint of too much awe.

Damian nodded. "I'll give you a tour later."

A small whimper came from the car seat and Gabriela knelt on the marble floor. "Look who's awake." She pulled the canopy back, took Claire out, and stood with the baby in her arms.

Damian held the little hand and smiled. "Welcome home, little Claire."

Claire grinned at Damian.

"Someone's happy to see you," Gabriela said to Damian.

"She's probably happier to be out of the car seat. Come on, let's get you two settled in."

Gabriela looked up at the staircase. "Which floor did you say we're on?" Any other day, she wouldn't mind climbing the stairs, but today was not it.

He chuckled. "We're on the third floor. Come this way."

He walked past the staircase and Gabriela followed him to find a small lift tucked in the corner. "Oh, thank goodness," she said with a relieved sigh.

Damian pushed the door open when they arrived. "There's a guest bedroom to the front where I had part of my home office moved to," he said gesturing to his right. "The bathroom for this floor is next to it. To this side is our suite, with its own full-bath, a small laundry room, and closets. Originally, it had a sitting room in the back, which I later turned into my home office, and now it's Claire's nursery."

They walked through the rooms as he talked about them, passing the beautiful bedroom with tall ceilings and decorated in neutral tones, and ending in the nursery.

Gabriela stopped at the door and her eyes widened. "This is the prettiest room I've ever seen."

113

The walls were painted a soft white and the classic wood furniture complimented the rest of the room. A fluffy, gray rug had been positioned on the floor between the upholstered chair and the crib, and the bedding in tones of pink and gray tied everything together. Board books and simple, classic toys adorned the shelves.

"You like it then?" Damian asked, leaning against the door jamb.

"I love it. When did you have this done?"

"My secretary found a decorator and they got started on it the day we married." He gestured at the changing table. "I had them stock diapers and wipes and a few other essentials." He gestured toward a monitor sitting on a shelf. "The baby monitor is wide range and will work throughout the house."

"Did you hear that, Claire?" She grinned at the baby. "Let's get you changed."

Gabriela changed the baby's diaper and then walked to Damian's bedroom, the one she'd be sharing with him. The bedroom, the bed, and everything else. To her, it still felt as if she were living in an alternate reality where she now existed as a wife and mother. Would the feeling ever fade?

After changing Claire into clean clothes and feeding her a bottle, Gabriela was ready to unpack and take a shower. She sat on an upholstered chair with the baby on her lap and looked around. Tall ceiling, light gray walls, a huge bed with a tufted headboard. It was simple and elegant, and almost too neutral.

Had Damian asked the decorator for an update in here as well? Any personal touches that might point to Damian's likes were conspicuously absent. Or maybe he didn't want her to infer his character from his personal objects.

He appeared at the door. "Let me take Claire so you can go take a shower."

Gabriela raised an eyebrow. "Do I look that bad?"

"Just a bit tired." He approached and took the baby from her. "This little girl didn't let you sleep on the flight."

"She didn't sleep much either," Gabriela said. "I'm surprised she's not ready for a nap yet." She stood and covered a yawn with her hand. "A shower sounds wonderful. Thank you."

After Damian left with Claire, Gabriela spent the next twenty minutes unpacking hers and the baby's suitcases, only to realize Claire needed a new wardrobe already. The little dear was growing too fast and a shopping trip was not only a good idea, but also a necessity.

In the bathroom, she found a soaking bath tub and a shower with a glass enclosure. Well, there could be no use of the bathroom while Damian took a shower. Or vice-versa. She'd have to talk to him about that to avoid any awkward situations.

As much as she longed for a relaxing bath, she bypassed the tub and took a quick shower instead. Next to a stack of towels, she found two white bath robes hanging on hooks, the fluffy kind that felt too good to pass up. With her hair wrapped in a towel, and her body cocooned in terry-cloth heaven, Gabriela sat on the bed and looked at the time on her phone. Could she afford a thirty-minute nap? Damian's mother was coming later, probably in the evening, or even after dinner. That would give Gabriela plenty of time for a short nap.

She passed a hand on the white pillow case, ironed just the way she liked it. What side of the bed did Damian take? Maybe he wouldn't mind if she took the side closest to the nursery, so she could hear better when Claire needed her. Before she changed her mind, she took her phone and set a timer for thirty minutes. It would be enough.

A few minutes later, a voice called out her name.

"Gabriela, time to wake up," Damian said.

She kept her eyes closed. "Five more minutes, please."

"Are you sure? My mom should be here in a half hour or less and I thought you might want to get dressed."

She reached out her arm and pawed for her phone until she found, then cracked open an eye. It read two hours later. Not thirty minutes.

She sat up in bed and clutched the robe closed with her free hand. "I set the alarm for thirty minutes. Why didn't it go off?"

Damian stood by the door with Claire in his arms. "Maybe you didn't hear it. You were tired."

"I'm sorry. I didn't mean for you to watch Claire while I napped."

"Don't worry about it."

"Give me fifteen minutes."

Damian nodded. "We'll be in the nursery."

Seventeen minutes later, dressed in slacks and a short sleeve blouse that didn't look too wrinkled, with hair in a low ponytail, and minimal makeup, Gabriela found Damian on the rocking chair, reading a book to Claire, who seemed to be enjoying the activity.

He looked up. "That was fast."

"I already took too long doing nothing."

"Resting is not doing nothing." The corner of his mouth curved in a smile. "That was bad English, but you know what I mean."

She did know what he meant, but wasn't quite sure she agreed with him. There was so much to do and learn.

Gabriela knelt in front of him and Claire and held the baby's hand. "What about this little lady? Has she been good?"

"As long as I'm holding her, she's been great. She hasn't taken a nap yet, so I'm hoping she'll sleep well tonight."

Gabriela stood and reached out her arms. "Can I hold her, please?" As ridiculous as it sounded, she'd missed the little one.

Damian handed her the baby and rose. "When my mother arrives, will you give us a few minutes alone so I can break in the news to her?"

That was a good idea. "Yes, of course. Where do you want me to be?"

"Just stay here. I'll come and get you." He moved toward the door but then turned back. "With my mom's return, we'll have to—" he stopped, as if looking for words. "She's going to see us together and assume we're normal newlyweds." A swath of color tinted his neck and he rubbed at it.

"You mean newlyweds in love," Gabriela said, guessing at his discomfort. "The kind who can't take their hands off each other."

This would be interesting, pretending to be in love with her new husband.

He nodded. "Maybe not that much. She knows I'm not a fan of PDA."

She frowned. "PDA?"

"Public display of affection. Kissing and touching in front of others."

"So, you don't want us to kiss in front of people?"

"Yes. No. I mean, sometimes we'll have to."

Have to? Did he find kissing her that repulsive? Gabriela swallowed the emotion that threatened to rise and choke her. She picked up a board book from the bookshelf and settled Claire on her lap. "I'll just follow your lead."

She certainly wouldn't be doing anything that led him to believe she was forcing him.

Damian's shoulders relaxed. "That's a great idea. Let's do that." His phone pinged and he got it from his pocket. "She's pulling up to the garage."

Before Gabriela had the time to say anything, he left and she heard him descending the staircase at a clipped pace.

For a few minutes, she focused on reading the book to Claire about farm animals, adding the different animal sounds as she told the story. She kept her voice steady, hoping she wouldn't hear Damian talking to his mother.

But those two little words wouldn't leave her mind—have to. He wouldn't kiss her unless he had to.

Not to worry, Damian Vaughn. She wouldn't be kissing him either.

When the sound of voices up the stairs finally registered with Gabriela, her first instinct was to jump and hide. Instead, she forced herself to remain seated, Claire against her with one arm and the book in her free hand. Calm. Serene. Approachable. Ready to face her new mother-in-law.

Up until now, even though they'd been in public since getting married, only Luke knew of their marriage. Reality had not fully set in.

Meeting Mrs. Vaughn was about to change everything.

Gabriela rose and reshelved the small book. She readjusted Claire in her arms and waited.

A set of quick steps approached first, high heels clacking on the wood floor, followed by Damian's steps, not as rushed, but firm as he always was.

Mrs. Vaughn entered the room and stopped short. She had to be in her mid- to late-fifties but wore a timeless elegance that made her look younger. Brown hair in a smooth bob. Expertly applied makeup. After an attentive look, the Portuguese features were there; her late parents were from the islands even though she'd been born in America.

Damian came in around his mother and walked over to Gabriela with a smile on his face. "Mom, this is Gabriela, my wife. And our daughter, Claire." He put his arm over her shoulders.

"My goodness, Damian," she finally spoke. "A wife and a baby. Just like that."

"I told you. Gabriela and I met last year."

Not a lie, but not the complete truth either.

She glanced around the room and then back at him. "You had your office redone into a nursery while I was in Millbrook."

He nodded.

"You're thirty-five years old and I'd begun to believe this would never happen. But you did it." She kept staring. "You married a Portuguese woman and you brought her baby too."

"Claire is our baby, not just Gabriela's," Damian said.

For a man who had plans to let Gabriela keep Claire at the end of their marriage contract, he sure staked his claim to her rather quickly.

Gabriela passed Claire to Damian and extended her hand to her new mother-in-law. "So nice to meet you, Mrs. Vaughn."

"Please, call me Linda. My dad wanted to name me

Deolinda after his mother, but my mother insisted on an American name, so they shortened it to Linda."

Linda Vaughn took Gabriela by the shoulders and leaned in for an air-kiss on each cheek. "I still remember my Portuguese greeting manners. My parents would be so proud. May they rest in peace." She did a quick sign of the cross.

The gesture brought a small smile to Gabriela's lips, reminding her of so many women in her own family who would have done the same thing and with the same words.

"And sweet baby Claire," Linda said as she approached Damian. "Can I hold her, please?"

"Of course." Damian handed Claire to his mother and the baby promptly started crying.

"What's the matter, little Claire?" Linda bounced Claire gently. "You don't know Grandma yet, but I know we'll be great friends."

Claire cried harder.

"I'm sorry," Gabriela said. "She's tired from the plane trip but hasn't taken a nap yet."

The more tired she was, the crankier she became.

Linda cooed at Claire over the sound of the baby's cries. "Some babies are just a little more high maintenance, aren't they? That's okay, sweetie. We love you just as much."

She passed the baby to Gabriela and when Gabriela held Claire up to her shoulder and rocked sideways in a soothing motion, the baby relaxed and gradually stopped crying.

Damian and his mother watched.

"Awe, she's a mommy's girl," Linda said with a smile.

"She likes Damian too," Gabriela added, still swinging Claire who wasn't completely asleep yet. Why did Gabriela feel guilty when Claire preferred her over Damian?

"Come on, mom," Damian said. "Let's go talk in the library while Gabriela puts Claire down for a nap."

The nap didn't come without some effort on Gabriela's part but Claire finally relented. Gabriela placed her in the crib and held her breath. After a few minutes with a stir from Claire, she grabbed the monitor and descended the stairs to join Damian and his mother.

She found them not in the library but in a dining room large enough and grand enough for a dinner party that might include her entire family. From the conversation, she gathered on the menu tonight was one of Damian's favorite dishes, lobster pieces on toasted bread, like some sort of warm sandwich.

By the time they finished eating, Claire's protesting sounded from the monitor.

Gabriela stood. "Thank you so much for dinner, Linda. It was delicious."

"I only plated it, but you're welcome all the same."

Damian came around and kissed his mother's cheek. "Thanks, mom. We'll talk more tomorrow."

Linda rose and hugged Damian. "It's good to have you back."

She then did the same to Gabriela. "And I'm so glad to have you in the family. I'm looking forward to getting to know you."

Gabriela smiled. "Thank you, Linda. You've been so kind." What a surprise Linda had turned out to be.

Before Damian suggested they take the staircase, Gabriela walked to the elevator, too tired to climb two flights of stairs when each floor was a length and a half taller than regular modern floors. As beautiful as the staircase was, it had been a long day.

They stopped at the entrance to their bedroom and waited for another sound from Claire. Gabriela turned down the monitor, now that she was closer.

"Your mother is not like I expected her to be," she said in a low voice. "You two are so different."

Damian turned to her and raised an eyebrow. "What do you mean?"

"She's an extrovert. So warm and welcoming. You're—" She hesitated for a moment before continuing. "You're so guarded. I never know what you're thinking."

Damian turned to watch her and she returned the look. "What?"

He cleared his throat. "Maybe I could say the same about you," he replied. His eyes dipped to her mouth once, twice.

Her cheeks heated and her breath quickened. She teetered on the balls of her feet and her chest tightened with a quick feeling that seared inside her. Everything in her clamored to be pulled to him.

But she held her ground, waiting for his next move, clasping the monitor in her hands until her knuckles stung.

After a lingering, electric moment between them, Damian took a step back from her. "Good night, Gabriela. I'll take Claire when she wakes up at two in the morning." Then he turned around and left toward the ensuite bathroom.

In her crib, Claire whined again, this time louder.

Welcome to married life and twenty-four-seven parenting.

Between Claire's poor sleeping and his hyperawareness of Gabriela sharing his bed, Damian's first night at home didn't go well.

The sound of her breathing, the scent of her skin, the heat of her body at the opposite side of the mattress—any little movement caused him to hold his breath and keep his body still, waiting for something he wouldn't admit to himself even in the dark of night.

Why had he thought he would be fine with Gabriela in his bed? After all, they didn't love each other, and had married only for mutual convenience. Two adults could behave and keep their word and their part of the contract. Easy as that.

But he was a man who had convinced himself for many years that he was better off without the complications of love and the entanglements of physical intimacy—until Gabriela Romano came along in his life.

The more he knew her, the more attracted he was to her—to her warm, brown eyes and the way she smiled at him, to the way she treated Claire as if she'd given birth to her, the way she'd openly accepted his mother, the leap of faith she'd made in leaving her old life to embrace the new—every day he discovered something new about Gabriela, and the attraction mounted.

Having her in his bed, at the reach of his fingertips, was the kind of bittersweet agony he'd remember till the end of his days. What a fool he was.

Instead of torturing himself, Damian had let Claire provide the perfect distraction and he'd risen out of bed to change and feed her through the night. Better than taking a cold shower and risk waking Gabriela and his mother. That would be an awkward explanation.

He'd be suffering the repercussions all day, already more tired at seven in the morning that he could remember being in a long time.

It was Saturday morning and they always gave the weekends off to Mrs. Harrison and James. It would be a quiet two days with only mom, Gabriela, and Claire. Maybe he could take them for a drive to show Lower Manhattan to Gabriela. Maybe they could stop at Central Park, if the weather was nice and Claire in a good mood.

In the kitchen, mom sat at the round table with the newspaper spread out on the surface. "You're up early," she said.

Damian brushed a quick kiss on her forehead. "Not really. I usually get up earlier than this on weekdays." He walked to the coffee maker and poured himself a mug of it.

"You do, but it's the weekend, and you have a new wife and a baby who kept you up most of the night."

"Oh, you heard that?" He pulled out the chair on the other side. "I didn't mean to wake you up. Sorry."

"You know I sleep light. Always have." She took a sip from her cup. "Maybe I can help next time. How would Gabriela feel about that? It would give you two more uninterrupted time together." She waggled her eyebrows.

"Mom, please," Damian said in reply, anxious to put a stop to her suggestive hints. "I'll check with Gabriela later."

"You'll check what with me later?" Gabriela asked as she entered the kitchen with Claire in her arms. "Good morning," she added.

She was dressed in skinny jeans and a simple top, her hair held back at the nape, and slippers on her feet. The dark semi-circles under her eyes belied her fresh appearance. Had Claire kept her up as well? Or did she have other reasons for sleeping poorly?

His mom sprang up from her chair with a wide grin. "Good morning, sweetie pie," she said to Claire. "Morning, Gabriela. Did you sleep well?"

"Yes, thank you. The bed is very comfortable."

Claire smiled back and mom cooed at her. "You're so cute, yes, you are."

Damian observed the exchange. "That's her saving grace, being so cute and adorable. She sure is a terrible sleeper." He stood, got a clean mug from the cupboard, and filled it with coffee for Gabriela.

"Would you like to hold her?" Gabriela asked.

"Gladly," mom said taking Claire into her arms. She continued the baby-talk in a sing-song voice. "Don't listen to him, sweetie. Your daddy holds the record for being a terrible sleeper."

"She's already been fed and changed." Gabriela took a sip and grimaced.

"Sorry, it's American coffee," Damian said. "We'll get a cappuccino machine."

Mom turned her attention from Claire and looked between him and Gabriela. "You two don't have to hold back on my account."

"Hold back what?" Gabriela asked.

"Hold back from hugging and kissing in the morning. I remember being a newlywed, you know." She winked.

As far as he was concerned, that was tantamount to permission.

"In that case…" Damian approached Gabriela, took the cup from her hand and set it down, then pulled her to him, wrapping his arms behind her back and waist.

She kept her eyes on him and he on hers, as if pulled to each other by an inevitable magnet. Slowly, her hands trailed a path on his skin up his forearms.

At some point, mom had left the kitchen with Claire, and he couldn't even hear the duo anymore.

They hadn't even kissed yet and already he burned with longing for her.

"Good morning, wife," he said in a low voice.

Gabriela's eyes tracked his lips and her mouth parted.

He adjusted his stance and she looked up at him. "Good morning, husband," she said in the same low tone.

Bending, he nudged the side of her neck, and her hands clasped him harder.

He should kiss her already. A real, deep kiss, not a hurried peck.

Just then, the phone in his pocket rang and vibrated. Gabriela dropped her hands from him and he let her go, swallowing a sigh of frustration.

He looked at the screen. "It's Luke."

Gabriela stepped back. "I'll go join your mom."

Damian answered the phone. "Your timing is astounding."

Luke chuckled. "Did I interrupt a moment?"

"That kind of tone doesn't endear you to me," Damian replied.

"Is this before or after seeing the paper?"

"What paper?"

"The New York Times, page fifty-seven."

Damian walked to the table. "Well, look at this," he said. "The Times is already open to page fifty-seven. And it's the wedding announcements section." That's what mom had been reading until Claire had distracted her.

"You're welcome," Luke said.

At the top of the section, a black-and-white photo of him and Gabriela on their wedding day, one of the ones Luke had taken, followed by the usual announcement verbiage. Short and to the point. "How did you get this in the Times so fast?"

"I dated a girl who works at the Times and she knows a guy in the Weddings department," Luke replied. "Plus, you were in the top ten most eligible bachelors in the People Magazine two years ago. The elopement of Damian Vaughn is big news."

That silly list. He'd never asked to be included, but the company's marketing department had told him it made for positive publicity so he'd consented to the interview and photo op. Mom had thought it hilarious.

"I figured it will save you from having to repeat it all the time at work on Monday," Luke added.

He was right. "That's a good point," Damian said. The less he had to say about his elopement, the better.

"Damian, I had the most marvelous idea," Mom said as she reentered the kitchen, still holding Claire.

"Is that Linda?" Luke asked. "Tell her hi from me. I'll see you on Monday."

"Till Monday." Damian disconnected. "Luke says hi."

Mom looked askance. "He was there for your wedding, wasn't he? You eloped and invited your lawyer but not your mother."

She could be dramatic when she wanted.

Behind mom, Gabriela hid a smile.

"He was there to help with the paperwork, including the prenup."

She shrugged. "That's fine, really, because now I have the perfect excuse to plan a reception for you."

Gabriela's eyes widened.

"We appreciate the thought," Damian said, "but we're fine without a reception."

"I'm going to insist." Mom passed Claire back to Gabriela and pulled out her phone from her pocket. "It'll be my wedding present to you. Besides, you saw the announcement in the Times, didn't you?"

Damian nodded as she continued.

"I assume Luke sent it in since you never think of those details. But now all of New York knows you got married and they'll be wondering why I don't like my new daughter-in-law if I don't throw a party."

"Mom—"

She sat down and started scrolling through her calendar app. "What do you think? In one month? We'll have it in Millbrook."

"I don't think—"

"Is that too long from now?" She continued. "Maybe two weeks then. But I'll need help. I'll call

Joanne. I'm sure she'll be happy to help me plan."

She dialed a number and then left.

Damian leaned against the counter and crossed his arms. "So, what are you doing two weeks from today?" he asked Gabriela.

She chuckled. "Going to your mom's party with you."

Damian shook his head and smiled. "Well, in that case."

He'd been voted out.

Mom came back in, still holding her phone to her ear. "Damian, dear, you don't have any plans this afternoon, do you?" She didn't wait for his reply. "Will you take little Claire, please? I'm taking Gabriela shopping."

Before he had a chance to say anything, Claire was in his hands and Gabriela left with mom, who threaded her arm through Gabriela's elbow as if they'd been friends for years instead of just a day.

So much for his quiet weekend.

On Sunday, Mom went to her friend Joanne's for more party planning. If anyone could pull off a reception-like party in two weeks, it was that duo.

Damian started out the day with enough ideas on how to spend it with Gabriela and Claire but somehow ended up taking a nap with the baby. Gabriela unpacked the rest of her suitcases, did several loads of laundry, and organized Claire's closet first, then hers, spending most of the day at the ironing board, despite him telling her she could use the laundry service that came by twice a week.

By bedtime, Claire was asleep in her crib, as surprising as that was. Damian hung back in the guest bedroom with his laptop until he was sure Gabriela was already in bed.

It was awkward, the way they took turns and pretended to be at ease with each other as they went about their routines. How much longer until a sense of comfort and familiarity grew between them?

Damian found Gabriela reading in bed with her bedside table lamp on, legs bent and the book resting against her knees.

She wore the same pajamas as the day before, soft gray pants and a matching printed top with thin straps. As pajamas went, it was perfectly modest and appropriate. But the sight of her bare shoulders and creamy skin had him swallowing the knot in his throat.

When he entered, Gabriela sat up against the headboard and put down the book.

He went around the bed to his side and sat on the edge of the mattress with his back to her. "You can keep reading, Gabriela."

"I should get some sleep before Claire wakes." She slid her legs under the sheets.

The slight rustling sound raised the hairs at the back of his neck. Damian took a breath and closed his eyes.

"Are you okay there?"

Darn. She'd heard him.

"Yes, I'm okay." He pulled the sheets back and sat against the headboard as well. "Just trying some new relaxation techniques I read about." And now he was lying.

"May I turn off the light?" She asked.

"Go ahead."

She extended her hand and clicked off the lamp.

His eyes gradually adjusted to the ambient darkness, punctuated by the small glows of night lights in their bedroom, the nursery, the bathroom, and the hallway.

On the other side of the bed, Gabriela's shape remained seated. Should he wait to lay down until she did it? Where was the instructions book for situations like this? And when would they start feeling more comfortable when alone with each other?

"Are you going back to work tomorrow?" Her question broke the silence.

"Yes, I am."

He'd been away from the office for too long.

"Hope your day will go well," she said after a pause. "Goodnight."

She turned toward to the other side and lay down.

"Goodnight, Gabriela."

How was he supposed to fall asleep with her in his bed?

CHAPTER SEVEN

*W*hen Damian arrived at the Vaughn studio complex on Monday morning, the news had obviously spread. People went out of their way to shake his hand and congratulate him.

Mrs. Gold, his secretary for over ten years, had the Saturday Times strategically placed at the corner of her desk, which he couldn't miss seeing on the way to his office.

"Good morning, Mr. Vaughn," she said.

"It's good to see you, Mrs. Gold." He greeted her with a smile.

"I had some wild ideas when you asked me to find a decorator for a quick remodel, but I never guessed it meant a new wife and baby. You sure know how to keep a secret, Mr. Vaughn. Congratulations and best wishes, sir."

"Thank you, Mrs. Gold. I'll pass it along to Mrs. Vaughn." That still felt weird, saying Mrs.

Vaughn and not meaning his mother, but his new wife.

"It's good to have you back, Mr. Vaughn."

He placed a small wrapped gift on the desk. "I brought a new piece for your collection." Mrs. Gold collected fine crystal trinket boxes.

She reached for the gift, unwrapped it and pulled it out to admire it against the sunlight. "This one is especially fabulous. Thank you."

"You're welcome," Damian replied. "Please hold off all calls until after lunch." He pushed open his door and looked back at Mrs. Gold. "I'm expecting Luke Blackbourne, so please send him in when he arrives."

Although he'd kept up with emails and correspondence, he still had a long list of new ones clamoring for his attention. The script-writing team had sent a dozen new scripts for him to read and over fifty pitches. How was he going to find the time to get through all those?

Damian rubbed his neck as he went down the list and prioritized the items. Maybe it was time to promote a couple of the writers to directors and expand the writing team. He'd always believed in training and delegation, but now more than ever he had to put those principles to work.

A knock sounded at the door. Damian glanced at the clock to see two hours had passed already and he could hardly tell what he'd accomplished in that time.

Luke came in and closed the door behind him. "How does it feel to back at work after the hiatus?"

He crossed the room, sat on the leather sofa, and placed his briefcase on the floor beside it.

Damian came around the desk and sat opposite Luke. "Everything feels the same, and then I remember I have a wife and baby at home."

Luke reached in his briefcase. "I got something to help you remember better." He pulled out a rectangle and handed it over to Damian.

It was a hinged frame in the same wood tones as the rest of his office, with two five-by-seven photos—one of him and Gabriela on the steps of the American Embassy, and the other of them with Claire.

The corner of Damian's mouth rose. They did look good together. The way Gabriela had coordinated her dress and Claire's outfit to his navy suit made the three of them look like a cohesive unit, a little family meant to be together.

"We look good," Damian said. "Thank you." He stood and placed the frame on his desk where he could see it.

"I sent frames to Gabriela and your mother as well."

Damian resisted an eye roll. "Great. One more reason for my mom to say how thoughtful you are."

Luke chuckled lightly. "I try my best. I sent you an email with all the photos I took that day."

Damian sat back down. "And to Gabriela, I'm sure."

"Actually, in addition to the email, I also sent Gabriela print copies." He grinned.

"Only prints? No photo album?"

"Nah. I figured you can do that yourself and score some husband points."

"I'll keep that in mind." Maybe he would for their one month anniversary. Gabriela was the kind of woman who'd remember dates and occasions and, even though their marriage relationship was different from most, he was sure she'd appreciate the gesture.

"Do you have any updates on Elsie Barr?" Damian asked.

Luke's behavior instantly changed from playful to serious. "I do." He pulled out a folder from the brief-case and set it down on the coffee table between the sofas and upholstered chairs. "That's the detective's report. Paul Rogers was a bust. He lost contact with Elsie after moving to California. In fact, the detective notes that Paul didn't know of Elsie's passing and was saddened to hear the news."

Damian picked up the folder and scanned the report. "What's the plan now?"

"The detective is already in New Jersey investigating her professional life. Since she left over a year ago, it's harder to find people now who worked with her then, especially without giving a clue to the reason."

"I'm sure it is."

"Elsie Barr was also a very private person. She didn't socialize out of the office or go out with friends. Having no witnesses to her life just adds to the problem."

"So many questions," Damian said.

Luke nodded. "I'm beginning to think we might not get answers to most of them." He took out his phone and turned the screen to Damian. "I hired a company to monitor your public image. It's early still, but the response to the wedding announcement has been positive, and that includes comments on the family picture posted on the company's social media."

"That's a relief," Damian said. "It means the plan worked."

"You've received some invitations for interviews and photo ops with your new family. I recommend you accept the one from Forbes Magazine."

"Pass the details to Mrs. Gold."

"Already have." Luke stood. "Sorry. I have to go. I have an appointment on the other side of town."

"Keep me updated," Damian said as Luke left.

Damian tried to go back to reading one of the scripts, but his attention was elsewhere. Elsie Barr filled his thoughts. Luke was right—they might never have the answers to why she'd named Damian as Claire's father. Was he ready to accept that?

Damian's phone chirped with an incoming text and he swiped at the screen.

It was Gabriela.

Just thought you should know. Two of my cousins are coming over to see me.

Damian pushed the button to call her instead of replying. "Hey, I got your text. Who's coming?"

"Hey, Damian," she replied. "You didn't have to call." Her voice sounded out of breath.

139

His concern rose. "Are you all right?"

"Yes, I'm fine. Claire is napping so I took the stairs from the ground floor to our bedroom." She took a breath. "I much prefer the elevator."

Damian smiled, relieved to hear she didn't sound worried. "Tell me what's going on." He kept his voice casual.

After a short pause, she replied. "I'm sitting now. And Claire is still sleeping. I woke to an email from Filipe asking for my new phone number. He'd tried to text me and the texts had bounced. I emailed him back with the new number. Then a few minutes ago I got a text from him saying he and Matias are in New York and want to visit. So I gave him the address after asking Mrs. Harrison for it."

"They're both in New York?" Was that a coincidence or just a bit too convenient?

"I know," Gabriela said. "They made it sound like it happened, but they're not fooling me."

"They must have seen the announcement then," he said.

"Yes, I figured as much. I'm in for a family scolding, I'm sure."

Damian glanced at the time on the computer screen. "Do you know what time they're coming?"

"When Filipe texted they had just landed and still had to go through customs and pick the rental car. I'm guessing an hour or two? How bad is traffic from the airport to here?"

"Depends on which airport they're at." If Damian left right now, he could make it home before Gabriela's cousins. "I'm coming home."

"You don't have to, Damian. That's not the reason why I sent the text."

"I know I don't have to, but I want to." He didn't know what her cousins intended to say or do but he should be there to support her.

"What about your work there?" she asked.

"I'm only catching up on stuff. I can do it later. I'll see you in a few."

"I'll be here," she replied.

It actually took more than a few minutes. A late-morning drive from Queens to Manhattan was an adventure on most days, but especially on Mondays at lunchtime.

When Damian arrived, he parked in the garage, leaving the driveway free for Gabriela's cousins.

He climbed the stairs from the basement to the kitchen and asked Mrs. Harrison to prepare a light lunch for four.

Then he sent Gabriela a text. I'm home.

I'm in the library, came her reply.

This time, he took the elevator and found Gabriela at the desk with the baby monitor right beside her.

"Is Claire still napping?" He asked.

Gabriela stood. "She'll be waking up soon, I'm sure."

"And my mother?"

"She left right after you did to meet with her friend for more party-planning."

"She's taking this party too seriously." Damian removed his suit jacket and draped it over the back of the desk chair, then loosened his tie and rolled his sleeves back.

Just then, the doorbell rang and the monitor crackled with a sound from Claire.

Damian and Gabriela chuckled.

"Why don't you go meet your cousins? I'll get Claire."

They parted ways at the landing and he bolted up the stairs then made his way to the nursery where Claire was beginning to show her displeasure for being alone when she woke.

As much as he'd envisioned his first day back at work to be spent at the office, he didn't regret the decision to come home early. The studio was a well-oiled machine, and it ran smoothly in his absence. He'd made sure of that in the past few years since taking over.

At home, he had responsibilities now, and Gabriela and Claire needed him.

By the time Gabriela descended the stairs, Mrs. Harrison had let the cousins inside.

"Filipe. Matias," she called.

They stood by the staircase and looked up when they heard her.

"Olá, cousin," Matias said.

They both smiled at her and greeted her with

air-kisses and hugs. Gabriela relaxed and returned the greetings.

Despite her calm behavior and words with Damian, she'd been worried about her cousins' arrival and their reactions to her. If they intended to rail at her, they had plans to do it in private.

"Gabriela, it's good to see you," Filipe said. "You look really good."

"Thank you. I recovered well and my health is much better." She motioned for them to follow her up the stairs. "Come on, let's talk in the library. The front parlor looks like a museum."

As beautiful as it was, that room was not one of her favorites in the house.

"This place is amazing," Matias said. "Does Damian Vaughn own it?"

"Technically his mother does, but it will be his one day." Whether Damian had plans to stay or go else-where, she didn't know. By then, she wouldn't be in his life anymore. Her heart squeezed and she turned her thoughts to something else.

When they arrived in the library, she sat on the upholstered love-seat and Filipe and Matias took the sofa opposite her.

Matias took the lead, as she'd known he would. "I think you know why we're here," he started.

Gabriela nodded. "I do. Are my parents mad at me?"

"I wouldn't say mad," Filipe replied. "More like disappointed. You're their oldest daughter and you chose to elope instead of inviting the family to the wedding."

A wave of emotion rose in her chest and Gabriela took a deep breath, fighting the tears. "I didn't mean to hurt their feelings. Or anyone else's in the family."

"Your parents just want to understand what happened," Matias said. "As do we. Are you alright? Why did you get married so fast and didn't tell anyone? You barely know him."

"We had to learn from an announcement in an American newspaper, like the rest of the world," Filipe added.

She should have guessed they read the New York Times.

"Is anyone in the family under the impression I was forced to marry Damian? That I'm here against my will?"

"We just want to know if you're happy, Gabriela," Matias said.

She sighed. "I don't even know if I should be angry or flattered that you two offered to come check on me."

"You parents want to know when you're coming back."

"Hello, everyone," Damian said as he entered the library with Claire in his arms.

Her new husband had impeccable timing, saving her from questions she didn't want to answer, didn't even have an answer to.

Gabriela rose from the seat and he walked straight

to her. He kissed her on the lips, an intentional kiss just a notch above a peck, brief and sweet and much too perfect.

"I missed you," he murmured, loud enough for her cousins to hear his words.

She hadn't expected that. Her cheeks instantly flamed and she took Claire from Damian, to shift the focus of the situation and to distract herself. The way her heart beat so strongly, for sure they'd be able to hear it.

She shifted to English, for Damian's benefit. "How's my little sweetie doing?"

Claire grinned at her and Gabriela's mood instantly lifted. She lived for those sweet smiles.

"She's changed and fed and ready to meet some family," Damian said.

Was that a wink? What did it mean? Had he noticed her reaction to his kiss?

Damian turned to Matias and extended his hand. "Hi, I'm Damian Vaughn. You're Matias, the oldest Romano cousin."

Matias returned the greeting. "I see Gabriela has informed you well about the family dynamics."

"She did, but I also remember seeing you at Filipe's wedding last year," Damian said. "I'm glad you two were able to visit."

Filipe stood and shook hands with Damian. "Damian," he said, his tone with a hint of a warning more than a greeting. "I send my cousin to your resort and you marry her? How did that happen?"

"The gate to our yard was left unlocked and open one day, and Gabriela ventured in, thinking it was part of the resort. I saw her and…"

"I saw him," Gabriela corrected, jumping in to continue the story. "Damian thought it was his garden that enticed me, but really, it was him." She tilted her head up to smile at him and he smiled back.

She sat down and settled Claire on her lap. She held the baby's hand and waved at the cousins. "Say hello to Filipe and Matias." Maybe that would diffuse the tension that had sprung up among the men.

Damian immediately joined her, sitting as close as he could and draping his arm on her shoulders with a natural ease that once again impressed her. Maybe he'd missed his true calling and should have been an actor. From his actions and words, even she was beginning to believe their marriage was one of love. He was so convincing.

But no, it was all part of the charade. Maybe she'd ask Luke for a copy of the marriage contract and keep it where she could read it often. She could use the reminder.

Like she'd hoped, Matias and Filipe turned their attention to Claire and even did some baby talk. It was easier for men to notice babies once they became fathers.

"Who does the baby belong to?" Matias asked.

"Claire is ours," Damian replied. "We adopted her."

With the new adoption papers, Claire's birth certificate had both their names as the parents.

"She's ours," Gabriela repeated with a smile, unable to keep the happiness from showing on her face. However this marriage with Damian turned out, she was Claire's mother forever and that was worth everything.

She leaned into Damian's side and he tightened his arm around her, then kissed the side of her head with a sweetness that twisted her heart. The two of them with Claire made the picture of a perfect family, a picture her cousins would report back to her family.

The wall phone rang and Damian rose to take it. "Thank you, Mrs. Harrison," he said then hung up. "Lunch is ready. Will you join us, please?" He asked Matias and Filipe.

The cousins nodded.

"We'll stay. Thank you." Matias said. "After lunch, will you join us in a video call to Gabriela's family? Her parents are anxious to see her."

Knowing her parents, they probably had called anyone in the family who was in town and now waited by the computer.

Damian joined her again, this time with a hand on her back. "That's a great idea." He turned to her. "I bet they'd love to see Claire too. She's their first grandchild, right?"

He now rubbed gentle circles on her back and the heat of his fingers through her thin blouse was much too distracting. "She is," she managed to reply.

After a delicious lunch of shrimp salad with toasted bread and seasonal fruit, they returned to the library where Damian set up the laptop for the video call. The large screen would work better than using a phone or tablet. Matias called a number and relayed the information for Damian's account and, at last, the connection was made.

Damian pulled out the chair for Gabriela and she sat, holding Claire at the same level as her face.

At once, several faces appeared on the screen, everyone talking in Portuguese. Her sister sat at the front, with her parents behind and her brother in the background.

"Gabriela," her sister said first. "There you are. Oh, look at the cute baby."

"Hello, everyone!" Gabriela replied.

Greetings back and forth took the next moment, a bit chaotic as everyone talked at the same time.

Off camera, Damian smiled as he could see the screen and her family trying to fit on the other side.

"Those are my parents, Pedro and Adelina, my sister Juliana and my brother Alexandre."

Gabriela took a breath, holding the tears back. It had been a while since she'd been to Porto to see her family, and she'd missed them more than she thought.

"Who are you talking to? Is it true you're married?" Juliana asked.

Gabriela grabbed Damian's forearm and pulled him down. "This is my husband Damian Vaughn and our baby Claire. We've adopted her."

He smiled and waved and greeted her family with a Portuguese olá.

On the other side, they all gasped at the same time.

Her mother covered her mouth. "It's true," she said, her voice trembling with emotion. "You got married and you have a baby."

"It's true, mãe," Gabriela confirmed, her own emotion catching her voice. "I did get married and have a baby. Isn't Claire so adorable? She's three months old."

"Oh, she's so cute," Juliana said.

They all agreed with her, cooed and made baby noises at the screen.

"How do we know he's really your husband, Gabriela?" Alexandre teased. "He could be some guy you grabbed from the street."

Juliana turned back and swatted his arm.

"Matias and Filipe are here, remember?" Gabriela said. Her cousins said hi off screen. "They can confirm Damian's my husband."

"It's true," Filipe said. "They're married."

"Prove it," Alexandre said. "Kiss him already."

"How old are you? Twenty-two or twelve?" Gabriela said.

Her parents and Juliana smiled but remained silent, and Alexandre would view that as a win for his cause.

Before she could tell her family the kiss wasn't happening, Damian leaned her way, took her face in his hands, and kissed her.

This man. His kisses.

They rendered her speechless.

Were they getting better or was she beginning to crave them more?

When he pulled apart and smiled, Juliana clapped, but Alexandre wasn't as easily impressed. "That doesn't count," he said. "No tongue."

This time it was mom who turned around to swat him.

Claire started fussing and Gabriela took one of her little hands and waved at the screen. "Say xau, Claire. Xau-xau." She handed the baby to Damian who left the room to entertain her.

Gabriela spent the next ten minutes answering her family's questions and at last said good-bye with promises of sending pictures and coming for a visit before Claire turned six-months.

She turned to Filipe and Matias. "Thank you for making that possible. It was fun to see them and talk to them. How long are you two staying in New York?"

"Luciana and her husband are home for a couple of weeks before she has to travel for a job, so we're going to see her tomorrow and leave the next day," Matias said.

"That's right, Luciana lives north of here, doesn't she? How far of a drive?"

Filipe pulled out his phone. "About two hours, depending on traffic."

"I should go visit when she's back," Gabriela said. She hadn't seen her cousin Luciana since Filipe's wedding. "Do you have her contact?"

"We do," Matias replied. "We also have a private

group on Facebook that Vanessa, Catarina and Jacinta started for all the family. Can we add you?"

"Yes, please do. I'd love to see what everybody's up to." She stood. "How about a tour of the house?"

An hour later, after showing her cousins all the floors and rooms, and catching up with them, Damian joined them in the foyer, with the baby monitor firmly in his hand. He wound his arm around her and rested his free hand on her hip.

As simple as the gesture was, it also claimed a kind of intimacy and possession that needed no words. Not between them and not to those around them.

She's mine, it said. *We are together.*

Her awareness spiked and a shiver ran up her arms. Gabriela willed her breathing to calm. She had no doubt Damian knew exactly what he was doing. The gesture was deliberate.

When it was time for good-byes, Damian dropped his arm from her and she immediately missed the weight of his hand.

Gabriela hugged Matias and Filipe, one at a time. "Thank you for coming. It was so great to spend time with you and to see my family."

"I'm glad we made the trip," Matias said.

"I'll be better at staying in contact," Gabriela promised.

"Good," said Filipe. "We'll hold you to it." He turned to Damian to shake his hand. "Thank you for having us, Damian. Congratulations on your new family. I hope you appreciate how lucky you are."

"I do," came Damian's firm reply. "Believe me, I do."

His conviction sounded sincere. Did he mean it?

Matias stepped forward and shook Damian's hand. "Welcome to the Romano family."

Gabriela descended the outdoor steps onto the sidewalk with them and waved as they pulled away in their rental car.

Damian waited for her to return inside and then closed the door.

"That was fun," he said. "I'm glad they came to see you."

"I am too. It was great seeing my family as well." Her tone came out more wistful than she'd intended.

She made for the staircase, but Damian took her wrist. "Gabriela, we can plan a trip to Porto whenever you want to. You're not trapped here in Manhattan."

Her eyes glanced at the spot where he touched her. He loosened his fingers and rubbed her skin as he let go, setting a chain of goose bumps in the wake of his touch.

"I think I'd like to go visit when Claire is a little older. It'll give her time to settle into a routine and for her system to grow. I read in a parenting book that babies are less prone to spitting up and being fussy by the time they're six months old."

Damian nodded. "Whatever you think is best."

Gabriela spent the rest of the day with Claire, part of it in the courtyard garden at the back of the ground floor. In the shade of the building, they sat in a swing, surrounded by the fragrance of flowers in mature bushes and spilling out of containers. At the back, a wall fountain trickled its relaxing sounds and enveloped the ambiance in its own cocoon of a quiet paradise. Hard to believe one of the largest cities in the country existed outside these walls.

She didn't see much of Damian until later, when they prepared for bed. In the four days since coming to the Vaughn Residence, as it was named, she and Damian had developed a routine of sorts, taking turns getting ready for bed. He kept a stack of non-fiction books from which he liked to read and Gabriela read her books on parenting on an e-reader instead.

Tonight was not much different. Gabriela sat in bed against the headboard and looked at Damian. He'd fallen asleep reading, and she took the book from his hands and set it on her bedside table. Claire would be due for a change and a bottle in an hour and Gabriela should rest until she heard her through the monitor, but sleep wouldn't come.

The events of the day kept playing in her mind— her cousins' visit, the video chat with her family, introducing Damian and Claire to them.

She'd be lying to herself if she said she didn't miss them. Her family, her cousins, her aunts and uncles and grandparents. Their get-togethers and family dinners, and especially the memories she had of her childhood summers spent with all of them. After moving from Porto, the distance had placed more space between her and them.

Her life in Lisbon, the life she led before going to Faial, was a million years ago. She no longer was that career woman who lived for her job; she especially wasn't the woman who'd arrived at Hydrangea Manor recovering from a complete hysterectomy, with her spirit broken and her heart shattered with the knowledge she'd never be able to get pregnant.

That Gabriela was a person of the past. The new Gabriela had a husband sleeping in the same bed and a baby girl in the next room. Despite knowing she'd never give up her new life, she couldn't help but wonder how well she fit in with Damian's.

There was one more thing keeping her awake—the way Damian had kissed her.

How was she to put that out of her mind?

CHAPTER EIGHT

In the next few days, Damian and Gabriela settled into somewhat of a normal routine. Every morning, just as he got ready to leave early to the studio in Queens, he'd peek in the nursery to see Gabriela on the rocking chair, still in her pajamas, feeding a half-asleep Claire. He'd wave at her and she'd smile back, hands full of baby and bottle.

That image stayed with him throughout the day, a domestic, cozy vignette that arose an emotion within him he never thought he'd have. Glancing at the frame Luke had brought with the picture of Damian and Gabriela only exacerbated those feelings, and sometimes he wondered how he got any work done.

In the evening, Damian and Gabriela had dinner together, sometimes with Mom, but mostly the two of them with Claire in the baby bouncer, who happily observed as long as she had Gabriela in her line of view.

How had he filled his hours outside of work before Claire and Gabriela had come along? Not yet married a month and already he couldn't remember how it used to be. He'd adjusted to married life so much quicker and better than he could have predicted.

The day after the Romano cousins visited, Gabriela seemed more subdued and pensive. Did she miss her family? Or, was it possible she might be thinking about the way he'd kissed her? It was almost all he could think of.

In all honesty, Damian had taken advantage of both situations to kiss her, hoping she'd confront him about it after Matias and Filipe left. But she hadn't brought it up—not the kissing and not why he'd done it.

Although those kisses had not been intimate and passion-filled, he knew her well enough to see the emotion they'd spurred in her. Gabriela wasn't immune to him, even if she pretended to be, and at least now he knew the attraction was mutual.

What to do with that knowledge was a different story.

On Friday, at the office, Damian's concentration teetered on the brink of useless. He'd asked Mrs. Gold to reschedule a meeting for Monday hoping he'd come back recharged and relaxed after the weekend.

"Mr. Vaughn," Mrs. Gold said through the intercom, "Mrs. Vaughn is on line two." After a short pause she said, "Your grandmother."

Damian winced. Nanna Vaughn. She had his cell number but she preferred the land line during office hours. He hadn't visited her, hadn't even called, and was now due for a scolding, which he totally deserved.

He picked up the phone and answered in his upbeat voice. "Nanna, what a nice surprise."

"I'm surprised you still remember your old Nanna. I had to learn of your elopement through my friend Muriel who read the announcement in the Times before I did. Imagine my surprise to find out my only grandson got married and has a child." She sniffled. "Good thing I'm well trained and recovered quickly. Muriel didn't even suspect a thing. Then your mother shows up with an event planner for a party happening next week without checking with me first. Fortunately, there's nothing on the calendar for that day. What do you have to say for yourself, Damian?"

"I'm sorry, Nanna," he replied in his most contrite tone. "I should have come to see you when I returned, or at least called. It's been so busy with getting back to work, and helping Gabriela adjust to life in Manhattan. And then the baby is still not sleeping through the night—"

"However valid those reasons are," she interrupted, "they don't excuse your behavior."

"You're right. They don't."

"I'm busy this weekend, hosting the New York Chapter of the Jane Austen Society. Muriel wanted to have it at her house but Highland Park is much better suited for it." She sighed dramatically. "Come early next week, on Thursday night. That will give your new wife and child the chance to get settled before the party, and we can spend some time getting to know each other on Friday. And don't say you have to work. You're the CEO of Vaughn Family Movie Channel and you can take a day off for family."

"It sounds like a great plan, Nanna," he replied sincerely. "We'll be there Thursday evening and stay until Sunday. I think Gabriela will love it there."

"Is that how you say your wife's name?" Nanna asked.

"Yes, Gabriela," Damian repeated. "And the baby's name is Claire."

"I'm looking forward to meeting them, Damian."

"Thank you for inviting us to come early, Nanna. I can't wait to be there and introduce my family to you."

After saying goodbye and hanging up, Damian remained in his chair. Spending three days in Highland Park would be heavenly. He'd always loved the estate and grounds, and the change of pace and scenery would be a welcome break for him and Gabriela.

His cell phone rang and vibrated on the desktop. Another Mrs. Vaughn; his mother, this time.

"Hey, Mom. How are you?"

"Damian, do you know you've been home with Gabriela for a week?"

"You're right. It's been a week already."

"You two are newlyweds and you haven't spent any time together," she continued.

"We do spend—"

"I know you have a young baby," Mom interrupted, "but you need to make time for each other."

"We absolutely should. I'll talk to Gabriela when I get home,"

"You don't need to. I already did," she said brightly. "As it happens, I'm free tonight and it'll be a treat to spend the evening with my granddaughter. I told Gabriela to dress up because you're taking her out for dinner."

"That sounds great, Mom, but I haven't made reservations to anywhere we'd need to dress up, and it's very last minute to get any."

"Actually, you have reservations to *Chez Pierre*." Her voice rose with excitement.

"How did you manage that? Chez Pierre has a standing wait list of three months."

"You can thank me later, Damian. Just be home by five to get ready and take your wife out for a night in the city."

Before he could thank her, she hung up.

As soon as he placed the phone on the desk top, it rang again. He glanced at the caller ID, ready to let the call go to voice-mail, but then smiled. The third Mrs. Vaughn—the one he'd been thinking of all day.

"Gabriela, hi. Is everything okay?" He sat back in his chair.

"Damian, I'm sorry to be calling you at work."

The corners of his mouth stretched in a smile when he heard her voice. Her accent was usually stronger when she talked fast or was nervous.

"Don't apologize. You can call me anytime. What's going on?"

"Linda said we're going out tonight and she's watching Claire, but I don't remember you saying anything."

"My mom's right. I'm sorry," he said. "I completely forgot to tell you we have reservations for tonight and she offered to watch Claire. Is that okay?"

"Oh." She hesitated before continuing. "Yes, of course it's okay. Linda mentioned something about dressing up?"

"Wear a cocktail dress, if you have one."

"I think I have something for the occasion."

After saying goodbye and hanging up, Damian held the phone for a moment, his eyes lingering on the photo of him and Gabriela, as he had before. Only this time, anticipation rose, for the night ahead in her company.

He'd have to thank mom for the reservations and for watching Claire.

By the time Damian arrived home, he was an hour late, courtesy of the miserably slow traffic on the way back from Queens. Maybe it was time to find a condo closer to the studio. He spent too much time on the road.

"There you are," Mom said as he exited the elevator on the third floor. "Gabriela is ready and waiting downstairs. What took you so long?"

He'd texted Gabriela and Mom saying he was late, but it had taken longer. "Traffic." He brushed a kiss on her cheek and continued toward the bedroom. "The three-piece suit?"

She nodded. "The steel gray one with the striped navy and silver tie. I'll tell James to bring the car around."

Twenty minutes later, showered and dressed, Damian arrived in the foyer. Mom held Claire and Gabriela was kissing the baby's cheeks and saying goodbye.

"My favorite girls," he said, smiling.

Mom and Gabriela turned at the sound of his voice and Damian stopped at the sight of his wife. She wore a navy dress, something that perfectly hugged her curves and then flared at the knees. A silver clutch in her hand, nude heels, and her hair in a low bun with wavy tendrils framing her face completed the look.

Gabriela looked him over and smiled, her expression relaxed and appreciative. "You look nice."

He strode toward her and took her free hand, then twirled her in a circle. "You look exquisite."

She chuckled. "You'll make me fall. I'm not used to high heels anymore."

Damian placed a steady hand on her waist and brought her flush against him. "I got you," he said close, watching her, so close he saw the moment she held her breath, eyes round and wide.

"Look at you two, already dancing and you're not even there," Mom said.

Damian dropped his arms from Gabriela and took her free hand in his. "We better get going." He tugged her toward the door and waved back at Mom. "Thanks, Mom, for watching Claire."

"Thank you, Linda." Gabriela added.

"Don't worry about Claire. She'll be fine. Have fun, you two."

Once in the car, he gave the address to James.

Damian glanced at Gabriela's hands, holding her clutch on her lap. What if he reached over and took her hand again? His fingers itched to touch her.

"Where are we going?" Gabriela asked.

"To Chez Pierre in lower Manhattan. It's French fusion with a dance floor to the side."

Her eyes widened. "Dance floor? I don't know how to dance."

"I do." He winked at her. "Don't worry. It's not a dance competition. Nobody will be paying attention to us anyway. You can always count on a couple of celebrities being there, especially on a Friday night."

"Celebrities? It sounds posh."

"Maybe a little."

When James stopped the car, Damian exited first and then handed Gabriela onto the sidewalk. He tucked her close to him as he navigated their way to the front door through a crowd milling behind the ropes guarded by a man. Damian showed him the reservation confirmation on his phone and the guy let them pass.

Gabriela raised an eyebrow. "Not only posh, but also exclusive."

"Definitely exclusive." Not everyone could afford the price per plate at Chez Pierre.

Once in the elevator, she relaxed but didn't let go of his hand, and Damian wasn't about to drop it either. He liked the way their hands fit together. He liked a lot of things about her tonight.

"Is it always like this?" she asked.

"They're probably waiting for a celebrity sighting."

At last, the elevator arrived on the destination floor and the doors slid open.

Damian pulled Gabriela's hand through the crook of his arm. "Are you ready?"

Gabriela's jaw slackened as she entered the room on Damian's arm. Lacquered and mirrored surfaces reflected the light from wall sconces and crystal chandeliers.

The ambiance was decidedly French in the elegance of colors and the subtlety of sounds. Nothing was left to chance as evidenced by each small detail. The overall effect was impressive.

"Monsieur Vaughn. Always a pleasure to see you, sir," the maître d' said with a strong French accent. "Madame Vaughn, welcome to Chez Pierre. Follow me, please."

She clung to Damian's hand as she walked beside him, feeling the eyes of those around them as they passed. They whispered about her, didn't they? Or maybe it was it her self-consciousness reminding her how much of an outsider she really was. Everyone else seemed at ease, except her.

Damian thanked the maître d' and pulled out the chair for her. The table was round and facing the corner of floor-to-ceiling windows, framing a blanket of city lights twinkling in the waning sunset and the city below.

Directly above them, suspended from the ceiling in various lengths, dozens and dozens of teardrop lights carried on the same mesmerizing effect of light and shadow.

"This place is incredible," she told Damian.

He nodded. "It does make an impression, doesn't it?"

"And the view." She could hardly find the words to describe it.

"You've been in New York for eight days already and you haven't had the chance to see anything yet, have you?"

Gabriela shrugged. "There will be time for that. Claire needs me and we're still adjusting to married life."

"As true as that may be, we should find time to spend alone," he leaned toward her, "and not just for the sake of convincing others of our relationship."

164

She nodded, not knowing what else to say. Did he really want to spend time alone with her?

A waiter came along to take their orders, and Gabriela busied herself with the menu while Damian asked the guy some questions. Focusing on the printed words was not working, as her attention strayed to the man beside her.

"Everything sounds good," she said after a moment.

"Are you in the mood for something familiar or do you feel brave enough to try something new?" Damian asked.

"I love trying new foods. What do you suggest?"

"The duck confit." Damian said confidently. "It's divine."

She closed her menu and returned it to the waiter. "The duck confit for me, please."

"You won't regret your choice," Damian said with a smile.

He was referring to the dish, but Gabriela couldn't help thinking about the choices they'd made with each other.

Every time she looked at him tonight, her heart beat faster. There was something about a well-dressed man that evoked an alluring appeal, especially when that man was Damian Vaughn, her husband.

Her husband.

It still took her by surprise, being married. Getting used to her new role of wife was proving harder than becoming Claire's mother.

Sometimes it hit her in the middle of the night, after feeding Claire. She'd return to bed and gaze at Damian's sleeping form, usually turned to the opposite side. On occasions, he'd turn in bed while she tended to the baby, and she'd return to find him facing her. How many times since the first night had she imagined how it would feel to sleep in his arms?

At least once every night.

"Why don't you make a list of places you'd like to see in New York?" Damian asked.

"I haven't thought much about it," she replied. She'd been fantasizing about him instead. What would he say to that if he knew?

"Please do," he insisted. "I'm serious. I'd love to show you some of my favorite spots too."

"That would be fun," she conceded. She might even get to know him a little better.

The soft sounds of a piano played the introduction to La Vie en Rose, and a moment later a singer joined, her alto voice beautifully complementing the lyrics.

"I like that song," she said.

"I do too." Damian stood and extended his hand to her. "May I have this dance, please?"

She hesitated. "I can't dance, remember?"

He took her hand and pulled her up. "Just this song."

Damian guided them to a corner, away from the middle of the floor, and she was glad he was sensitive about her feelings. He lifted her hand in his free one and settled an arm around her waist until they stood close to each other. Even in heels, Gabriela was still shorter than him, but closer than wearing her everyday flats. She rested her other hand on his upper arm and their bodies aligned.

Awareness coursed through her, a consciousness of every point of contact between them; his skin and his scent; of the warmth of his body. Even their breathing had synchronized.

Gabriela closed her eyes and sighed. What she would give to keep this moment forever—to feel this safe and content and in complete harmony with this man.

Damian gave her hand a squeeze and nuzzled his head closer to hers. "I was right," he whispered in her ear.

Goosebumps burst on her skin, trailing down the side of her neck. She tipped up her mouth and whispered back, "About what?"

He took a quick breath. "I knew I'd love dancing with you."

Emotion lodged in her throat. Instead of saying anything, Gabriela reached up and brushed her lips on his jaw.

She hardly noticed when the song ended. Damian relaxed his hold on her and then let her go to join others in clapping.

On the way to their table, he grasped her hand and leaned in. "I'd like another dance before we leave."

"I would too," she said.

As soon as they took their seats, two waiters approached with their dishes.

The food was equally impressive—visually stimulating, well-seasoned, and perfectly cooked.

They kept the conversation flowing throughout the meal, with casual topics and funny anecdotes and, after their charged dance, the easy mood helped the tension soften. Like banked embers, it smoldered under the surface and it would surely fan to life at the lightest contact between them.

After sharing dessert and paying the bill, Damian led Gabriela to the dance floor. The singer had left, but the pianist still played and a few couples swayed to the music.

"One dance before we go," he said.

She smiled. "I think I stepped—"

"Damian? Damian Vaughn, is that you?" A feminine voice interrupted from behind them.

Damian's body tensed immediately and his expression turned from playful to guarded. After a quick breath, he laced his fingers with Gabriela's and they turned around.

"Hello, Portia," he said in a neutral voice.

"It is you." The woman was tall and willowy, with light blonde hair styled in a pixie cut and a red dress that left little to the imagination.

Who was she and why did she put Damian on edge?

Completely ignoring Gabriela, she leaned in to kiss his cheeks, but Damian stepped back and placed his arm around Gabriela.

168

"Have you met my wife?" He asked the woman then turned his face to Gabriela. "Sweetheart, this is Portia Grantwood. We knew each other in Yale. Portia, this is my wife Gabriela."

If Gabriela hadn't been watching the exchange between Damian and Portia Grantwood, she would have missed when the woman's eyes went large for a brief moment.

"Well, well," Portia Grantwood said. "So the rumors are true. You did get married." She glanced at Gabriela and then resumed looking at Damian. "I'd say we did more than know each other at Yale," she added with a suggestive smile.

"If you'll excuse us," Damian said. "Have a good night."

The farther away they walked from the woman, the more Damian relaxed and, by the time they reached the elevator, he exhaled deeply.

This time, it was Gabriela who threaded their fingers together as they rode down, hoping she could offer him a measure of comfort.

"I'm sorry we left before dancing," he said.

"I'm not worried about that. Who was she?" From Damian's reaction, there had to be more to the story between him and the woman named Portia.

"I did know her at Yale." He looked to Gabriela. "She pursued me quite doggedly during my senior year, despite my insistence I wasn't interested."

"Not a friend then."

169

He shook his head. "Not a friend at all. I'm sorry for cutting our night short. I wasn't expecting to see her and it rattled me a bit." The corners of his mouth stretched in a quick smile that didn't reach his eyes.

"No need to apologize when it's not your fault." Maybe a distraction would work better. "How about driving the long way home so I can see a bit more of Manhattan at night?"

His mood lifted and his smile widened. "Why didn't I think of that? I'll send James a text to bring the car around."

Gabriela liked the idea of prolonging the night for a bit longer. As much as she missed Claire, the time spent with Damian tonight had been magical, and she wasn't ready for it to end.

When they arrived at the lobby, the crowd outside the building had grown. In addition to the man guarding the entrance outside, another one had joined inside and checked the reservations of arriving guests.

Damian took her hand and halted. "Let me see how long before James pulls up." He got his phone and sent a text to the driver.

Gabriela stood beside him, not looking forward to wading through the crowd.

"Is this a busy night or is there something going on?" Damian asked the man.

"A little busier than a normal Friday night," the man replied. "Big D made a post on Instagram and pinned Chez Pierre as the location."

"Big D?" Damian asked, voicing her own question.

"The Emmy-winner rapper," the man replied matter-of-factly.

Damian checked his phone again and typed a quick reply, then slipped the phone back in his pocket before taking Gabriela's hand. "Let's go. James will be pulling up soon."

"Sir," said the man checking the reservations. "If you'd like to avoid the front door, take the second hallway on the right and the door at the end. It exits onto the alleyway where the deliveries are made."

They thanked him and made their way as he'd indicated.

"Thank goodness," Gabriela said once they were out of earshot. "Walking through that crowd would not have been fun."

Damian grimaced. "I'm sorry. This wasn't the way I wanted this night to go. First Portia and now this."

She tugged at his hand until he looked to her. "That's not what I'll remember about this night, Damian. Not at all."

His expression turned playful. "Let me guess. You really liked the duck."

"I think you can easily guess what I really liked." As if anything else could ever make her forget dancing with him.

"Hold onto that thought." Damian pushed the door open and poked his head out, then dialed a number on his phone. "Can you turn around? We're in the alleyway by the delivery entrance. Thanks."

Gabriela stepped out with Damian, and she pushed her arm through his, keeping close to him. Although it wasn't completely dark, the alley was less illuminated than the street up ahead and a swell of nerves threatened to rise.

"Such a glamorous way to end our date, isn't it?" Damian teased.

She appreciated the humor in his voice. "I did ask to see Manhattan at night."

Damian chuckled. "I aim to please. Your own personal tour of the best alleys in the city."

As they neared the sidewalk, a dark figure rounded the corner and stopped in front of them. "Say cheese."

A flash of light fired in their faces. Gabriela let out a small scream and turned her face away as Damian stepped in front, with his back to her.

"Not cool, man," Damian said, his voice grave and deep. "Get out of the way and leave us alone." He kept walking with her hand in his and she followed as close as she could, hanging on to his arm.

"I'm just doing my job, Mr. Vaughn," the man said. "You're not Big D but I'm sure someone will pay me well for photos of the new Mrs. Vaughn."

After a scurry of movement, the man came around to her side and called out her name before firing the flash in her face again. She flinched.

As Damian turned to shield her from the paparazzo again, the man grabbed at her elbow, pulling her away from Damian's side. The flash went off for a third time.

Damian growled. "Leave her alone." He pulled back his arm and swung a punch at the guy.

Gabriela gasped.

At the last minute, the guy jumped to the side and Damian's fist scraped the guy's jaw and hit the camera sideways, making contact with part of the lens's body.

Damian flexed his fingers then fisted them again, his brow furrowed and his eyes dark.

The guy righted himself, checked the lens, and rubbed his chin. Then he smirked before turning around and leaving.

Gabriela stepped forward and held on to Damian's arm just as James pulled up to the sidewalk in the black sedan. "Come on, Damian. Let's go."

CHAPTER NINE

$\mathcal{D}$amian took the stairs from the lower level to the first floor and veered toward the foyer.

How could an evening that had started so well end so badly? His knuckles smarted and he flexed his fingers again. Stupid paparazzo.

"Damian, wait, please," Gabriela said, coming up behind him.

He stopped and waited for her to catch up. She placed her clutch and her heels on a console table nearby and approached him in her bare feet.

"Let me see your hand." She picked up his hand before he offered it to her, turning it to inspect his fingers.

"I'm—"

"Don't apologize again," she interrupted. "None of it was your fault."

For a moment, he could only concentrate on Gabriela's skin against his, on the way she so tenderly held his hand.

"It doesn't look like there's anything broken, but let's get those scrapes washed and disinfected." She turned to leave but then turned back as he stood there. "In the kitchen."

Being as late as it was, Mrs. Harrison had already left for the day. Mom was upstairs with Claire and hopefully wouldn't hear him and Gabriela in the kitchen. He'd rather not have to explain to her what had happened after they left Chez Pierre.

He shed his suit coat, his vest and tie and rolled his shirt sleeves back.

"Is there a first-aid kit around here?" she asked.

Damian walked to the butler's pantry and retrieved the box, then returned to the sink where Gabriela washed his hand with warm water and soap.

"Has this happened to you before?"

"Scraping my knuckles in a fist fight?"

"Being accosted by paparazzi photographers." After a second wash, she patted it dry with paper towels.

"Not to this level of invasion. They usually have long lenses and most of the times I don't even realize I had my picture taken until it shows up somewhere online. I don't know what the deal was with this guy." He'd been in their faces, especially Gabriela's. "How hard did he grab you? Let me see your arm."

"I'm not done here." She reached for the disinfectant and dabbed it on his knuckles. "This might sting."

"Just a little." He held back the flinching. When she was done, he repeated his request. "Can I see your arm?"

176

"I'm alright." Her voice was firm, but her eyes belied something else.

He took her elbow for a closer look. "Will you tell me if it bruises?"

Gabriela met his eyes and nodded. "I'm okay, Damian. Thank you for defending me."

"Of course," he replied.

Was it vulnerability he saw in her eyes? Had Gabriela been scared by the incident?

If he raised his hands, he could pull her close for a hug, and reassure her he'd always defend her, but as he debated what to do, Gabriela waded the used paper towels and threw them in the garbage, putting some distance between her and him. He leaned his back against the center island and slipped his hands in his pockets.

"I'm assuming you don't want to tell Linda what happened."

"I don't. What do you think?" Knowing his mom, she would only worry unnecessarily.

"I agree. Let's not tell her. At least not tonight."

"I do need to call Luke and tell him what happened." The pictures the paparazzo had taken would be published by morning, if not before, and Damian wanted to know if there was any legal recourse for them.

Gabriela glanced at the time on the microwave digital display. "Why don't you go on ahead to our bedroom and I'll get Claire from Linda."

"That's a good idea." He grabbed his tie and suit coat, and draped them over his arm.

When they stepped into the elevator, she handed him her shoes and clutch and parted ways on the second floor and he continued on to the third, fatigue already setting in. What an evening.

He set Gabriela's silver clutch on top of her dresser, then went through the motions of undressing down to his white under shirt and suit pants, and stood barefoot as he sorted out the night's events, one by one. Was there anything he could have done for a different outcome?

A few minutes later, the elevator pinged and Gabriela stepped out with a bright-eyed Claire.

"This little missy woke up when she heard my voice," Gabriela said, slipping off her shoes.

Indeed, Claire was wide awake and smiling, as if she'd planned it all along.

"Will you hold her while I get out of this dress?" She passed the baby to him and, although Claire didn't start crying as she did at times in his arms, her smile faded into a little frown. No doubt about it, she was a momma's girl.

Gabriela walked into the bathroom and closed the door. Damian strolled to the windows, telling himself it was his job to distract Claire when, in reality, he knew it was him who needed the distraction. The mental image of Gabriela undressing filled his imagination far too quickly, especially when fueled by the memory of dancing with her earlier in the evening. She fit well in his arms. Her curves, her planes, all of her.

When she came out, she wore her pajamas, her face was scrubbed clean of makeup, and her hair piled up on top of her head in a big, messy bun. She hung the dress in her closet and then walked over to them, feet bare and arms open.

"Thanks, Damian." She took Claire. "I'm going to change her, give her a lotion massage, and see if she wants a bottle."

"Do you need any help?"

She shook her head. "Spending time with her will help me decompress."

"I'll call Luke from the guest bedroom." He gestured toward the opposite end.

Gabriela nodded absently as she walked to the nursery, talking to Claire in low tones, and Damian watched her leave. At times, the bond she had with that child took him by surprise, how quickly and deeply it had developed.

He grabbed his phone and dialed Luke's number.

"Hey, man, it's Friday night. You should be on a hot date with your wife," Luke said when he answered the phone.

Damian entered the room and walked straight to the double windows overlooking the back of the building. "We did go out and it was great." And it had been pretty hot. "But it didn't end so well."

Damian told Luke about his and Gabriela's run-in with the paparazzo after they left Chez Pierre.

"That's crazy," said Luke. "Would you be able to identify the guy?"

"Easily. I took a good look at his face." He'd been pretty close to the man. "I'm wondering if there's anything we can do about this."

"It's too late to stop him from selling the photos."

"I should have called the police on the spot, shouldn't I?" Damian let out a frustrated sigh. "I didn't even think about it. I was worried about Gabriela and wanted to bring her home as fast as possible."

"Which is totally understandable. I would have done the same thing. Do you want to press charges against the guy?" Luke asked.

Damian hesitated. Would it make a difference if he did? "Maybe I should talk to Gabriela first." He had more than just himself to think about.

"That's a good idea. Talk to her and see what she thinks. In the meantime, I'll talk to a buddy of mine who knows more about this kind of situation."

Damian thanked Luke and ended the call.

At some point during the conversation, Damian had taken a seat on the upholstered chair and he remained there for another moment. Although he'd known he'd have to think of Gabriela and include her in his decisions, when he married her, this was the first time he'd done it so naturally and without a conscious effort.

Their lives were entwined. However long their marriage lasted, they'd be a part of each other's lives for a while.

But he was starting to think a while wouldn't be enough.

Gabriela turned to the other side in bed and met a pair of bright blue eyes and a wide toothless grin directed at her.

Unable to resist, she smiled back at Claire and leaned in to kiss her sweet little cheeks. "Good morning, you little rascal. How did you get here?"

Had Gabriela brought the baby to bed herself during the night and now couldn't remember? Claire did not sleep through the night—that was a milestone yet to happen—and Gabriela had changed her and given her a bottle at two in the morning. But she couldn't remember anything else after that.

She went up on her elbow and peeked over at Damian, who slept with his back to them. Had he brought Claire to bed?

As Claire was content to lay between them, Gabriela played simple hand games with her, relishing the quiet time. The clock read six-fifty-two and she wasn't in a hurry to get up. Saturday mornings were meant to indulge in a slower pace.

The memory of the night before came to her—the dinner, the dancing, the amazing location. How dreamy her time with Damian had been, especially dancing in his arms. Just thinking about it raised her heart rate. Close proximity to him increasingly brought her off balance, and, from the way he'd responded to her, Gabriela was sure the attraction was mutual.

Would Damian bring it up to clear the air between them? Or should she? What was the protocol in such a situation?

As if there was any. She chuckled lightly at the idea. Other than the provisions and agreements they'd set up in the marriage contract, they'd been winging it so far, and they'd keep winging it for the time to come. In any case, thinking of every variable would have been impossible.

A few minutes later, Damian stretched and turned around, and she watched him as he woke up. His sleep-wrinkled face, his drowsy eyes, his rumpled hair—he was adorable in the morning. Most days, she was feeding Claire by the time he left for work.

After blinking a couple of times, his eyes focused and a slow smile pulled at the corners of his mouth. "Morning," he said, looking straight at her.

"Good morning. You wouldn't know how this little stowaway got here, would you?"

Damian chuckled and supported his weight on his elbow. "I do know."

The T-shirt he wore bunched around his bicep and Gabriela couldn't help but notice his well-defined arms.

"She woke up around five something. I changed and fed her and put her to sleep, but she woke up crying an hour later." He took Claire's hand. "I tried calming her down but she wasn't having it and I was too tired. So I brought her here and she fell asleep immediately." His expression was one of satisfaction.

Gabriela tsked him. "That's a big no-no."

His eyebrow rose. "Is it?"

She nodded. "Now she knows she doesn't have to sleep alone." Hopefully, one time didn't form a habit and maybe Gabriela wouldn't have to retrain Claire to sleep in the crib again.

"You can't blame her, can you?" Damian said. "She just wants company. Sleeping with someone is a lot better than sleeping alone."

Gabriela's neck heated. "Is it?" Were they still talking about Claire sleeping in their bed?

"Don't you think so?" For a quick moment, his gaze was intense, but then he looked to Claire and tickled her tummy. "Tell mommy sleeping alone stinks."

Mommy.

That was her. She was the mommy of this beautiful baby. How had she come to be so lucky?

Damian glanced at her while he played with Claire, smiling wide. How did he feel about sharing the bed with her? He used to have it all to himself.

It was a large bed and they each kept to their sides; it wasn't hard to do. But, at times, when he turned in his sleep, Gabriela imagined him reaching over and spooning with her. She imagined how that would feel; how he would lift her hair from her neck and kiss her behind the ear, and what would happen after that.

It was the kind of imagination she quickly squelched. It wouldn't lead anywhere.

Damian sat up against the headboard and placed Claire on his legs with his knees bent. "We should do something fun today."

Gabriela sat up sideways in bed, facing them, and crossed her legs. "What kind of fun?"

"A family outing of some kind. Something to help us forget the way last night ended in a fiasco."

It had been the perfect night until the end. "I choose to remember the good parts." She rubbed her forearm and Damian's eyes followed the gesture.

"How's your arm?"

She turned the elbow out and was surprised to see two round bruises had formed overnight.

Damian frowned. "We need to take a picture of that." He picked up Claire and set her down on the mattress again, then reached to his bedside table and grabbed his phone. Holding her fingers in one hand and the phone in the other, he photographed her arm from different angles.

After he put the phone back, Gabriela took his right hand. "How are your knuckles?" His skin was a bit scuffed up, but there was no visible swelling.

"Already healing." He pulled his hand back. "It's you I'm concerned about. I'm sending the pictures to Luke. If he says there are grounds to file charges against the guy, will you consider doing it?"

Despite his carefully worded question, she sensed this was an important issue for him. "If you and Luke think I should, then I will. Ask him what I need to do."

Damian nodded. "I will."

Claire chose that moment to start protesting, kicking her legs and showing her displeasure vocally.

Gabriela picked her up. "Are you feeling neglected, little one? And probably hungry too." She rose from the bed and cradled Claire in her arms. "Why don't you take a shower while I change and feed Claire and then you can watch her while I get ready."

Damian stood and started making the bed. "Does that mean a yes for going out today?"

"Yes, let's go do something fun. What do you have in mind?"

"How about the New York Aquarium? It's in Brooklyn."

"The aquarium sounds great." Gabriela walked to the nursery with Claire and Damian followed them. She liked the idea of a family outing, just for the three of them.

When his phone sounded from the bedroom, he turned back. "Let me see if it's Luke."

Gabriela changed Claire's diaper, dressed her in an adorable little outfit, and placed the largest bib she could find around her neck in case of a spit up. She walked over to the rolling cart in the corner, a feeding station she'd set up in the nursery so she and Damian didn't have to go down to the kitchen on the ground floor every time Claire needed a bottle. This house was enormous. After preparing a bottle, she sat on the rocking chair with Claire,

Linda came in from the hallway, holding her tablet in her hands. "Gabriela." She took a step inside and stopped, then glanced at the screen a few times. "Did you and Damian have any intention of telling me?"

Gabriela's eyebrows knit together. "Telling you what?"

Just then, Damian returned through the door that connected the nursery to the bedroom, clasping his phone tightly in his left hand. "That was Luke and I'm afraid I have bad news."

He stopped short at the sight of his mom. "Oh."

Linda held up the tablet with the screen turned to him. "Let me guess. Luke told you about the pictures."

"The pictures?" Gabriela asked. Then it dawned on her. "Oh no." The encounter with the paparazzo last night. "The pictures are out?"

Damian nodded. "There's more than just the ones he took." He held up the phone to her.

Linda put down the tablet and took Claire from Gabriela, then continued feeding her. "Is this why you went straight to your bedroom when you got home yesterday?" She looked up at Damian.

"We didn't want you to worry," he replied.

Gabriela walked over to him and took the phone to see the photos. The website was called Celebrity Watch and it featured the newest posts at the top. She scrolled past one from this morning about a movie star jogging in Central Park and found the one she wanted, titled *CEO of Vaughn Family Movie Channel* and his new wife. She clicked on it.

The brief commentary talked about Damian and his elopement with Gabriela, then mentioned their night out and dinner at Chez Pierre, which apparently was their first public sighting as a couple. "What does it matter if it's our first outing in public? Do people really care about this?"

Damian shrugged. "Some people want to know what the rich and famous do."

Linda put down the bottle and propped Claire on her shoulder, then patted her back. "They're obsessed with following celebrities and the paparazzi fuel that."

There were rows and rows of pictures, starting with them exiting the back door to the building. The harsh flash only accentuated their shock in the first picture, her dismay and Damian's unmistakable anger in the ones that followed. It was clear the way he'd tried to shield her, but the photographer had been relentless.

After a few of those, the perspective shifted to show a wider angle and the altercation between Damian and the photographer. "There was someone else taking pictures on the other side of the street. Did you notice anyone else?" She asked Damian.

"I didn't. He must have had a long lens."

"It mentions his name. Alan Smith."

He nodded. "Which makes it easier for us. Now we know who he is. Luke said we should go in to the closest precinct and file assault charges against him." He held out his hand for the phone. "Don't read the comments, please."

Gabriela returned the phone, curious how bad the comments really were. Did people mention her? Was that what Damian didn't want her to read?

"I'll watch Claire if you want to go now," Linda said.

"Thanks, Linda," Gabriela said. "That will be so much easier for us."

Thirty minutes later, after showering and getting dressed, Damian and Gabriela left for the precinct. Luke was waiting for them when they arrived, and they went in together.

"I'm here for moral support," Luke said. "You don't really need me for this."

They met an officer, explained the situation, and he interviewed them in turns. The officer took their contact and explained the case would be sent to the prosecutor's office to decide whether to file charges. In the end, it was simple and didn't take half as long as she'd expected.

"That was anti-climactic," Gabriela said once they were back outside.

"Did you expect more drama?" Luke asked in a light teasing tone.

"I don't know what I expected, but I'm glad it's done."

"This part is done," Damian said. "We'll have to wait for what the prosecutor's office says. If they decide to file charges."

After they said goodbye to Luke, Damian called James to drive them back home.

This fascination the public had with what others did—she couldn't understand that. Did it really matter to others that Damian's family was well-off and that he was the CEO and heir of the family business?

"Have you had your picture in the tabloids before?"

Damian glanced at her. "Several times. My parents and grandparents as well. I'm sure if I hadn't married you, the public interest and backlash about Claire would have been a serious issue for me and the company's image."

Gabriela disguised a sigh. At times she almost forgot why Damian had married her. They'd been getting along really well so far, had worked out a rhythm between the two of them to parent Claire. Sure, they didn't act like newlyweds did, but Gabriela liked to think they'd developed a friendship, or at least an easy camaraderie. Hadn't they?

She'd come to know Damian in the past few weeks and he was a good man. A genuine one. He treated everyone with kindness and respect, and acted like Gabriela and Claire were his family. What if she couldn't have a marriage in the real sense of the word? She'd known what to expect from the beginning, had read the contract, line per line, had signed her agreement at the bottom of the page. Dreaming about more was only setting herself up for disappointment.

When they arrived at home, Gabriela placed her hand on Damian's arm and held him back. "If you don't want to go to the aquarium, we can stay home. I don't mind."

"Do you want to stay home or are you worried about being in public?"

She hesitated. She did want to go but not at the cost of their privacy. "What if people recognize us from that post on Celebrity Watch?"

"We can't stay home all the time, Gabriela. I think we should go and enjoy ourselves and forget about yesterday's fiasco for today." He took her hand, squeezed her fingers and smiled at her.

She smiled back. "Let's go see the aquarium then."

At least now, she had an excuse to wear something other than yoga pants and T-shirts.

Less than an hour later, they parked at the New York Aquarium. Gabriela unlatched Claire's car seat while Damian retrieved the stroller from the back of the car. This time, he drove instead of having James do it. She and Damian wore sunglasses and hats, and she hoped that would be enough to disguise them from unwanted attention.

The afternoon weather had warmed since this morning, and the sun shone much too brightly in the vivid blue sky. The hat and sunglasses would definitely serve for more than one purpose.

After paying for the tickets, Damian pushed the stroller and Gabriela took the map. They chose to visit the indoor attractions first, where they could stay out of the sun and the public eye.

The movement of the stroller soon lolled Claire to sleep and she napped peacefully as Damian and Gabriela visited the indoor displays before moving to the outdoor ones.

"I'm glad we came," Gabriela told Damian. "It's been a while since I did a day trip to the aquarium. Or even the zoo." Not since she was a kid and mom and dad took her and Juliana and Alexandre on the annual trip to the zoo when they visited family in Lisbon. Porto didn't have a zoo.

Damian kept pushing the stroller. "It feels good to do something different, doesn't it? When I was growing up, Nanna Vaughn and Grandpa used to take me to the Central Park Zoo in the summer months."

As they finished seeing the penguin display, Claire woke up in a bad mood.

Gabriela unbuckled her from the car seat. "All right, little missy. We hear you." She grabbed the diaper bag from the back of the stroller. "I'm going to change her," she said to Damian. "We'll be right back."

Claire didn't like having her diaper changed, especially right after waking up cranky, so Gabriela moved quickly and met Damian outside.

He took the diaper bag and returned it to the back of the stroller. "There's a picnic area a few yards away under the shade. We could stop there to feed Claire."

Gabriela carried Claire propped up and looking out, her little hands grabbing on to the blouse Gabriela wore today. She was growing too fast and, more and more of lately, she didn't like being held in a cradle position.

After the trip to the zoo, Gabriela and Damian spent the evening in the backyard garden, prolonging their easy, relaxed day.

An almost perfect day.

Although Claire fell asleep early, she woke up soon after Damian and Gabriela retired to bed.

Damian pushed the blankets away. "I'll get her."

Through the monitor, Gabriela heard his steps and heard him leaning over the crib, whispering to Claire as he picked her up.

Then came the terrible sound of retching.

Gabriela bolted out of bed just as an, "Oh no," came from Damian.

She turned the lights on in the nursery and found Damian holding Claire, both of them covered in milk spit up.

"Aww, poor thing," she said, approaching them. "She's going to need a bath."

A look of relief filled Damian's expression as he handed Claire to Gabriela. "I'll go take a shower in the other bathroom."

Gabriela quickly bathed Claire, dressed her in clean clothes, and held her in the rocking chair until she fell asleep. After gently placing the baby back in the crib, she returned to her side of the bed, just as Damian walked in to his side.

He wore pajama pants and nothing else. Barefoot and shirtless.

Her eyes widened for a moment before she turned off her bedside lamp and slipped under the sheets.

He was well toned, for sure. Shoulders, biceps, chest with enough hair not to hide his skin, a defined back.

Did he work out or was what she'd seen the product of good genes? Probably both.

If she were honest with herself, she'd imagined what he'd look like without a shirt. Now she didn't have to.

Damian got into bed and turned off his bedside lamp. "Good night," he said.

"Good night," she squeaked, then cleared her throat.

Gabriela tried to go to sleep, but every time she closed her eyes, it was shirtless Damian she saw. She turned to the other side, toward Damian. The low light in the bedroom was enough to let her see his shape, as he lay down facing the ceiling.

This would make for a long night.

Knowing he was only an arm's length away from her, not wearing a shirt, didn't help in her efforts to fall asleep.

"Damian." She called his name softly. "Are you still awake?"

"I'm awake." His voice sounded farther away than he was, as he faced the window.

"Would you please go put on a T-shirt?"

"What?" He turned around to face her. "Why?"

She paused for a moment, looking for a neutral way to say it. "It's distracting me."

This time he came up on his elbow. "*I* distract you? Says the lady who wears spaghetti strap pajama tops to bed."

Gabriela swallowed. He'd noticed? "I wear

a comfortable pajama set that happens to have spaghetti straps. I'm not topless."

"Maybe sleeping without a top is more comfortable for me. It's practical too. If Claire spits up on me again, I can just hop in the shower. No harm done to the shirt."

As he talked, he moved closer to her and, in the filtered light from the French doors on one side, and the night light on the opposite wall, their eyes met.

Immediately, the mood shifted, charged with a sudden energy that filled the air between them.

Her heart sped up and her fingers itched to touch him.

Damian supported himself on one arm and with the other, he caressed the side of her face.

"I don't want to do anything to violate our contract." Damian hovered over her, his eyes intent and his lips—

Don't think of his lips. Gabriela made a last, valiant effort to rein in her emotions.

"But I'd be lying if I said I wasn't attracted to you," Damian continued. "Or that I didn't enjoy kissing you."

"I'd be lying, too," Gabriela admitted. Sure that he heard her heart beating so loud.

"So, is kissing—all right?" The uncertainty is his voice endeared him to her all the more.

"It's better than all right." She reached her hands up to pull him down and touched the side of his neck.

From the nursery, Claire wailed, her cry echoing through the monitor.

Damian shook his head. "Of all the times…"

Gabriela rolled away from under him. "I'll get her this time."

If Claire hadn't cried just now, what would have happened between Gabriela and Damian?

CHAPTER TEN

*I*t was finally Thursday. After his last meeting in the early afternoon, Damian said goodbye to Mrs. Gold and met James in the building's underground garage. As soon as he arrived home and finished packing, he and Gabriela and Claire would leave for Highland Park. He was looking forward to the drive to Millbrook upstate.

After the events of last Friday night and Saturday, the week had passed in a mood of awkward tension between him and Gabriela. Even though she hadn't blamed him for any of it, Damian felt responsible. He'd failed her and Claire, hadn't protected them, had not taken their safety as seriously as they needed.

And so they tiptoed around each other, much too carefully and stiffly. He hoped the long weekend at Highland Park would bring back the easiness between them. The party mom had planned was scheduled for Saturday, but for the rest of the time there would be no paparazzi, no public eye, no looking over their shoulders for any of that—it had to work.

It had been a while since he'd visited Nanna. She rarely came to the city anymore and he got lost in work and life, which had a way of interfering with his best intentions. Best intentions always fell short.

But now that he had Gabriela and Claire in his life, it was important to him that Nanna met them.

The thought stopped him cold.

Neither Gabriela nor Claire were intended to stay in his life permanently. As calculated as it sounded, they were more like transient fixtures, passing briefly for a specific purpose. Why did it sound so analytical?

And why did it matter to him that they met his beloved grandmother?

He brushed the thoughts away, not ready to deal with them.

As soon as he got home, he took the elevator to the third floor, shedding his tie and suit coat on the way.

"Gabriela?" He called as he stepped into the hallway.

"In the nursery," came her reply.

He detoured to the bedroom where he left his briefcase, the tie and suit coat. In the nursery, Gabriela held Claire on her hip and packed the baby's weekender bag with her free hand.

"Has she been difficult today?"

"No more than usual."

Damian approached and took Claire in his hands. "Oh look. Progress. No cries and no frowns from Miss Claire here. Is she finally tolerating me?"

Gabriela smiled. "You're grossly exaggerating. It was never that bad."

"Everyone knows she only has eyes for you. See?" Even as he spoke, Claire had turned to where Gabriela stood. "I actually agree with her. You're much prettier to look at than I am."

Gabriela blushed, a small smile pulling at the corner of her mouth, but she didn't reply to his comment. He'd noticed how she had a hard time accepting his compliments. Maybe he ought to give them more often.

She added a receiving blanket to the bag and zipped it closed, then carried it in one hand as she walked to their bedroom. "I've already packed the diaper bag and mine. Linda left this morning and took my dress and your tuxedo."

"That makes it easier for us, since the back seat is for Claire."

"Yes, that's what she said."

"We're actually driving up in the Escalade since it has more room. The car's trunk is not large enough for all the bags and the stroller."

"The extra room will be nice." She added Claire's bag to the line-up where the other bags waited by the door, and gestured to his closet. "I hope you don't mind. I packed some of your essentials, to get you started."

Damian approached her, handed Claire back to her and kissed Gabriela's cheek. "Thank you. Of course I don't mind."

She blushed again. "You're welcome." She shouldered her purse and the diaper bag, then glanced between the bags, the stroller and the car seat, all in a row by the door.

"Go on ahead. I'll bring them all down." He'd make them all fit in the elevator in one trip.

"Thanks, Damian."

Twenty minutes later, with the trunk loaded and Claire safely installed in the back seat, they took I-87 and drove north. Traffic out of the city was slow, but once they cleared the city limits, he was able to make the posted speed limit.

"Tell me more about your grandmother and her home," Gabriela asked.

"She lives in Highland Park in the small village of Millbrook. It belongs to the Wharton side of the family, who made their fortune in metallurgy. Nanna is the last of the Whartons." That was a simplified version, but enough for now. He'd tell her more later.

"Do you spend a lot of time there? What's it like?"

"I spent summers there when I was growing up. Climbing trees, catching tadpoles in the pond. You know, boy things." Damian glanced at her and smiled.

"You were just like Matias and Filipe, always getting in trouble, and leading the younger kids into trouble."

Damian shrugged. "I didn't have any cousins, so I had to entertain myself. Later, when I was older, I went horseback riding and swam a lot."

"Your grandma has horses? How big is the place?"

"She sold off the horses some time ago. I don't have time to visit for longer periods of time as I used to." A pang of guilt reared up. When was the last time he'd come to visit Nanna? "As for the estate, it's not as large as some of the neighboring ones. Only fifteen acres."

Gabriela turned to him with wide eyes. "Fifteen acres?" She pulled out her phone and did a search. "That's over six hectares. If you're calling that small, what do you consider large?"

"Some estates are over twenty-five and thirty acres. A few are fifty or more. In comparison, Highland Park is small."

The look of surprise in her face didn't abate.

"I'm glad we came today," Damian said. "We'll have the time to go on a tour tomorrow."

"Is this a tour on foot?" She asked, her voice teasing.

Damian chuckled. "If you want. Or we can take the golf cart."

"That might not be a bad idea." After a pause, she asked, "Does your mother like it there? She seemed excited before she left."

"Mom loves Highland Park and she visits more often than I do." Anticipating Gabriela's next question, he added, "She and Nanna Vaughn get along well."

"I'm glad they do. That could have easily gone the other way."

Damian nodded. "They have both suffered loss, and the man they have in common has brought disappointment to them."

The rest of the drive went smoothly, with Gabriela commenting on the landscape. Seeing her fresh perspective on a trip he'd done countless times was a reminder of how easy it was to take for granted the surrounding beauty.

They passed the gates and the long driveway and at last the house was visible.

Gabriela brought a hand to her mouth. "Goodness, Damian. This place is incredible."

He smiled as he parked the vehicle, pleased with her reaction. "I'm glad you like it. Highland Park is really special to us." That was an understatement.

Mom met them in the foyer when they arrived and promptly went to Claire. "How's my grandcutie?" She got the baby out of the car seat and held her up in her arms.

"She slept the whole way," Damian said. "She'll be cranky."

"Not for Grandma, she won't," Mom replied, already smiling and playing with a happy Claire, who apparently only had issues with him.

Gabriela had set down the diaper bag and turned to take everything in, coming to a stop in front of the staircase. "This curved staircase. Wow."

When she noticed him and Mom watching her, she blushed. "Sorry. I sound like a tourist. When I was a kid, I watched Gone With The Wind and always imagined what it would be like to make a grand entrance in a long dress." She shook her head lightly. "Don't mind my ramblings, please."

Mom smiled. "I think you'll have your dream fulfilled on Saturday."

The party. "Oh boy," Damian said. Knowing Mom, she'd probably gone all out with the planning.

"Let me show you the nursery," Mom said to Gabriela, who picked up the diaper bag and followed.

Damian came up the rear with the rest of the bags, leaving the stroller and car seat by the entry closet. "Where's Nanna?"

"She's resting. She said she'll see you after dinner."

Instead of turning towards his old bedroom, Mom continued down the second floor's hallway.

"You're putting us in the old suite?" The second-largest suite had been occupied by Mom and Dad when Damian was growing up but, after their divorce, Mom had moved to a guest suite and made it her own.

"It was Nanna's request. She had the sitting room next to it turned into a simple nursery."

Still holding Claire, she went in first and opened the door wide. "Look, Claire. This is your bedroom."

"This is adorable," Gabriela said. "I love it."

The old sofas and upholstered chairs had been removed, making the space seem much larger than he remembered. Behind them, a small wardrobe and dresser with a changing pad took the whole wall, followed by a bookcase and a rocking chair in the corner. The crib was set up against the opposite wall. Everything was done in soft tones of creamy white and pastel colors. On the shelves, he recognized some of his baby toys and books.

As Mom had said, it was simple, but extremely well done and nothing left to chance. It seemed as Nanna had expectations for more visits from them. He blew out a breath.

"It looks different," he said lamely as he set down Claire's bag by the wardrobe. "When did Nanna have this done?"

"When she found out you got married and had adopted a baby girl," Mom replied. "She asked me for help in collecting some of your baby things, and then I brought a designer from the city. Once the old furniture was removed and the walls painted, it was easier to get a clear vision of what to do." She turned to Gabriela. "Don't worry about the paint. We had the walls painted in non-toxic low VOC paint which doesn't have any fumes."

While Mom took Gabriela around the nursery reminiscing about his old baby stuff, Damian took his and Gabriela's bags to their bedroom. The furniture was the same but the linens and curtains had been updated, much to his relief. Even the artwork had been replaced and the bedroom as a whole didn't resemble the same one where his parents had slept in.

He'd have to thank Nanna later for her sensitivity. This would make the stay much easier for him.

Mom and Gabriela spent the rest of the afternoon together with Claire, and he didn't see them again until dinner, which they set up in the eat-in kitchen. He knew Nanna had a cook and a maid, but maybe they had the night off as he didn't see them around.

He and Gabriela and mom took turns holding Claire, as they didn't have a high chair.

"I'm going to buy a high chair online and ask Cathy to bring it up when she comes tomorrow."

"Who?"

"Cathy's the event planner. She's arriving tomorrow with the decorators and the catering crew will be here early on Saturday."

Damian raised an eyebrow. "Decorators?" He should have known Mom would plan something grandiose.

"Not a word from you, Damian Walter. It's not our fault you went and eloped. This is just a reception party. That's all." She covered Gabriela's hand. "We're not mad at you, dear. Just him."

Gabriela opened her mouth as if to say something, but then just smiled.

Great. His wife sided with his mom and grandma, holding him responsible for something that had been out of his control.

Mrs. Finch showed up as they finished the meal. "Mr. Vaughn, your grandmother has asked that you and your wife come to see her when you're done."

Damian stood and introduced her to Gabriela. "This is Mrs. Finch, Nanna's personal assistant. Thank you, Mrs. Finch. You may tell Nanna we'll be up in a few minutes."

Gabriela and mom cleared the table and Damian held Claire, who seemed quite content.

When they were done, Damian set his hand on Gabriela's back and they walked to the service elevator.

"Who else lives here, other than your grandmother and her assistant?"

"Mrs. Finch is more than Nanna's personal assistant. She's a registered nurse and also acts as a secretary when needed. Besides being a companion. If things haven't changed, there's a full-time gardener, a cook, and a maid for everyday upkeep. A cleaning crew comes once a week for the rest." He was probably forgetting someone.

The door to Nanna's suite was slightly ajar and he knocked on the jamb.

"Come in, Damian," Nanna replied.

Just before entering, he took Gabriela's hand and twined his fingers with hers. "Follow my lead," he whispered in her ear.

Gabriela inhaled quickly, then leaned away to meet his eyes. For a moment, he wanted to explore all the possibilities he read in her gaze. But the timing wasn't right. Not with a baby in his arms and his grandmother inside the room.

He pushed the door open and entered. "Nanna," he said.

As he approached her, Gabriela dropped his hand and took Claire from him, stopping a few paces behind him.

Nanna sat in her favorite upholstered chair, the same one he remembered from long ago. Damian leaned down and kissed her on the cheek, and she lifted her arms around his neck. Was it his impression or did she feel smaller, more frail? He didn't want to think about her age.

He turned to Gabriela. "This is Nanna Vaughn, my grandmother. Nanna, this is my wife Gabriela and my daughter Claire." Every time he introduced them, a sense of pride filled his chest, one he didn't want to examine too closely.

Gabriela extended her hand. "I'm so glad to meet you, Mrs. Vaughn."

"Oh, no, my dear. Not Mrs. Vaughn. With three of us now, it gets too confusing. Just call me Nanna Vaughn." She pulled Gabriela close and kissed her on each cheek. "Damian's Portuguese grandparents have been gone for some time, but I still remember the proper Portuguese greeting."

Damian's shoulders relaxed. They'd get along just fine.

Nanna turned to Claire and smiled. "Look at those intelligent eyes. She's a doll, Damian, but looks nothing like either one of you."

"Well, she is adopted," he commented. "We're not keeping that a secret."

"Are you planning to adopt more children?" Nanna asked. "Or are you busy working on the old-fashioned way?"

Damian glanced at Gabriela who looked at him and blushed. She shifted Claire to her other arm, not saying anything.

"It's too early to discuss that, Nanna," he said. "We'd like this one to sleep through the night for a while first."

"You're not getting any younger," Nanna said. "The older you get, the less stamina you have to deal with babies."

"We'll keep that in mind."

"Raising kids is hard work," she added. "I'm still trying to understand what you were thinking in adopting a baby in the first place."

He could always trust Nanna to get to the crux of an issue. "Sometimes a situation comes your way and you take it, even if you never planned for it." That was true about a lot of things in his life lately.

Gabriela took a seat on the sofa facing Nanna and held Claire on her lap. Damian joined them. A sudden feeling of inadequacy washed over him. Just a few minutes ago he'd been proud to introduce Gabriela and Claire, as if he had any part in their greatness. Gabriela was practically raising Claire by herself. He helped and participated, but the bulk of the work was hers. And Claire's cuteness had nothing to do with him.

As for Gabriela, the more he got to know her, the more he discovered what an amazing woman she was. How many people would have left their old lives behind and adapted so well as she did? At every turn, there was something new, and she never complained about any of it.

In reality, what was he doing? His marriage to Gabriela was a sham, an out-of-necessity arrangement with an expiration date. Claire would go with her, not him. Neither one of them was his to keep, no matter how much he pretended.

Their first night at Millbrook surpassed Gabriela's expectations. Claire slept for five hours straight and had easily returned to sleep after a diaper change and a bottle.

Maybe it was the change of scenery, a quite literal one. Or maybe the clean air and the sounds of nature. Whatever the perfect recipe was that had provided such a calming rest, Gabriela was ready to embrace this change and take it with her when they returned to the city. Or maybe she could suggest to Damian that they visit Highland Park more often and for longer periods of time.

This long weekend trip reminded Gabriela of the times she and her siblings had gone from Porto to the grandparents' farm in the countryside to spend summer with the cousins. In relation to Manhattan, Millbrook was the countryside, but the similarities ended there. From what she'd seen of Highland Park, it was a veritable mansion with magnificent rooms. Damian had promised her a tour today and she was looking forward to that.

He'd left early to meet with the estate's overseer. As Damian had explained, the man managed the buildings and grounds to make sure everything was kept in good running condition.

Gabriela fed and dressed Claire, enjoying their time in the beautiful nursery. Nanna Vaughn's words about babies easily came to Gabriela's mind. Would she and Damian adopt again? Nanna had advised them to have more children while they were young, as it would be easier on them.

But more children and easier weren't in their future. Separation and divorce were. And only a month into the charade, Gabriela had realized how many people would be affected by that. Why hadn't she thought that through better before she'd signed up for this? It wasn't just her heart that would break, but Damian's mother's and grandmother's likely as well.

His grandmother's question had caught her off guard, the subject of more babies was something that had never and would never come up for discussion between them. She wouldn't have to explain to Damian why they'd have to adopt again, and why she couldn't get pregnant. Her secret was hers to keep.

As was Claire when this was all over. For some reason, this thought didn't bring the joy it had only a few weeks ago. She loved Claire and wanted nothing so much as to be her mother forever. Nothing so much, except perhaps Claire's father. He hadn't figured as much into the equation at first. But now her heart had plans her mind hadn't thought of.

She was doing a poor job protecting her heart.

When Gabriela came down, she found Linda and Nanna, and Mrs. Finch, in a bright room facing west. The main wall was entirely made of French doors and large windows, making it the perfect room to be used at this time of day.

A chorus of good-mornings greeted her. Linda stood and came around the table, and reached for Claire.

"Come see what arrived by special courier," she said excitedly. "Cathy won't be in for another hour and I was too impatient."

Gabriela followed her to the next room where a high chair stood by the wall.

"Bring it over by the table," Linda directed.

Once in place between two chairs, she strapped Claire in. "The seat is reclined and I put the tray away until she gets older."

Linda took her seat on one side and Gabriela on the other, with Claire in the middle, content to look around.

Gabriela joined in for breakfast and took a plate of scrambled eggs and a latte from the cook.

"Do you have plans for today?" Nanna Vaughn asked.

"Damian said he'll take me on a tour of the house and the grounds," Gabriela replied.

"Where is Damian?" Linda asked.

"He left early to meet with the overseer."

"Mr. Pepper," Nanna said. "We can't run Highland Park without him. Or his father and grandfather before him."

For a few minutes, Nanna Vaughn talked about how many employees Highland Park used to have in the old days. "His children didn't want to follow in his steps, like the generations before. When he retires, we'll have to find someone else. Of course, I won't be here to worry about that."

"Who won't be here?" Damian asked as he entered the room.

He wore dark jeans and a black T-shirt and Gabriela couldn't remember seeing him with such a carefree expression. He smiled at her and she followed him with her eyes as he went around the room, greeting Nanna and Linda.

"I won't be here," Nanna replied. "I was telling your wife about the need to hire a new overseer when Mr. Pepper retires. You'll have to worry about that."

"No need to be morbid, Nanna," Damian said. "You still have a lot of good years left in you."

"I've been waiting for you to marry and have a child." She shrugged.

Damian glanced at her but didn't comment. He tickled Claire's feet. "Look at the big girl in the high chair." Then he leaned down and brushed a kiss on Gabriela's cheek. "Good morning," he said quietly in her ear.

The little hairs in the nape of her neck rose instantly.

"Good morning," she said in the same tone, smiling. When she looked around, she found the others staring at them.

"Don't hold yourselves back on our account," Nanna said.

"Hold what back?" Damian asked, voicing Gabriela's own question.

"You don't have to kiss demurely in front of us," Nanna replied with a wink.

Linda chuckled. "I agree. You're newlyweds. Aren't pecks on the cheek a bit tame?"

Was teasing newlyweds a global pastime? First her family, and now Damian's. Gabriela turned to him to see his reaction.

"If you insist," Damian said to his mom. He took Gabriela's face in his hands and his lips descended on hers.

Only this kiss was not like the other times he'd kissed her in front of others—firm, strong and almost too personal for an audience.

The sides of his thumbs caressed the skin of her jaw and, just as Gabriela found herself parting her lips, craving more, Damian pulled back and straightened. "Was that better, Nanna?"

Nanna cleared her throat. "Much so."

Gabriela returned to her breakfast, pretending to carry on as before while her heart clamored to jump out of her chest. Had it affected him at all or was it all a game?

After taking a cup of coffee and a plate of eggs from the cook, he sat beside Gabriela, telling Nanna about his time spent with the overseer.

Slowly, her racing heart calmed, her flushed cheeks cooled and the prickles at the back of her neck faded. She even managed to join the conversation as if nothing had happened.

"Gabriela said you're giving her a tour?" Linda asked Damian.

He glanced at Gabriela and then at his mom. "I want to show her the house this morning, and the grounds this afternoon."

Linda turned to Gabriela. "You're going to love it."

"You're getting the special guided tour, from top to bottom," Damian replied with a smile pulling at the corner of his mouth. "It includes the attic and the dungeon. And that's just the inside."

Linda picked up her phone and swiped at the screen. "Cathy's here with her crew." She stood. "We have a lot of work to do. I'll see you all later." She leaned over Claire. "I'll see you soon, little cutie."

Claire responded with a wide toothless grin. It was wonderful to see her more and more social as she grew older.

Nanna Vaughn and Mrs. Finch soon excused themselves, leaving Damian and Gabriela at the table.

In the nearly empty room, and without the others to act as a buffer between she and Damian, Gabriela's tension rose. In the presence of company, the rules were clear—they were newlyweds and expected to act as such.

But in privacy, and without witnesses, knowing how to treat her only-in-paper husband became a source of apprehension—kindness, always. But how much familiarity? Sharing a bed didn't make them any more married when it was only a place to sleep. How ironic that the one person who was supposed to be the most present in her life was also the one with whom she felt the least certainty.

As Damian shifted in his seat, Gabriela stood from her chair and unstrapped Claire. Then her gaze fell on the table. "Should we help clear the breakfast dishes?"

Damian stood and tucked in the chairs. "Someone will come along and do it after we leave."

She nodded. Old habits were hard to break, and she wasn't used to leaving plates on the table, even if it was someone else's job to clean them. She'd just have to keep reminding herself this was her life for the time being. When the contract was over, she'd return to her normal.

They started the tour at the front of the house. Damian led her to the foyer and, from there, he showed her the front parlor, the music room, and they peeked in the salon, where Linda and a younger woman directed some workers.

"The party will be here tomorrow night," Damian said.

The present activity confirmed his words, as furniture had been pushed to the walls and decorations abounded everywhere.

As they went throughout the rest of the ground floor, they took turns carrying Claire.

Damian gestured to the staircase. "Many a time I was caught sliding down the banister," he said with a chuckle.

She could almost see him then, what with the way his eyes twinkled when he share the memory. "Were you punished?"

"Do scoldings count?"

She smiled. "Nobody had the heart to chastise you."

They visited all the rooms, whether large or small, and he kept true to his word by adding tidbits about the family history and showing her other places where he'd gotten in trouble as a child.

After the attic, with soaring views of the property and the river beyond, they returned to the library, which had also served as Damian's grandfather's office and still contained many of his favorite things.

Damian sat behind the mahogany desk with Claire on his lap while Gabriela lingered over the book spines and the glass case with artifacts collected on long ago trips.

"One of my oldest memories is playing on the window seat with miniature toy soldiers while Grandpa worked at this desk. I must have been four," he said wistfully.

On a second pass around the room, a thin volume caught Gabriela's attention and she pulled it out.

The dusty little book with its familiar drawings brought a smile to her face. "Is this a first-edition of The Little Prince?"

"Most likely, and probably not the only first-edition either. Nanna loved to read and Grandpa loved to buy her books."

As Damian told more stories of his childhood, Claire fell asleep to his voice and Gabriela continued to explore the amazing room. It quickly became one of her favorite places at Highland Park.

After the kiss and awkwardness at breakfast, Damian was back to his relaxed self, much to Gabriela's relief. Talking about his family and his memories of growing up brought him out of his mood and smoothed the worry from his expression. She liked this version of him much better.

On their way back, they passed Linda carrying an armful of artificial flowers.

"Do you need some help?" Gabriela asked her.

"Absolutely not," she said with a smile. "That's not what you came for. You two go spend some family time together."

"Don't take it personally," Damian said, after his mom had hurried on along. She loves doing things like this but has little excuse to do them for a long time."

They ate lunch by themselves. Linda was still busy with preparations for the party and Nanna Vaughn stayed in her suite with her companion. Afterward, with Claire fed and changed, Gabriela and Damian returned to the foyer at the front of the house.

He retrieved the baby stroller from the closet. "With this little peanut in tow, I thought we should cut the outside tour short and stick to the immediate grounds. I hope you don't mind."

Gabriela buckled Claire in the stroller. "I don't mind." That was reality with a baby. "The little miss is in charge, aren't you, Claire?" Claire grinned. "She's completely in agreement, as you can see."

Damian chuckled. "She's a little tyrant and she loves it."

Damian showed Gabriela the courtyard, the swimming pool, the rose gardens, and the glass greenhouse. The visit turned even shorter than they'd planned, as Claire's tolerance to sit in the stroller for a long period of time proved to be much too thin. By the end, Gabriela had to carry a cranky Claire while Damian pushed the empty stroller back to the house.

"I'm sorry she's not feeling well," Damian said. "Maybe we can try again on Sunday. We don't leave back to Manhattan until after lunch."

"I'd like that," Gabriela said. "We'll see if Miss Claire will cooperate with us." If only they could stay for a whole week instead of a long weekend, then Damian would have the time to show her all the places at Highland Park. Already she loved the house and grounds, and perfectly understood why Nanna didn't go to Manhattan when she had paradise here.

Claire's mood didn't improve for the rest of the day, and Gabriela couldn't figure out what troubled the baby. What if she didn't get better by the time the party started? Gabriela had planned to bring down a portable crib for Claire so she could keep her close by while she and Damian mingled with guests.

Maybe that wouldn't be a good idea if whatever was ailing Claire didn't go away.

In the evening, Gabriela tiptoed out of the nursery and left the door barely ajar. She stood still, waiting for any sounds, but none came. Claire was finally asleep. What an ordeal that had been. Poor baby.

When she turned, she found Damian coming from the direction of the elevator.

"Is she sleeping?" He asked.

Gabriela touched a finger to her lips and Damian nodded. He took her elbow and led her to the other end of the hallway, toward the staircase.

"Did you turn on the monitor?" Damian asked.

Gabriela pulled her phone out of her jeans' pocket and opened the app where she could see live video feed of Claire sleeping soundly.

Damian looked over her shoulder, one hand still on her elbow and the other on her lower back.

A string of shivers stole up her back and Gabriela took a low, calming breath, concentrating on acting as normal as possible. The way he stood so close to her was not helping.

"Perfect," he said. "I saved you a plate from dinner. Come on."

He took her hand and they descended the staircase. Once in the kitchen, Damian retrieved a covered plate from the refrigerator and placed it in the microwave. After being done, he took it out, pulled the film away, and placed it on the table where a setting for one was already laid out. Gabriela sat down and he took the closest chair to her.

"Thank you. This is wonderful," Gabriela said after the first forkful of ravioli. "I'm sorry I missed dinner with your mom and grandma."

"No apology necessary. They know how it is." After a short pause he added, "I have a surprise for you."

"What kind of surprise?" His hesitation piqued her interest.

He rubbed the side of his jaw, the tell-tale sign he was nervous, but his eyes shone bright with a touch of enthusiasm.

"First, I have to confess I had two surprises planned. But the more I thought about the second surprise, the more I realized you'd probably want to have some input in it."

Smart man. He was right on that one. "I'm intrigued. What is it?"

"It's about a babysitter for Claire during the party tomorrow. I think we'll enjoy our time much better if we don't have to worry about her."

"I have been worried about that," Gabriela confessed. "Hopefully Claire will be feeling better tomorrow, but even if she isn't, I like the idea of having a babysitter watch her, someone to be there with her."

"I was hoping you'd agree with that."

"Did you find someone trustworthy?"

"I did. I'll show you the list of babysitters and we can choose one tomorrow morning."

Gabriela finished her dinner, rinsed the plate and utensils, and placed them in the dishwasher. "Where's that surprise?"

"In the basement." He smiled.

"Which you conveniently left out of the tour this morning."

"You noticed." He gestured toward the back of the

kitchen. "This way. These are the service stairs. They go from the basement to the attic."

Gabriela followed him. The staircase was only wide enough for one person and illuminated by artificial light, unlike the wide main stairs at the front of the house with large windows and sweeping turns.

The bottom landing and hallway were brightly lit as well.

"There's an exercise room, storage and mechanical rooms, and probably other rooms I can't remember. But this one is my favorite." Damian stopped in front of a solid wood white door with a small golden plaque that said screening room.

"What's a screening room?" She asked.

He opened the door wide and flipped on the switch as they entered. Despite the light fixtures being on, she couldn't immediately see what was inside other than fabric-covered walls and dark ceilings.

As Gabriela's eyes adjusted to the ambient light, three rows of upholstered recliners flanking a center aisle became visible.

"Is this a movie theater?"

Damian walked on ahead to the front and turned on the screen and more lights. "My grandpa liked calling it the screening room because it was here he screened so many of the first-cuts produced by the company."

"Do you still do that?"

"I do all that kind of work at the studio. This room is for entertainment only. I had the sound and image systems redone a few years ago with new technology. I think you're going to like it."

The seats were wide enough for two people and Damian led her to the one at the front. Gabriela took her phone out of her pocket and placed it face up on the cup-holder to keep an eye on Claire. After sitting himself next to her, he pulled out a lever on the side until the back reclined and the bottom popped up as a footrest.

"Very comfortable," she said.

"The trick is to not fall asleep while watching a movie," Damian said. "But this is a great one. No chance of sleeping through it."

Gabriela chuckled. "Let me guess. Is it one of the company's movies?"

"Yes, it is. Not only do you have to watch it, you also have to promise to like it," he said in a mock serious tone.

As the movie started, the lights in the room faded, leaving on a track of tiny lights on the floor to mark the way out.

"I can't promise anything. Claire didn't sleep well last night."

"I'm sorry," he said. "I'll get up with her tonight."

The screen brightened the whole room and *The Vaughn Family Movie Channel presents* appeared in large letters.

"I'll be okay." Gabriela glanced at Damian and found him watching her, his eyes bright and large, his expression tender and warm.

A fluttering sprung in her stomach, the warm feeling spreading and setting her heart on a wild beat.

He raised his arm and softly whispered, "Come here."

Ignoring all the warning bells ringing loudly within her, she shortened the distance and settled against him, fitting perfectly at his side with his arm around her shoulders and his hand coming to rest on her upper arm. In a natural gesture, she rested her hand on his chest. His breath caught and his arm tightened on her, then he leaned in her direction and kissed the side of her forehead.

Gabriela looked up and he held her gaze.

What was happening between them?

Neither one of them needed to remind the other of the obvious—they were alone. There was no one else around for whom they had to pretend, no one to impress. They both knew it. Her awareness of him, of the way they sat so close to each other, the way they touched, the firmness of his chest and the scent of his skin—all of him and all of her and nothing else.

Slowly, ever so slowly, Damian bent his head and his lips parted. Gabriela straightened and met him halfway until their lips touched. At last.

Unlike the other times they'd kissed, this kiss was slow, deliberate, unhurried.

His hands splayed her back and brought her even closer. Gabriela wound her arms around his neck and, as their mouths turned into the perfect angle, she parted her lips. Immediately, Damian deepened the kiss.

A glorious shiver passed through her. If he felt anything close to what she did right now, they'd for sure combust in a swell of feelings and emotions, all of them too grand to contain inside.

More. Don't stop.

"Yes. Yes." Damian whispered in her ear, his voice rough and ragged, marking the side of her neck in a string of hot little kisses.

Had she really said the words out loud?

"Are you sure?" came another whisper from him in between more kisses.

Did he even have to ask?

A loud rattling noise interrupted them. They stilled, as if the noise would pass them over and continue on to somewhere else if only they remained immobile, their mingled breaths quiet and expectant.

When it rang again more insistently, Gabriela disengaged her arms from Damian's neck and reached for her phone.

"Claire's awake," she said, the alert clear and unmistakable on the small screen. "She's awake," she repeated, more to herself than him.

Damian let out a deep sound, more groan than sigh, and scrubbed his face in a long movement laden with something she recognized too well—frustration.

CHAPTER ELEVEN

After leaving the screening room to attend to Claire, Gabriela had found Damian asleep by the time she returned to bed. And in the morning, when she woke up to baby sounds over the monitor on the bedside table, he was already gone.

For two people married in name only, with a contract that declared their intentions to stay away from anything physical between them, they had certainly indulged in the most passionate kiss of her life. Even Damian's for-display-purposes kisses had paled in comparison, not to mention the few kisses she'd received from men before.

But more than the beginning kiss was what happened after. Or rather, what hadn't happened. If Claire was a baby with better sleeping habits, how far would have they taken their make-out session? She clearly remembered wanting more, even asking for it out loud, and Damian had said yes.

What would she say to him when she saw him next? How awkward would it be between them again?

Relationships were never easy but theirs was even more complicated than normal. The more they knew each other, the closer they grew. The attraction had also grown stronger and she was now sure it was mutual. But the nature of their marriage, the reason behind it, the expiration date on their contract—that was their reality.

She changed and fed and dressed Claire, then quickly dressed herself and made her way to the breakfast room, where she found Nanna Vaughn and Mrs. Finch.

"Good morning," she greeted them, then pulled the high chair from its place and strapped Claire in. "Did Linda and Damian already eat?"

"We haven't seen them. I assume Linda is with the event planner, worrying too much about getting everything perfect for tonight." Nanna took a sip of her drink. "Did you not see your husband this morning?"

"He left without waking me up." Could Gabriela blame him? She might have done the same.

Nanna's expression softened. "His grandfather was considerate like that." For a few minutes, she told stories of her husband and the little things he'd done for her.

Gabriela only half-listened, mentally going through her list of Damian's kindnesses toward her, which were too many to enumerate. How had she not noticed until now? Of course, leaving the bedroom before she woke was his way to avoid an embarrassing situation for the both of them, wasn't it?

After breakfast, she placed Claire in the stroller and went for a walk in the rose garden. The day before, during her tour with Damian, Gabriela's glimpse of it had been brief and she was now anxious to see it with more time.

The morning was clear and already warming, with a bright blue sky that rivaled the one in Manhattan. But as blue and bright as it was over Highland Park, it was the Lisbon sky she missed the most.

Damian had said they could visit Portugal any time she wanted but it wasn't the right time yet. One day she'd return.

She pulled down the canopy on the stroller to shield Claire from the sun. The rose garden was a rectangle plot between the east side of the house and a row of Italian cypress trees, designed in simple lines of low hedges and rose bushes in myriad colors. In the center, a stone fountain happily gurgled along with the buzzing of bees and, under the shade of an arbor of climbing lavender roses, a park bench beckoned to Gabriela. She removed Claire from the stroller and sat with the baby on her lap.

Life wasn't perfect, but this moment was. A glorious little slice of time, just her and this baby she adored, cocooned in the scent of flowers and the happiness of being together.

For these few minutes, Gabriela could pretend that everything else in her life was as wonderful, that her husband wanted her just as much as she wanted him, that their marriage was more than a list of stipulations and deadlines. She could pretend she fit into his life and that living in grand houses and spending the weekend at the family estate was normal.

Pretending was easy, wasn't it?

So she stayed on the bench, humming lullabies and telling stories in Portuguese, until the sun chased away the shade and Claire demanded her lunch.

Not ready to face Damian and not wanting to talk to anyone else, Gabriela entered through the back door where she left the stroller, and ducked into the elevator unseen.

Claire fell asleep after being changed and fed. She even stayed in the crib and didn't fuss, didn't wake up. Gabriela hovered for a while, waiting to see what happened, but the baby slept on. Maybe it was the fresh air, or maybe the walk through the gardens; whatever the reason was, Gabriela hoped it wasn't a one-time occurrence.

At lunch, she and Damian met in the kitchen to talk about the babysitter for tonight. Linda reminded them to stay away from the salon and the catering kitchen, and Gabriela agreed since she had no desire to go where all the busyness for the party's preparation was.

Nanna Vaughn and Mrs. Finch had been at lunch as well and, with everyone around, Gabriela and Damian didn't have a chance to talk in private.

It suited Gabriela just right. She wasn't ready to discuss the kiss with him. It could wait until after the party, or even after they returned to Manhattan.

She didn't see Damian again until later, when the babysitter from the agency arrived at five in the afternoon. He met the young woman in the foyer and brought her up to the nursery, where Gabriela sat with Claire, playing on the rug.

"Gabriela," Damian said, entering the room. "This is April Strindberg."

April looked to be in her early twenties, dressed in sensible pants and flats, and had a friendly expression.

Gabriela sat up but April came forward. "Please, don't get up on my account." She joined Gabriela and Claire on the rug, and shook Gabriela's hand. "It's a pleasure to meet you, Mrs. Vaughn."

Then she leaned over Claire and smiled wide. "Hello, Claire, how are you?"

Claire didn't smile back but didn't start crying either, and Gabriela marked that as a success.

She stayed with April for a while, telling her about Claire's routine, showing her where everything was. Damian slipped out of the nursery at some point, and Gabriela didn't notice, so focused she was on getting everything set up for April. Maybe Gabriela was nervous; she could admit that. It was the first time leaving her with a babysitter. It was normal to feel this way, wasn't it? Especially with the babysitter staying until morning so they could stay at the party as late as they wanted.

When Gabriela returned to the bedroom, she found Damian shaving in the bathroom, with the door ajar. He wore a pair of old jeans, hung low on his hips, and a white tank undershirt showing off his shoulders from the back. His biceps flexed with his movements and her heart skipped a beat at the memory of his arms tightly wound around her when they'd kissed the night before. She let out a soundless sigh.

There was something intimate in the simplicity of watching a man getting ready, a kind of vulnerability in his gestures, with his guard let down during such mundane tasks. He stood barefoot on the marble tile and the sight of it only brought the sense of closeness she had with him, like any other husband and wife who lived together. It was comforting to her they had that, despite everything else they lacked.

Damian caught her eye in the reflection of the mirror and slowed. Gabriela didn't break the eye contact as he finished shaving his chin, rinsed the razor, turned off the water and wiped his face on a white towel.

Then he turned around to her. "Do you need to get in the shower?"

She shook her head. "I did this morning."

A knock sounded at the door.

"Come in," Gabriela said.

Linda opened the door and kept her hand on the knob. "Let's go, Gabriela. Time to get ready." Her makeup and hair were already done, but she hadn't put on her evening dress yet.

Gabriela made her way to the door and looked back at Damian before leaving. "I'll meet you back here in thirty minutes."

"One hour," Linda corrected. "Wait for her at the bottom of the staircase," she said to Damian.

He nodded at them.

In the end, the one hour was barely enough. Linda had hired a stylist who did makeup and hair and she worked on Gabriela non-stop from head to toe.

Gabriela would have preferred less fussing but Linda wouldn't have let her get away with it. When she stood in front of the mirror in Linda's dressing room, Gabriela could agree the final effect had been worth all the work.

"You look amazing," the stylist said. "You look absolutely striking in this dress."

"I knew you would," Linda agreed.

After trying on so many dresses when they had gone shopping, Linda had chosen an A-line ankle-length chiffon with a princess scoop neckline, and beading and sequins on the bodice and sleeves.

With her hair artfully arranged in a low messy chignon with tendrils and dramatic makeup, Gabriela felt like an actress in a vintage movie. "I look so different," she said.

"I wish I could be there to witness when Damian sees you," Linda said. "But I need to finish getting ready. I'll find you later."

Gabriela didn't move. "I should take the elevator instead. I'll trip in these heels."

"Not the same effect," Linda said. "You'll be fine."

Gabriela thanked the stylist and Linda, and walked out to the hallway. The sounds of music rose from the floor downstairs and she peeked over the banister. It sounded like some guests had arrived as well.

Then she stilled. In the center of the foyer stood Luke talking to a man with his back to her, a man she would have recognized anywhere. Because he was hers. For a little while at least. For tonight, when she could pretend all she wanted. Gabriela walked forward and stood at the top of the stairs.

Luke removed an envelope from his front pocket and handed it to Damian, then said something with a serious expression. When he looked up, his face relaxed. He tapped Damian on the arm and gestured with his chin up in her direction. Damian turned as she started descending with a firm hand on the banister, just in case.

His expression lightened and his eyes pinned her with a smolder that made her blush.

Goodness.

That look.

This was her moment, much better than any movie that she'd ever watched. Descending the grand staircase in a long dress with a man admiring her with unmistakable appreciation. Not just any man, but the one she was married to.

Her heart skipped, completely surrendering to her feelings for him. Pretending to herself she could resist him was a lie. She only had to hide it from him.

When she arrived at the bottom, he held out his hand to her. She clasped it and he looped her arm through his elbow.

He continued watching her and Gabriela smiled at him.

Damian looked dashing in a slim-fitted black tuxedo and immaculate white shirt. He'd styled his hair back and the close shave he'd done earlier accentuated his jawline and made her wish she could feel his smooth skin with her fingertips.

He leaned close and whispered in her ear. "You've been holding out on me, Mrs. Vaughn."

He'd used an earthy cologne, subtle, masculine. Gabriela found herself pulled in his direction.

"About what, Mr. Vaughn?" she whispered back.

"Red is your color." Another whisper. "You look absolutely amazing, Gabriela."

The genuine approval in his eyes sent a warmth radiating from her chest. "Thank you, Damian." She squeezed his upper arm. "We'll have to find more occasions to dress up. I love seeing you in that tuxedo."

His eyebrows quirked up and a small smile tugged at the corner of his lips. "Thank you. The monkey suit is not my favorite, but if you like it, I'll wear it."

As they made their way toward the salon, the sounds of music reached her ears.

"Where did Luke go?" she asked, after noticing his absence.

"I don't know. I have eyes for you only." He half-winced, half-chuckled and she recognized he was nervous. "That was cheesy. Sorry. But the sentiment is true."

"You keep that up and I'll be blushing all night," she admitted.

"Maybe that's my plan," he teased.

The doors to the salon had been opened wide and they paused at the entrance.

"Your mom went all out, didn't she?"

"I guess we're getting a wedding reception after all," Damian said, looking around.

The adjoining room to the salon had been laid out with long tables for a sit-down dinner, everything richly decorated in tones of white, cream, and soft gray, with twinkling lights and discreet greenery.

His expression was unreadable, and she couldn't begin to guess what he thought of such extravagance.

Other than Damian's family and Luke, Gabriela didn't know any of the one-hundred-fifty guests who'd been invited to the dinner. Instead of sending invitations to her family in Portugal, Gabriela had told Linda she would plan a party for them when she visited, but she couldn't help wonder if the chance for it would come.

Linda introduced them as Mr. and Mrs. Vaughn and offered a toast in their behalf, and Nanna Vaughn was the first to raise her glass.

Several times during the five-course meal, Damian touched Gabriela in different ways—squeezing her fingers, taking her elbow, brushing a hand on her shoulders—as if he couldn't spare the loss of contact with her for too long. But he had to be doing it for show, hadn't he? With so many people watching them, putting on their façade in the most natural way was important to keep their charade as real as possible. It was all about that; nothing more. She had to remember that.

Gabriela smiled through dinner. Damian did as well. It was a fairy tale—a beautiful, happy, fictional one.

When dessert was done, they stood and led the way to the salon for dancing. At the far end, a band transitioned from background music to dancing tunes. Damian walked her to the center of the room and drew her close, one hand around her waist, the other firmly gripping hers.

"I should have known there would be dancing and asked you to practice with me," she said. "I still don't know how to dance," she said.

Damian bent his head toward her. "Nobody's watching."

She chuckled lightly. "Everybody's watching."

"Because you look amazing and they're all jealous of how lucky I am."

Gabriela pulled back a little to look into his eyes. "You don't have to say things you don't mean when nobody else can hear you."

He slowed down and his expression turned serious. "I always mean what I say, Gabriela. You do look amazing and I'm truly lucky to have you."

She swallowed hard. "Thank you," she said softly. "I'm the lucky one." What else could she say without confessing her feelings for him?

His gaze dipped to her lips and his eyes darkened.

She was in trouble if he kept doing that as well.

The band segued into a brass version of a popular song, a romantic ballad, and they kept dancing—or rather, Damian danced and made it look like she knew how to do it as well.

"Are you happy, Gabriela? Do you have everything you need?"

He was full of questions she couldn't answer. They still hadn't talked about *The Kiss*, as Gabriela had come to name it, but everything else seemed to be fair game tonight.

"What more could I want?" Even as she answered his question with one of her own, she knew the answer—she wanted her marriage to him to be real.

She wanted to see the way he looked at her with unmistakable feelings, with a depth of emotion she would never doubt, with her heart full and her mind brimming with unforgettable memories.

After a moment, Damian held her closer. "If we had a song, this would be it."

Again, she didn't know what to say. She didn't doubt he meant it; his tone and expression were genuine. This time, she was saved from replying when a middle-aged couple interrupted and asked Damian for an introduction.

Gabriela smiled wide at the man and his wife, grateful for the distraction and for the chance to shield her tender emotions from Damian.

The more she pretended, the easier it became. But at what cost?

Damian was in trouble.

The longer he held Gabriela in his arms, the more he wanted her. Not just for tonight, not for the one year of the contract—forever.

That he was taking advantage of the situation tonight—keeping at her side through dinner, holding her close while dancing—and didn't care enough to stop it, should have warned him back, but it didn't. This party his mom had organized, extravagant as it was, it was also the perfect excuse for his closeness to Gabriela.

And she was responding to him. Maybe not in words, but her gestures, her body language, all but proclaimed her willingness.

He was so in trouble.

After dancing for the length of two songs, guests started interrupting them. Old friends of the family, a distant relative or two, but also politicians and celebrities with whom Damian had dealt in the past. Mom had obviously curated the guest list.

These people were curious about his Portuguese wife, and he couldn't really blame them. Damian smiled, made introductions, and watched Gabriela charm everyone without even trying. How long until he and she could politely slip out? He would rather spend his time with Gabriela, especially on a night when Claire wouldn't interrupt them.

As he planned an escape, Nanna caught his attention and motioned for them to follow her out of the salon. How timely.

Nanna herded him and Gabriela into the library. "Sit down, Damian. We're going to have a little talk." She turned to Gabriela. "You two, Gabriela. This is for the both of you."

Gabriela nodded, and sat next to Damian, the two of them across from Nanna Vaughn in her favorite wingback chair, like the throne it was.

"Can't this wait until later, Nanna?" Damian asked. "There's a party going on."

"You can spare a few minutes." Nanna paused and raised her eyebrows at them. "You two haven't consummated your marriage yet."

Damian's eyes widened. "Nanna," he exclaimed. "Please. That's private."

"I can tell these things, you know," Nanna Vaughn continued. "There's an aura of repressed sexual tension between you two." She waved her finger between Gabriela and him.

He glanced at Gabriela, expecting her to react, but her amused expression was evidence enough that she wasn't taking Nanna's comments too seriously. At least, Nanna had had the good sense of leading them away from the salon, and there was no one else around in this room or he'd be a lot more embarrassed by her comments.

Nanna gestured at them. "So what's the holdup? You two are married." She cocked her head. "Unless you're not."

"I can assure you, we are married, Nanna," Damian insisted. "Legal in both countries."

"Then it's a sham wedding." She turned to Gabriela. "Are you in trouble with Immigration? Like that movie where they had to get married so she's not deported. Maybe that's the problem."

"There's nothing wrong with Gabriela's immigration status. Luke already helped us get the paperwork started for her to apply for a green card and we're waiting for the appointment to be set."

"I don't understand you then," Nanna said. "You marry a beautiful woman who's the mother of your child, and you don't even—"

"I think you're imagining things," Damian said.

"That's not fair, Damian. Just because I'm eighty-five doesn't mean I'm senile."

He leaned forward toward her. "I'm sorry, Nanna. I didn't mean to offend you."

She sniffled. "The body is slow, but the mind is still very much sharp. And my intuition never fails. You won't admit to anything, but I know there's something not right between you two."

"There's nothing to admit, Nanna. We got married in Lisbon and I brought my wife home." That much was true.

Gabriela slipped her hand into his and squeezed his fingers. Was she telling him to calm down?

"I know you got it in your mind when you were younger that you had to live a celibate life on account of your father's many mistakes and poor examples, but I always thought that was utter nonsense. You're completely different from your father. Take your new wife and make sweet love to her. You can thank me later for the advice."

Damian stood and pulled Gabriela with him. "I appreciate the talk, Nanna, but we should probably get back to the party. There's a lot of people we haven't greeted yet."

"You do know how it's done, right?" Nanna asked. "If not, I know of this book with some beautiful photographs—"

Damian held a hand up. "We're fine, Nanna. No book necessary."

Nanna tilted her cheek and he bent down to drop a kiss. "We'll see you later."

Gabriela kissed Nanna on the cheek in the Portuguese way.

"Don't let him push you where you don't want to go, dear," Nanna said to Gabriela.

"I won't."

What was that about? Did Gabriela know what his grandmother meant with that? He had no clue.

"Bring baby Claire to see me in the morning," Nanna called out as they left.

Once in the hallway, Damian found the closest exit

to the courtyard at the rear of the house and away from the salon. "This way," he whispered to Gabriela.

They still held hands, and he pulled her behind him until they reached a Cyprus tree and took a seat on the closest park bench.

Gabriela burst out laughing. "Your grandma is quite the character," she said at last.

"I'm sorry. I didn't know she was going to pull that." Damian chuckled. "Nanna's usually quite proper, but once in a while her conversations veer to the inappropriate."

"Do you think she meant it?" Gabriela asked. "That she knows we have a marriage of convenience that hasn't been consummated?"

Damian choked at her frankness and had to pause to clear his throat. "You sure know how to get to the subject as well."

"Those were her words, not mine."

"I can't see how Nanna would know anything," he said. "She's bluffing, trying to get a rise out of us."

"But why would she do that?"

As Damian struggled to find an answer, his phone vibrated in his pocket.

"Is it the babysitter?" Gabriela's voice bordered on anxious.

He swiped at the screen. "No, it's mom. She wants us to come to the service door right now."

They stood from the bench.

"What is it? Did something happen to Claire? Or Nanna?"

Damian took her hand. "It's my father."

How he was able to say the word without contempt in his voice surprised him.

His father's presence at Highland Park, today of all days, could only mean trouble. What was he doing here? And how had he gotten in?

They made it back in silence, Damian's chest tightening with each step, the questions swirling in his mind. As they approached, Gabriela gave his fingers a squeeze and the gesture relieved some of his tension. She was there beside him, it said.

The scene at the service entrance was oddly quiet and anti-climactic. Damian had expected more commotion.

Two men in black suits and earpieces flanked the door, their stance firm. If two security guards were here, there would be others inside the house and on the property. Mom had truly thought of everything.

Mom stood just inside the door and his father had taken a seat on a low wall and smoked a cigarette. How typical of him, to disregard their wishes when he knew that his son, his ex-wife and his own mother didn't like smoking of any kind on the grounds.

"I'm sorry I had to bother you, Damian," mom said.

"It's not you who's bothering me," he replied.

Walter Vaughn looked the same as the last time Damian had seen him. He was still an attractive man, and he had always used his looks to his own advantage and the detriment to others. Tonight, he wore a black tuxedo with a white bow tie, never a black one.

At the sound of their steps, his father stood and dropped the cigarette butt. "There you are, D—"

"Pick that up." Damian gave him a wide berth and stopped by the door. Gabriela stood to his side, holding on to his arm, more to support him than to shield herself. It amazed him how her contact and warmth kept him grounded. If not for her, he would have already clocked Walter Vaughn.

"What?" His father asked.

"You littered. Pick it up."

Walter scoffed. "My mother keeps employees for that." He ground the worn cigarette into the gravel. "I came to see you and your mother had these goons stop me from entering." He cocked his head and paused. "Is that your new wife? You did better than I thought."

How did he manage to offer a twisted compliment and a veiled insult at the same time? That took a warped kind of talent.

Damian remained silent. That comment didn't deserve an answer.

"Aren't you going to introduce me?"

"That's unnecessary," Damian replied. "I'm sure these gentlemen have asked you to leave, after mom already asked you to leave, and I must insist on the same. Leave. You're not welcome here and you weren't invited."

"I don't need an invitation to come see my new daughter-in-law and granddaughter. Where's the baby? I want to see her too."

"That's not going to happen, either." Damian would make sure of that, whatever it took.

Damian nodded at the security guards and they stepped forward.

Walter Vaughn slipped his hands in his pockets. "Hold the gorillas back. I'm going." The corner on his mouth rose. "I got what I came for." He held a hand up. "Always a pleasure to see you, Linda. And a real pleasure to see you, new-Mrs.Vaughn." Then he turned and walked away.

One of the men in black followed him, the other stayed by the door.

Damian's shoulders relaxed, as he let the tension seep out from him. Why did he always feel like he'd aged years after facing the man?

Gabriela touched his arm. "Was he drunk?"

"He could be, but he knows how to hold his liquor." Damian let out a breath. "I'm sorry you had to witness his display."

"It's not your place to apologize," Gabriela said.

She was right, of course, but he still felt somewhat responsible. He should have known Walter Vaughn wouldn't have let this opportunity pass without his personal brand of interference. He was that kind of man.

Gabriela looped her arm through Mom's and he went to them, draping his arm over Mom's shoulders. Together, they rejoined the party which was going on the same as before. Such a relief.

After Mom left to greet some old acquaintances, Luke walked up with a raised eyebrow.

"Is everything okay?" he asked.

"Walter was here," Damian said.

Luke's eyebrows shot up.

"I made sure he left," Damian rushed to add. "Let's talk about it tomorrow. I don't want to ruin the rest of the party."

Luke nodded. "Yes, of course."

Damian and Gabriela mingled and danced and talked and, when the band announced the last song of the night, he pulled her in for one more turn around the salon and held on tight to her.

He couldn't shake the rest of the strain the earlier situation had put on him but dancing with her nulled the sharp sting. Holding Gabriela was the balm he needed. How was he going to convince her she had to stay in his arms until the night ended?

In the elevator, Gabriela leaned into him and removed her shoes. "We can't forget to thank your mom. It was a lovely party."

Damian draped his arm around her shoulders to better support her. "It was." His arm tightened on her. "Thank you for staying at my side, especially during the unpleasant business of my father showing up uninvited."

She looked to him. "Where else would I be, Damian?"

Such trust in her eyes. What had he done to deserve those words, that look?

The elevator arrived and they stepped out.

"I'm going to take a peek at Claire and the babysitter," Gabriela said.

Damian took the shoes from her and went to their bedroom, loosening the bow tie on his way there. He put Gabriela's shoes in the closet, took off the tuxedo coat and draped it on the back of a chair, then removed the cuff links and white shirt, the belt, the socks and shoes. Down to his black tuxedo pants and white tank shirt, Damian sat down on the upholstered bench at the end of the bed. He stretched his arms over his head and rolled his neck.

Gabriela returned. "They're both sleeping." She stopped when she saw him, her eyes lingering on his shoulders, arms, then dropping to his feet.

Suddenly, the air in the bedroom felt too hot. Damian swallowed.

After a brief moment, she continued, "Thanks for hiring the babysitter. I know I was nervous about it, but I have to admit it was nice to not worry about Claire." She reached for her earrings and removed them, then turned around and placed them on top of her dresser.

"You're welcome. I'm glad it worked out." At least that had gone well. "You should take the chance to sleep all night."

"I'll try."

He walked to the door connecting to the nursery and made sure it was locked.

Gabriela watched him but didn't comment.

Here they were, alone, with no interruptions, sharing a bedroom and getting ready to share a bed. He was even half-undressed already. Gabriela still wore her dress, her bare feet and ankles peeked from under the hem. He'd seen her barefoot before, but not while wearing a red evening dress that looked amazing on her. Her toenails were painted in a matching red and a fantasy ran wild through his mind.

He should put a break on those thoughts.

She sat in front of the mirror and started removing the pins from the back of her head, locks of hair untwisting in long tendrils down to her shoulders.

How could something so simple as tumbling hair cause his pulse to speed up like crazy?

Before he lost his mind—and his control—Damian went in the bathroom and changed into his pajama bottoms.

When he returned, Gabriela was nowhere to be seen. "Gabriela?"

"In the closet," came her answer.

She must be removing her dress.

Damian sat on the bed, against the pillows and headboard, and picked up his phone from the bedside table to give his hands something to do.

She came out a minute later, still wearing the dress, and stopped in the middle of the room.

Damian looked up. "Is everything all right?"

"Would you mind unzipping my dress, please?" Gabriela asked. "I was trying to do it myself and I think I got it stuck."

Was that a trick question? He wouldn't mind, even though he should. The way he felt at the moment, touching her was not a good idea. "Sure," he replied.

"Thank you."

Was it his impression or did she actually blush?

Damian stood, put down the phone down, and came around the bed.

Gabriela turned her back to him and held her hair in one hand.

At the sight of her exposed neck, his breath caught.

She turned to look at him over her shoulder. "Unless you can unzip with your mind, you'll have to touch it."

"I'm assessing the situation." Now he was, as he bent to get a better look. He grabbed the zipper's pull. "It's stuck all right." There was also no wiggle room. The dress fit Gabriela like a glove. "If you don't mind my asking, how did you get it zipped up?"

"I had help from the stylist your mom hired."

Damian tried again. His fingers touched her neck and her skin rose in goose bumps.

This was going to take longer than he'd thought. He stood so close, he couldn't think of anything else but her. The heat and scent emanating from her body. All his senses on high alert, perception raised.

"I'd rather not damage the dress to get out of it," Gabriela said.

"Have some faith," he said. "If not in me, then let's ask Google." He grabbed his phone, did a search and read the suggestions. "Hang on." Then he walked to the bathroom, scratched the top of a soap bar with his fingernail, and returned to Gabriela.

After rubbing a tiny amount of soap on the teeth, the zipper slid down effortlessly.

Too much so.

The sides of the dress opened up, sliding off Gabriela's shoulders.

"Oh," she said, crossing her arms in an attempt to stop the dress from falling off her frame.

Damian placed his hands on her, one on her shoulder blade, the other on her waist.

"Thank you," came her whisper.

"You're welcome," he replied in the same tone.

They didn't move. Gabriela still stood with her back to him, her hair draped to one side. Damian stood exactly behind her, their clothes touching, if not their bodies.

Unable to hold back, he bent his head and brushed a kiss on her skin, in the space between her neck and her shoulder.

This time, it was Gabriela's breath that caught.

After a moment, he placed another kiss, took a step closer, and encircled her waist with his arm. Her hand came to rest over his.

"I wish I had the words to convey to you how beautiful you are to me."

"Shh," she said, turning in his embrace until they faced each other. Gabriela wound her arms around his neck and brought him down for a kiss. Intimate, commanding.

More than a kiss. So much more.

Was this really happening?

"Are you su—"

"Don't say anything," she cut him off, her urgent whispers fanning the side of his face in between burning kisses. "Don't think. Just do."

Tomorrow, he would say all the things to Gabriela.

Tonight, he would just do.

CHAPTER TWELVE

*W*hen Gabriela woke up the next morning, Damian wasn't in bed with her.

She stayed under the sheets for a while, her mind full of memories of the hours they had spent together and her heart brimming with a new kind of love for him. A long night of lost sleep and heightened senses, the kind that blurred all the lines together to form a new shape of reality, a new path in their relationship.

Did he feel as different as she did this morning?

Gabriela waited but he didn't return. Sounds from the nursery reminded her of her responsibilities. She took a quick shower, dressed, and retrieved Claire before the babysitter had to leave. Still, no sign of Damian.

Where was he? She sent him a text but he hadn't replied to that either.

Little by little, a knot of anxiety threatened an appearance, even as she tried to push it away.

251

She made her way to the breakfast room. Linda, Nanna Vaughn and Mrs. Finch sat at the table and Gabriela joined them.

"There you are," Linda said. "Did you sleep well without interruptions from Claire?"

"Yes, it was wonderful." Gabriela shouldn't assume for Damian, but she hoped he felt the same way, wherever he was. "I want to thank you, Linda, Damian and I both want to thank you for the beautiful party."

Linda smiled. "You're so welcome. I'm glad you liked it. It was so much fun to organize."

"I know how hard you worked on it and everything was so well done and turned out just amazing. Even—" Gabriela stopped herself and glanced at Nanna.

Nanna waved her off. "No need to stop on my account. I already know my reprobate son made an unwelcome appearance. Too bad I had already retired to my room or I'd have given him a piece of my mind. He likes to get a rise out of us, especially Damian."

"Speaking of Damian," Gabriela said. "I can't seem to locate him this morning."

Linda wiped her mouth on the cloth napkin. "He left early this morning on some business."

Damian had left? Without saying anything to her? The knot in her chest grew and tightened.

Gabriela recovered quickly, not wanting her mother-in-law and Damian's grandmother to know how much his departure affected her. "That's right. I think I remember him mentioning something."

Nanna Vaughn and Linda exchanged a look but didn't say anything. Thank goodness they both kept their good breeding and social manners from interfering. If it had been Gabriela's Portuguese family, they would have asked all sorts of nosy questions.

Gabriela kept up the small talk through the rest of breakfast for as long as she could, her mind too occupied with all the possibilities and scenarios, her hope sinking with each passing minute.

At the first opportunity, she stood from the table and grabbed Claire. "I'm going for a walk before I start packing."

Linda looked up from her tablet. "At what time are you leaving for Manhattan?"

"I'm not sure, but not too late. I want to give Claire a chance to settle down from traveling before her bedtime. Do you want me to wait for you?"

"I don't know when I'll be ready," Linda said. "You go on ahead and I'll see you at home."

Gabriela placed Claire in the stroller, strapped her in, and pulled down the canopy. She walked through the rose garden, but didn't stop. Once she had gone far enough away from the house, she found a bench in the shade, pulled the canopy back on the stroller and straightened the seat so Claire had a better view of her surroundings.

She sat for a moment, with the phone in her hand, getting the courage to dial Damian's number. What if he didn't answer?

At last, she pushed the button with the speed dial for his number.

He picked up on the second ring and Gabriela exhaled in relief.

"Hi, Gabriela. How are you?"

The normality of his voice threw her off, as if they'd seen each other an hour ago instead of last night. "I'm—good. I didn't see you this morning."

"I left early and I didn't want to wake you up. You didn't see the note?"

"What note?"

"The note I left on your bedside table."

"I didn't see it. I'll have to look when I go back to the bedroom. I'm in the garden with Claire."

"How is she doing?"

"She's doing great. She likes to be outside. Where are you?"

"I'm on the way to the airport. There's an issue with Sabine Chamberlain and I need to be in Hollywood. You know how are actresses are."

Sabine Chamberlain was an A-List celebrity actress, one of the best paid in Hollywood. And no, Gabriela didn't know how actresses were. Damian never talked about his job, about the work at the studio, what it entailed. She knew he was the CEO, and also had other responsibilities as the heir to the family business, but what that really meant on a professional level, she had no idea.

Damian continued. "There's a chance we might be able to cast her in our next movie and I have to be there for the talks and negotiations."

"Of course," Gabriela said.

"With all the distractions, I forgot to tell you about it," Damian said.

Had he forgotten or was he making up an excuse? There had been nothing on his schedule for today or the next week, not after the party.

And what did he mean with distractions. The party? Or her?

"I asked James to come to Highland Park," Damian said. "He'll take you home to Manhattan whenever you're ready. Listen, I have to board. Can I call you later?"

"Of course," she repeated.

"Have a good day, Gabriela."

"Bye, Damian," she said, but he'd already hung up.

He hadn't avoided her, like she'd feared, but he hadn't brought up their night together either. He'd barely been personal at all, but was distracted and somewhat aloof. Why had he left so abruptly and without waking her up? Did he have regrets of their night together?

Gabriela didn't have any. They were married, in every sense of the word now, and their relationship wouldn't be the same as before. But that was good, wasn't it?

She had hoped for more of a connection between them, and his behavior confused her.

When Gabriela returned to the bedroom to finish the packing, she looked for the note, on the bedside table first, then under the bed, where she found it, almost halfway under.

It was a simple sheet of lined paper, folded in half, with only three lines of handwriting.

Gabriela,

I'm sorry to leave without talking to you, but something came up and I have to go to California. I'll call you when I get a chance.

Damian

P.S.—Last night was amazing.

She read the last line again. That didn't feel like he had any regrets and, although that was comforting to her, she still had so many questions.

After lunch, she left to Manhattan, having promised Nanna Vaughn she would return for a visit, even if Damian didn't have the time to accompany her and the baby. Gabriela made the promise, wondering, deep down, if she was in any condition to make such an assurance to the old lady.

Returning to the house in Manhattan without him didn't feel right, like part of the family was missing.

She was such a fool, falling for a man who didn't love her back.

Damian didn't call back later like he'd said he would. Should she worry about the lack of communication from him? Surely, if something bad had happened, the news would have reached her already.

Her phone rang early on Monday morning. Gabriela turned over and hurried to get it when she saw Damian's number on the screen.

"Damian, is everything all right?"

"Hi, Gabriela. I'm sorry I'm calling so early." He sighed wearily. "Everything's fine."

She glanced at the time. "Aren't you three hours behind?"

"Yes, I am. I wasn't able to call last night and I have a full schedule today, but I wanted to tell you I'm thinking about you and…Claire. We'll take more when I get back."

"When are you coming back?"

"I'm not sure yet, but I'll let you know. Have a good day, Gabriela."

"You too, Damian."

After he hung up, she looked at the phone for a moment, then rolled on her back and stared at the ceiling.

It was barely past six in the morning, which meant three in California. Why was Damian up so early? Or had he stayed up late? Whichever the case, that had been a strange phone call.

She was now wide awake and unable to go back to sleep. Claire would wake up soon and it was probably time Gabriela resumed the routine she'd worked to establish since moving into Manhattan. Claire needed the predictability of a schedule and so did she. Four days in Highland Park had been—mostly— wonderful, but placing their lives on hold in Damian's absence would only make it harder on a day-to-day basis.

On Tuesday. Gabriela was in the nursery with Claire, sorting through laundry, when a knock sounded on the open door.

She turned to find Luke.

"May I come in?" he asked.

She waved him in. "What a surprise, Luke." She put the lid down on the hamper to continue later. "If you came looking for Damian, he's in California."

Luke picked up Claire from the crib and sat on the glider chair with her. "Yes, I know. I'm leaving today to join him for a couple of days."

"Business can't wait until he returns?" she asked.

"Not this particular issue," Luke replied. He picked up a toy and held it up for Claire.

Before she talked herself out of it, Gabriela found the courage to ask him what she really wanted to know. "When is he coming back? Do you know?"

He looked up at her from playing with Claire. "He didn't tell you?"

Damian hadn't told her he was leaving, let alone when he was returning. Somehow, she managed to keep the resentment from her voice. "Not in so many words. When I talked to him on Sunday, he was on his way to the airport but didn't mention how many days he'd be gone."

"I'm sure he'll tell you next time he calls," Luke said.

Despite his casual tone, his brows furrowed. Did he know something he couldn't say? She wouldn't ask. It wasn't fair put him in the middle of her problems with Damian.

"I'm sure he will," she agreed. She even half-believed it. Damian would have to call her at some point, wouldn't he?

After an awkward pause, she turned to the shelves and straightened the board books, giving her hands something to do.

"I actually came by to see you," Luke said.

Gabriela turned around, unable to hide the curiosity.

He stood and shifted Claire to his left arm. Then he reached into his inside coat pocket with his right hand and withdrew an envelope. "This is for you."

She took it from him, undid the flap and took out the first piece of paper. As she read the words at the top of the page, her heart jumped. City of New York, certification of birth.

Claire Adelina Romano Vaughn. Father, Damian Walter Vaughn; mother, Gabriela Adelina da Silva Romano.

Adelina after Gabriela's mother.

"Is this for real?"

Luke chuckled. "Yes, it's real. I wouldn't be giving you a fake birth certificate. Her social security card is also in there. Keep them both in a safe place."

It must be the other paper in the envelope. "I will. Has Damian seen this?"

"No. These are the originals and I brought them to you. I'll tell Damian when I see him."

Gabriela's eyes swam with unshed tears making it hard to focus on Claire's full name, on her own name listed as the mother.

She was officially a mother, so declared by the city of New York.

"Are you okay, Gabriela?"

She nodded, eyes still fixed on the page, her fingers covering her trembling mouth, even as the first tear rolled down her cheek.

"You're crying."

"These are happy tears. You have no idea how much this means to me," she said, wiping a tear with her fingertips. "Thank you for bringing it over."

"You're welcome," Luke said. He stepped forward. "I should be going."

"Here, let me get her from you." Gabriela put the birth certificate back in the envelope and tucked the envelope under her arm, then took Claire from Luke.

"Is there anything you need, anything I can do for you before I leave?"

His concern was genuine, she knew that, but Luke couldn't get her what she and Claire needed.

"Thanks for asking, but I'm fine. We are fine, aren't we, Claire?" Claire smiled, making Gabriela believe her own words even more.

Luke watched them with a calm expression, but she couldn't help wonder what went through his mind.

They went down together in the elevator and she walked him to the front door.

"Have a good trip, Luke," she said as he stepped out.

He paused before descending the front steps. "Any messages for Damian?"

They both knew she and Damian could text and call at any time for him to find out how Gabriela and Claire were doing. Simple as it was, that was all it took.

In truth, she couldn't force him to pick up the phone and call, any more than she could force him to love her.

"Tell him not to worry about us."

LOS ANGELES, CALIFORNIA

Damian entered his office and removed his suit coat, then loosened his tie. After sitting through another two-hour meeting for an issue that could have been easily resolved in thirty minutes, he was fed up with the politics of the movie business. What would it take to ditch the rest of the meetings on his schedule for today?

He stretched and rubbed his neck, already knowing the answer to his own question. As much as he disliked his trips to L.A., he was there because his presence was required.

Well, there was another reason.

In reality, he didn't know what he was doing. He'd left New York at the first chance, even when this trip hadn't been on the schedule for some weeks.

What he'd said to Gabriela on Sunday, that he'd forgotten to tell her about it, had been a lie, and she knew it. With the party mom had organized, his schedule had been clear.

But he'd lied about it, and quite easily as well. And after his early phone call to Gabriela this morning, she was probably wondering what was going on with him.

If only she knew what a mess he was.

Once more, Damian reached into his pocket and retrieved the letter Luke had given him when he'd arrived at the party at Highland Park on Saturday evening. At the time, Luke had said it was half the puzzle. Damian had put it in his pocket and completely forgotten about it until the next morning when his phone alarm rang. He'd scrambled out of bed to turn it off and had found it in the tuxedo's coat pocket, along with the envelope.

Only then had Damian opened the long, white envelope to find a smaller one inside addressed to him.

A letter from Elsie Barr.

Even now, his heart sped up at the sight of his name. He took the letter out, already knowing what it said, having read it so many times, and scanned the contents. As before, his eyes stopped at the one paragraph where Elsie explained the issue of Claire's paternity.

Once again, he read that part, over and over, as if reading it could make him understand it any better.

But the shock hadn't abated. Not yet, and maybe not for a long time.

It still didn't excuse his behavior, leaving Gabriela with a hasty note and no explanations.

What could he say, especially after the night they had spent together? How was he to face her when he was struggling?

Maybe he'd made things more complicated by giving in to his passion for her.

Their marriage contract loomed in the back of his mind, the agreement they'd made for a marriage in name only, and their signatures on the paper. This was another issue he'd been trying to understand.

If he were honest with himself, his attraction for Gabriela had been building for a while, like a fuse waiting for the spark to set it—the touches between them, the kisses in front of others, the give and pull they'd ignored so many times.

But on Saturday night, they had both been will-ing—very willing—participants, and it had been more than physical. So much more.

He'd lain awake for some time, even after Gabriela had fallen asleep curled up next to him, thinking, analyzing his feelings, trying to make sense of what this meant for their relationship. Then the alarm had rung, he'd found the letter, and everything had changed. Instead of going back to bed and waiting for her to wake up in his arms, Damian had left before sunup, before he had a chance to talk to her.

How everything could change so quickly.

He shook his head and took a deep breath. He had to apologize to Gabriela, and not only for leaving. But what would he say? *I'm sorry I slept with you?*

He wasn't sorry; not at all. *I'm sorry I'm not sorry I slept with you?*

I'm sorry I left without talking?

That would probably be a good start.

One thing was sure—Nanna had been right about the unresolved sexual tension between them. After one night together with Gabriela, the tension remained. One night was not enough, and the desire and passion clamored for more.

A knock sounded at the door and Damian straightened in his chair. "Come in."

The studio's secretary opened the door. "Mr. Blackbourne is here to see you, sir."

Luke entered with a briefcase in his hand. "I found you."

"I didn't know I was hiding from you," Damian said.

Luke took a seat on the sofa and Damian joined him on the upholstered chair opposite. "Not me, but someone else."

His best friend was taking his wife's side. "She told you?"

"She told me nothing. I inferred from what she didn't say. And then I talked to your mom who confirmed you left on Sunday without talking to Gabriela."

"I left her a note," Damian said.

"But you didn't tell her why you left," Luke countered. "I assume this has to do with the letter from Elsie Barr?"

"It does." There was more to it, but Damian wasn't willing to spill all the private details of what had happened between him and Gabriela. "You didn't tell me how you got hold of it."

"The investigator found out that Elsie left her neighbor a letter and a box for you. I went to see the old lady and was able to persuade her to give me the letter, with the promise I'd hand it over to you. She still has the box and you'll have to pick it up in person."

"What's in it?" Damian asked.

"I don't know but my guess is Elsie left something for Claire. Did she say who Claire's father is?"

He nodded. "She did."

"That bad?"

"I'll let you read it as my lawyer." Not that Luke would divulge information, but Damian needed the protection under the law, if it came to that.

Damian reached for the letter and handed it to Luke. "Read the fourth paragraph."

Luke took a moment to read it. "Well, that answers a lot of questions." He returned the sheet to Damian. "What are you going to do?"

"I'm not sure yet, but this information can't get out."

"I agree."

"I'm glad I held off on the paternity test," Damian said. "The less people involved in this, the better."

"Did you tell Gabriela you have a letter from Elsie Barr?"

Damian shook his head. "I needed some time alone to think about all this."

"And you had to fly all the way across the country for that?"

"I have meetings," Damian replied in a tone that lacked conviction.

"Nothing pressing. By the way, I went by the house this morning to deliver Claire's birth certificate. It moved her to tears."

"Gabriela?"

"Yes, she cried when I gave her the certificate," Luke said. "You know I never know what to do with crying women."

"Is she okay?"

"I asked her that and she said she was. I also asked her if she had any messages for you and her reply was, tell him not to worry about us. Her exact words."

Was there something he should worry about? "What does she mean?"

Luke raised an eyebrow. "I thought you'd know. Are you going to tell me what's going on?"

"It's complicated." To say the least.

"It always is." Luke rose and picked up his briefcase. "When are you getting back?"

"I'm not sure." Damian rubbed his temple. "I need to get this business with Sabine Chamberlain done first."

"Sabine Chamberlain is a brat and you can have someone else sit in for the negotiations."

"Maybe she's a brat but her movies sell and that's what we need. If she wants to talk to me, then I'll do it."

Luke walked to the door and Damian followed. "Fair enough. I won't tell you how to do your work." He paused before leaving. "Remember you have a wife and baby at home."

"You're the one person who knows they're not mine."

"If that's how you want it to be." Luke walked away, smiling at the secretary as he passed by.

After a moment, Damian closed the office door and lay down on the long sofa, with an arm over his eyes.

Darn Luke. He always knew what to say to get to him.

Sure, Damian had a wife and baby at home—a baby who wasn't his and a wife under contract.

A wife whose kisses he couldn't forget, whose caresses and embraces he didn't want to put out of his mind. Her scent, her shape, her smile. The way she'd looked at him during their night together.

Those memories were imprinted in his mind, in his heart.

Enough.

This self-inflicted torture led him nowhere. Work didn't get done with him laying down and reminiscing over his regrets.

Damian stood and walked to his desk to check his schedule and his to-do list. Luke's visit had thrown him off center, even though talking it over with him had helped.

When he picked up his phone to sync the calendar application, his attention fell on the picture he'd chose for the screen's wallpaper, him with Gabriela and Claire at the US Embassy in Lisbon. On their wedding day. Luke had taken a lot of pictures that day and in this one Gabriela looked to Damian with a hopeful smile.

Just the sight of her on the small screen set his heart racing.

He missed her. More than he had the right to.

The memory of those few, precious hours they'd had together on Saturday night was enough to bring the clarity he needed, at least for a little while.

Before he could talk himself out of it, Damian sent her a text message.

I'm sorry I didn't call before. Been kind of busy.

Excuses, however true they were. He was only as busy as he made himself to be.

When a reply didn't come, he added another message.

How are you and Claire doing?

This time, he got a reply. Hi, Damian. We're both doing fine. Don't worry about us.

Why did that line make him uneasy? The more she told him not to worry, the more he believed he had a reason to, as if the phrase was a premonition of something ominous.

Or maybe that worry was just a manifestation of his guilt, for leaving Gabriela without saying goodbye, without telling her he was falling for her.

What a mess he was.

I should be home soon, he typed.

Good luck with your business dealings, came her reply.

Damian stared at the screen for another moment. She didn't even ask when he was coming home.

He deserved that.

Somehow, he found the concentration he needed to get back to work. At least, he didn't have any more meetings today.

Two hours later, his secretary knocked on the door and handed him a document-sized envelope.

Inside, Damian found a letter from the company's publicist director saying she'd procured a last-minute invitation for him to attend The Popular Movies Awards on Friday at the Chinese Theater.

Damian groaned. He hadn't had plans to attend but now he was in L.A. and out of excuses.

CHAPTER THIRTEEN

On Friday, when Gabriela came down to the eat-in kitchen with Claire, she found Linda having breakfast.

"Good morning," Gabriela said.

"Good morning," Linda replied. She rose and reached for Claire. "I missed you, my little grand-cutie." Claire grinned her adorable toothless grin and Linda's smile grew wider. "You're getting cuter every day." She pressed a kiss to Claire's wispy hair. "She's so precious."

Gabriela could only agree, her own wide smile joining Linda's. "She is, isn't she?"

"Go ahead and have your breakfast," Linda said. "I'll hold her."

While Claire settled contentedly in Linda's lap, Gabriela walked to the kitchen and got a plate of freshly-scrambled eggs from Mrs. Harrison. She took a seat next to Linda, who was talking and cooing at Claire, much to the baby's delight.

"How are you fairing with Damian's first business trip? Linda asked. "It is the first one, isn't it?"

Gabriela nodded. "Yes, it's the first time he's taken a trip since we married. I'm doing all right. We both are."

"I'm glad he waited a few weeks before leaving on business, though I'm surprised he left on Sunday from Highland Park."

"I'm sure it couldn't be avoided," Gabriela said. What else could she say to her mother-in-law? Other than the phone call on Sunday and the brief texting on Tuesday, she hadn't heard from Damian and didn't know why he'd left so abruptly.

But not knowing his reasons didn't stop her from wondering if his departure was directly connected to the night they'd spent together. That was the only matter that had changed between them and she was sure that was it.

An important factor in their relationship—it had changed everything.

The whys kept turning in her head. Why wouldn't he talk to her?

"I give thanks every day that my son didn't turn out like his father," Linda said.

Gabriela stopped with the fork in midair.

Linda continued. "Three days after we got married, Walter left on his first business trip." She added finger air quotes with one hand to the last two words. "I was young and naïve and I believed anything he said." She shook her head, more to herself, it seemed.

"It continued even after Damian was born. He was a month-old baby when Walter went to a movie premiere with the flavor-of-the-month actress. It was all over the tabloids. In fact, if you google his name and the name of the movie, you can still find the pictures online." She sighed. "It was a hard awakening for me."

"I'm sorry," Gabriela said.

"I'm sorry for my young self." Linda went on with her narrative while she played finger games with Claire. "A hard lesson to learn. I didn't deserve Walter's behavior and Damian didn't deserve a father like that."

"Damian is lucky to have a mother like you," Gabriela said.

Linda smiled. "His Vaughn grandparents helped a lot, thank goodness. Walter broke their hearts as well, and they were committed to helping raise Damian. I worried about him for a long time, having that kind of example in his life. But when he was at Yale, he wouldn't go out on dates. At first, we thought he didn't want distractions or didn't have time. And those were reasons too. It wasn't until later that we found out about his self-imposed celibacy. He was determined to be the opposite of Walter."

Gabriela finished her breakfast while she listened to Linda talk about Damian. It was a kind of insight she'd been curious about, and she was content to sit in the very kitchen where he'd been raised, trying to imagine the younger Damian. Despite his family's affluence, he still had problems like any other person.

"When he turned thirty, I despaired he would ever marry. But he did." Linda smiled wide and patted Gabriela's knee. "I admit I was disappointed when I found out you two chose to elope. But, since he brought you and this sweet, adorable baby home, I can forgive him for that. I couldn't be happier to have you both here."

If Linda only knew why Damian and Gabriela had eloped. What would she say to that?

"You've been so kind and welcoming to me," Gabriela said. "Getting used to this new life would have been a lot harder without you around."

Those first few days had been rough, she could now admit to herself, as she'd tried to fit into Damian's high-society life as his wife while mothering a baby with cranky moods, all in a new country with different customs and social expectations.

After living for so long as a single, independent, career woman, spending her days indoors with a baby had been an adjustment. She'd gone from dressing up and working in the office, with plenty of stimulating conversations with other adults, to wearing T-shirts and sweatpants, changing diapers, and playing pat-a-cake with Claire.

It was all for love.

"You're welcome, Gabriela. It truly is my pleasure. Just rest assured you have nothing to worry about Damian's trip to Hollywood. He will never act the same way his father did." She rose and bounced Claire in her arms. "Okay, that's enough serious talk

274

to last all month. Do you have any plans for today?"

Gabriela carried the plates to the sink. "I had planned to spend some time with Claire in the garden out back when the weather cools down a little. Read some books in between feeding and diaper changes. That kind of thing." Just another ordinary day.

"Have you been to the botanical gardens? We should make a day out of it." Linda shifted Claire to her other side and led the way to the elevator. "Let's go pack a diaper bag and call James to come pick us up."

Gabriela followed Linda to the nursery, relieved with the idea of going out and doing something different and out of the routine.

Despite Linda's assurances, a small niggle of worry about Damian stole into Gabriela's heart. His absence only aggravated her concerns. How long would he stay away? They had agreed to live together as a married couple for a year, but what if he had changed his mind and was ready to separate now?

The outing to the botanical gardens turned out to be the perfect distraction to the end of a slow week. Too much time to think wasn't a good thing, especially when Gabriela filled in the gaps with her own theories. Those what-ifs wouldn't leave her alone.

Despite the busy day, Claire slept well, and only woke up once in the middle of the night. Gabriela returned to bed after feeding and changing her, but weird dreams chased her until early morning. She dreamed Damian was a famous actor who'd just won the most prestigious award, and he was surrounded by photographers and cameramen, and young actresses wearing long, red dresses, all clamoring for his attention.

That image was still in her head by the time she woke up, and it left her unsettled for a few minutes. She shook the feeling, rose and did some stretches and breathing exercises on the floor by the balcony, enjoying the alone time before Claire needed her again.

Gabriela's eyes strayed to Damian's side of the bed. Today marked one week since she'd seen him last. Last Saturday at Highland Park had gone so well for them, even with Walter Vaughn's interruption. She and Damian had danced, had kissed, and had spent the night together like husband and wife. Perfect and magical.

Had there been any signs that she'd missed, intoxicated as she'd been with Damian's touch and the passion between them? How could something that had felt so right and real lead to confusion and uncertainty?

Afterward, she sat on one of the upholstered chairs and pulled out her phone to catch up with the news. For a second before swiping at the screen, the old hope to see a message from Damian flared up in her chest. But it quickly fell into a wave of disappointment, like it had every morning since he'd left—no texts, no emails, no messages of any kind.

What if she shared a picture of yesterday's trip to

the botanical gardens with him? That might lend him a reason to reply.

Gabriela scrolled through the photo album on her phone and finally settled on one of her holding Claire, one of the pictures that Linda had taken, with smiles and a colorful wall of flowers in the background. She added the caption *your girls* and then hit send.

He'd been the one to use the expression first and would hopefully remember that, instead of thinking Gabriela too forward in her assumption.

Why did relationships have to be so complicated? Theirs was a special kind of complicated.

A notification popped up from the Facebook group for the Romano family. Vanessa and Jacinta had started it, connecting the family and making it easier to check on everyone. Gabriela hadn't visited the group in some time, what with the emergency surgery and the subsequent trip to Faial.

And then she'd met Damian.

After spending a few minutes in the family group, she returned to the main feed and scrolled, looking for news headlines. A particular one caught her attention.

Like father, like son: Damian Vaughn follows in his father's footsteps.

Gabriela clicked on the link and the full article popped up, with a side-by-side comparison of his father with a woman beside him, and then Damian with a young woman beside him. They were both dressed in formal clothes

Under the photos, the article continued, *Damian Vaughn, looking cozy with Sabine Chamberlain, just like his father did thirty-five years ago.*

Her vision blurred and an oppressive feeling burst from her heart, in searing hot circles of anguish and grief. For a moment, she couldn't breathe. Her hand flew to her chest, and she sat there staring at the screen, at the black letters on a white background, at the full color photographs, uncannily similar in pose and content.

Side by side, Damian looked too much like his father at the same age. The irony wasn't lost on her. For a man who'd been trying so hard to break away from being compared to his father, this was the ultimate comparison.

After the initial shock, a feeling of stupor took over, a numbness too large to deal with at the moment.

In the nursery, Claire whined, letting it be known she was now awake.

Gabriela turned off the phone and stood. What she needed was something to do. Lots and lots of work to keep her distracted.

And maybe a change of scenery.

Damian gripped his phone inside his pocket, as if it could change anything.

This was a different kind of torture, subjecting

278

himself to reading and watching a news article that should never have been published.

Like father, like son: Damian Vaughn follows in his father's footsteps.

That caption and the accompanying pictures haunted him.

At The Popular Movies Awards pre-show dinner, he'd found himself seated next to Sabine Chamberlain. She'd been the one to initiate a conversation about a possible contract with Vaughn Family Movies, and had asked a lot of questions. Despite the setting not being ideal, Damian had been eager to answer her questions.

He'd known there were photographers on the floor, but didn't remember when one of them had stopped by at their table, at the exact moment when he and Sabine appeared to be having an intimate conversation.

It was true they had been talking, but it wasn't private, let alone suggestive as in the picture.

Once again, a photographer had done a thorough job of messing up his life in a public, humiliating way. The press and the public always remembered his failures better than his successes.

He'd seen that picture of his father with an actress before. In fact, there were more pictures like that one —different venues, different times, different women. But this particular one of Walter Vaughn at an awards dinner in Cannes was the almost-perfect match to the picture of Damian and Sabine.

If only Damian hadn't been so engrossed in talking business with Sabine Chamberlain.

Luke was the one who'd told him about the article, how it was trending on the social media websites, how Sabine was giving interviews about it, capitalizing on five minutes of fame.

What a nightmare of a situation.

How could he even begin to explain this mess to Gabriela? There was too much at stake and he couldn't figure out where to start, especially after he'd left without talking to her.

Damian stayed until Monday to see the new movie contract signed with Sabine. In typical Sabine fashion, she was late and then dragged the meeting for as long as she could. He stayed until all the legalities were done and the contract filed, and then caught a red-eye flight from Los Angeles to New York, arriving just after six in the morning.

He'd texted James to come get him and, by the time they rolled into Manhattan, the fatigue caught up to Damian. The last three days had taken a physical toll. An emotional one as well, if he were honest with himself. Ignoring his problems only worked for so long until everything came crashing down on him.

He climbed the stairs quietly, not knowing if Mom and Gabriela were already up but, as he arrived on the landing, he found Mom exiting her room.

"Damian," she said.

"Hi, mom." He greeted her with a hug.

"I didn't know you were returning home today."

He nodded. "We signed the contract yesterday and I caught a red-eye flight."

"You must be exhausted."

"I'll be okay. Is Gabriela in the bedroom or in the nursery with Claire?"

"She's with Claire but not in the nursery."

"Downstairs in the kitchen?"

"No, Damian. She left yesterday."

Damian frowned. "Left where?"

Mom shrugged. "I don't know where she went. I only helped her get to the airport."

"To the airport? Why didn't you stop her from leaving?"

"Why would I stop her? She's an adult, free to make her own choices. It's not my place to stop her or tell her to stay."

Damian rubbed the side of his chin, trying to make sense of what was going on. "Did she say why she left?"

Mom fixed him with a stare. "She saw the headlines like everyone else in this country."

"And she drew her own conclusions," he said.

"You didn't call and you didn't text, Damian. What was she supposed to think?"

That blasted online magazine.

How was he going to explain everything to Gabriela with her gone?

Just when he thought it couldn't get any worse, it did. It was a bigger mess than before.

He walked into his bedroom and wheeled his suitcase to the walk-in closet. Gabriela's side was nearly empty. She'd left behind some formal clothes, including the red evening gown.

In the nursery, Claire's favorites toys were gone as well as her clothes. Damian opened the flap of a cardboard box marked donation and inside found baby outfits that no longer fit Claire.

Just like that, the two of them were gone from his life.

This was what he'd wanted, right? He hadn't planned on a wife and daughter. He'd been doing fine before they came along. He'd do fine by himself again.

A lie if he'd ever told one. But how was he supposed to fix this mess? How was he to convince Gabriela that he loved her and wanted her to stay? That nothing had happened in L.A., that he wanted to take their marriage contract and shred it. That he had no intention of giving her up after a year, or any time at all.

But why should she believe him? And if it was possible, why even try? It would only mean more hurt. For him. Gabriela, even Claire.

What was he going to do about the memories? All the moments he'd spent with Gabriela and Claire as a family—the meals they'd shared, evenings together, the car drives and outings. Their weekend at Highland Park. When he and Gabriela read in bed before sleeping, even when they'd gotten up in the middle of the night to tend to Claire.

He missed them.

He missed Gabriela with a fierceness that squeezed his heart and didn't let go.

The next few days passed with the inevitability of everyday life. He went to the office, had meetings, worked long hours, went home and slept, and repeated it all the next day.

True sleep eluded him. He lay in bed, sometimes he got up and walked, fiercely missing Gabriela on the other side of the mattress. He even missed Claire waking up in the middle of the night. The empty crib and the lack of baby sounds in the house weighed on him, and their absence spoke with a loudness and intensity that he tried to ignore.

But try as he did, he couldn't pretend they'd never been there, he couldn't forget them.

Luke came by the office on Friday before lunch. "You look like crap."

Damian glared at him. "Thanks. Great to see you too," he replied in a monotone voice.

"Grab your jacket. We're going out to lunch."

For a brief second, Damian contemplated resisting Luke. But that would take too much effort. Damian stood from the chair at his desk, put on his suit jacket, made sure he had his phone and his wallet, and followed Luke to wherever he planned to go.

A half hour later, they sat on a bench in the roof patio of another office building at the studio lot, eating burgers with fries and onion rings.

"I thought you were cutting back on junk food," Damian said in between bites.

"Call it a cheat day," Luke replied. "Comfort food is comfortable for a reason."

Damian nodded. Instead of drowning his sorrows in alcohol, he smothered his burger in cheese. It tasted better anyway.

"Your mom says you've taken to roaming the halls at night," Luke said when they were done eating.

Damian let out a long breath. His sleep schedule was conditioned to waking up at two in the morning to feed Claire. "I didn't mean to wake her. I'll be more careful."

"That's not what she meant, and you know it. Why can't you sleep?"

"I keep going through all the scenarios. Things I did; things I didn't do."

"That's regret talking," Luke said. "You can't change what's in the past."

"That's the problem, isn't it?"

"It's only a problem if you can't move forward. Learn from your mistakes and make different choices."

Damian turned to Luke. "You're full of wise counsel today."

"It's on the house. I've already clocked out for the day."

Little by little, Damian relaxed. The food, the company, the setting—simple things that contributed to changing his mood, if not lifting it.

"This was a good idea," he said.

Luke nodded. "We should do it more often."

When they arrived back at the office, Luke stopped Damian before he left.

"Have you been to New Jersey?" Luke asked.

"Not yet."

"You need to go see Elsie Barr's neighbor. I have a feeling it will bring about changes. As for Gabriela, that's in your hands, man."

Luke was right. Again.

On Saturday morning, Damian rose early and went for a run along the lower Manhattan loop just as the sun broke out over the horizon. He hadn't run outdoors in a while, and wasn't in the best of shape, but he soon found a balanced rhythm and kept a steady pace. Running helped him clear his mind and he could use all the clarity that came his way.

Later, after a shower and breakfast, he took the Lincoln Tunnel to New Jersey. When he arrived at the address Luke had given him, he locked the car and stood on the opposite side of the street. Was nine in the morning too early to knock on an old lady's door on a Saturday?

After a few minutes, the curtains moved at one of the windows and Damian crossed the street. He didn't want anyone thinking he was stalking.

The building had four stories and no elevator. Mrs. Maryann Holden lived on the second floor.

When he knocked, a voice sounded from the other side. "Who is it?"

"Damian Vaughn. I'm here to collect the box Elsie Barr left for me."

The door opened a crack, held back by an old chain. "Let me see your driver's license."

Damian retrieved his wallet and pulled out his license, then held it up in front of the chink.

"Closer. I can't see it that far."

He complied and two small fingers reached out and took his license.

Damian stared after it. Would that move turn into a problem for him?

After a moment, the door closed, the chain rattled, and the door opened again.

A short woman with gray hair waved him in. "You sure took long enough to come by, Damian Vaughn." She locked the door once he was in.

"I didn't know I was supposed to until recently."

"Yes, that lawyer man." She walked over to an old roll-top desk and brought out a small envelope.

Mrs. Holden walked back and returned Damian's driver license. "Take a seat."

As soon as he did, she gave him the envelope.

Damian tore it up to find a small key and nothing else. "That's it?" He asked. Why would Elsie leave a key for him and no instructions as to what it opened?

Mrs. Holden opened a drawer in the large bureau to retrieve something, then walked over with something in her hands, which she promptly placed on Damian's lap.

It was an old-fashioned cash box, a black metal one with chipped corners. The lock turned easily when he inserted the key.

"Elsie told me repeatedly I could give this box to you only. Confirming your ID was just a precaution."

Inside, another envelope, resting on a bed of other small objects. This would take some time and this was not the place to do it.

He closed the lid and stood. "Thank you, Mrs. Holden. I won't take any more of your time."

She followed behind him to the door. "What about Elsie's baby? Do you know what happened to her?"

Should he tell her? Damian wrestled with the decision for a moment before replying. "The baby's doing fine. She's healthy and happy and has an amazing mom who loves her."

Mrs. Holden smiled. "What a relief. I'm so glad. I know Elsie's glad too."

Those words stuck with Damian as he drove back to Manhattan. Instead of going home, he went to the office, where he could find the privacy he needed with no one around on a Saturday morning.

After reading the letter, Damian sat there looking at the contents of the box, full of small items and photos Elsie had left for Claire. Elsie had trusted him with the most precious thing in her life, and how did he measure up to that confidence?

He thought back to all the times he'd spent with Gabriela and Claire. Why had he thought he was like his father? Sure, he'd made mistakes but he hadn't tried to hide them. He was ready to move on and ask for forgiveness.

Luke had been right. Elsie Barr's letter touched Damian in ways he couldn't have imagined.

He was ready for change. And it was past time he got his family back.

CHAPTER FOURTEEN

Gabriela walked the pathway through the gardens at Hydrangea Manor, her custom for the past week. Today a gentle rain fell, but she paid it no heed, the fresh scent of rain lost on her as was the stunning landscape. The beauty of her surroundings had not soothed, as she'd hoped and as it had on her last visit. Recovering from surgery, even as extensive as hers had been, was proving far simpler than recovering from a broken heart.

She checked the stroller's canopy and rain guard. Claire was dry and showing signs of discontent. Time to return home.

When she'd left Manhattan, Faial had been the only possible destination. Her apartment in Lisbon had been sold right after she married Damian, and she wasn't ready to go to her parents in Porto. They

289

would inevitably ask too many questions, the kind Gabriela wouldn't want to answer. Maybe, in time, she'd go for a visit and introduce Claire to her grandparents and the rest of the family.

So she'd come to Damian's house and the manager at the manor had opened the doors and given her a key for the simple reason that she was Mrs. Vaughn.

For the time being, Gabriela didn't have any plans. It was just she and Claire, day to day. Some of it hadn't been easy, and still wasn't. Claire continued to hate traveling and flying, and was finally settling down to the new location and time zone. It didn't help that she'd started teething. After spending most of the day in a cranky mood, she'd finally calmed with the walk in the stroller.

Gabriela changed her, fed her, and then sat on the rocking chair with a book. After reading, she held Claire until she fell asleep and then moved her to the crib.

When she returned to the living room, the gentle rain had developed into a storm. Other than the sound of it, everything was quiet. She missed Linda and their conversations. It had been nice to have another woman to talk to.

She especially missed Damian—she missed seeing him when he peeked in on her and Claire before going to work, and his greeting when he returned home at the end of the day. She missed the way they sat in bed at night, each reading from their own current list, before going to sleep. She missed his smile, the way he talked to Claire, his presence.

Was love supposed to hurt like this? And why did it feel like a weight on her chest?

Gabriela pushed the questions away. She grabbed the book she'd been reading and sat in the large upholstered chair, her feet on the ottoman. A cup of lemon balm tea sat on the side table, cooling to the right temperature.

Outside, rain fell with purposeful intent, in unrelenting, continuous sheets. Gabriela eyed the gas fireplace. How early was too early to turn it on ahead of the upcoming fall?

At first, the sound barely registered. Gabriela paused for a second, but then continued reading and sipping her tea, dismissing it as coming from the rain outside. Then the door opened, steps shuffled in, and the rain sounded louder until the door closed.

Gabriela frowned and stood. It could only be Damian. He was the only who'd use a key to enter instead of knocking.

Her heart pounded in her chest, and she let out a long, shuddering breath.

She walked to the front door, anticipation and anxiety warring within her.

Damian stood on the entry rug, wet and dripping on the floor. His eyes locked on her, and neither one said anything.

She'd seen him last at Highland Park. She wanted to be mad, but it was so good to see him, even bedraggled and tired as he looked. A wave of relief washed over her that he'd come. She'd feared he wouldn't, not for a while or even at all.

Maybe he was here to tell her he wanted a divorce, but until he said so, she'd wait for him to explain what had happened in Los Angeles.

Gabriela crossed her arms over her chest, lest she stepped forward and threw them around his neck. How much she'd missed him.

"Is Claire asleep?" He kept his voice low.

She gestured to her right. "In the master bedroom. I moved the crib in there."

Damian inhaled deeply and kept his eyes on her. "I'm sorry I didn't tell you I was coming but I didn't want to give you the chance to leave."

Would she have? She didn't know what her reaction would have been.

He remained in the same spot, watching her with something akin to hope.

When she couldn't find the words to say anything, his shoulders sagged and he passed a hand through his hair. "Could you get a towel for the floor?"

"Why don't you go change out of those wet clothes? I'll take care of the floor."

It would give her the time she needed to get used to the idea of his presence, for the hard talk that lay ahead between them, whichever direction it took.

Damian nodded. "Thank you, Gabriela." He left down the hallway toward the guest bedroom, a suitcase in tow.

She retrieved the mop from the cleaning closet and dried up the water trail. Not knowing what to do next, she returned to the living room and sat on the same chair, book on her lap, as if she could do any sort of reading.

What if he wanted something warm to drink? She rose and filled the coffee pot with water, then turned it on. This late in the day, he wouldn't want a cup of coffee, but a decaffeinated one would be nice. Maybe he wanted something to eat too.

As she looked in the fridge, Damian came in, looking much better than before, and already changed into his favorite pair of old jeans and his Yale sweatshirt.

"I made you a cup of decaf." She picked it up and set in on the counter.

"Thank you." He walked over and picked it up. "This will hit the spot."

"Would you like something to eat?"

He shook his head. "No, thank you. I'm okay."

"How did you know I was here?"

"I called the manager and made up some excuse."

The moment grew awkward. Gabriela walked around the island then returned to the same chair, curling her legs under her.

Damian took the sofa across from her, took a sip, and then set down the cup on the coffee table.

She rubbed her palms against her pants, then caught herself doing it, and folded them on her lap.

He reached in his back pocket and took out an envelope. "We found Claire's real father."

Her breath caught.

He pushed the envelope in her direction. "This is a letter from Elsie Barr. I'd like you to read it."

What was in that letter that he'd traveled from New York to the Azores to deliver it?

Gabriela reached for it. She removed a single sheet of lined paper, written by hand on both sides.

Dear Damian,

I don't know how well you remember me. We were in the same graduating class and I dated Paul Rogers. You and I ran in the same circles but never had any classes together.

You're probably wondering why I named you the father of my baby, Claire. As I write this letter, with Claire sleeping by me, I know I'll die soon. I'm enjoying my last days on this earth with my baby as much as I can, trusting I have made the right decision for her future.

I always admired how different you were from the other boys. Well, sure, you were a teenage boy and still did typical boy things, but you had a maturity about you, a personal integrity that came naturally and with subtlety. You never flaunted it, and I'm sure most people didn't notice that about you. But I did. Then, years ago, when you took over your family's company and turned it around from ruin, there was an article in a magazine that I came across.

When the time came to choose Claire's father, I remembered that interview and the things you'd said.

Unfortunately, Claire's birth father is not a good man. We met at a company party and I knew from the beginning who he was, and that should have been enough as a warning— he does have a reputation—but I was a fool. He's charming, attractive, and very successful. He's also ruthless, hypocritical, and unscrupulous. In a moment of weakness, I fell for his charms, and that was all it took.

I don't regret Claire. I never will. I don't regret that I chose her life over mine. But knowing that I won't be here to raise her, and knowing how that man is, I couldn't have named him her father. I don't want him to ever find out he has a daughter, and I don't want her to find out who her birth dad is.

His name is Walter Vaughn.

You are so much the opposite of him that I could only name you as Claire's father. I hope you'll honor my wishes and never tell him about her.

*I know you will do what's best for Claire,
whether you keep her or find someone
else to raise her. You have the heart to do
what's right for my baby. Don't ask me how,
but I believe that.*

*I'm leaving a box of mementos and photos
for Claire. Earrings that belonged to my
mother, my father's watch, a picture of my
parents on their wedding day, another of the
three of us when I graduated high school, and
a few precious photos of me a+nd Claire. You
will also find my medical records in a flash
drive, and other official paperwork, and some
other trinkets. I labeled them so she'll know
their meaning.*

*The other letter I wrote for Claire. Just make
sure she'll read it when she's old enough
to understand.*

*It's my wish that Claire's parents will one day
tell her about her first mother who loved her
so, so much, and who wants her to be happy
and healthy and grow into a good woman.*

Thank you, Damian. I trust you.

Elsie Barr

Gabriela put the letter down, covered her face
with her hands, and cried.

So much love, so much sadness in those words.

Damian got up and brought back a wad of paper tissues. She took them and mumbled a thank you in between sobs.

Life wasn't fair, was it? Gabriela was Claire's mother because this woman she'd never met had lost her life through a terrible disease, and the only person she'd trusted was Damian.

What an incredible gift.

After a few moments, her crying subsided. At least, for now. She'd probably be crying every time she read the letter or thought about it.

She placed it flat on the surface of the coffee table, then folded it carefully and put it back inside the envelope. "You need to make a digital copy of this letter and laminate this original so Claire can have it when she grows older."

"That's an excellent suggestion." He didn't move to take the letter back.

"Do you have the box?"

"It's in the car," he said. "I'll bring it in tomorrow so you can see all the items mentioned."

She let out a breath. "It must have come as a shock to find out Claire's birth father is also yours." She'd felt that shock as well.

Damian nodded. "I wasn't prepared for that revelation."

"At least now you know why she put your name on the birth certificate."

"Yes, it did explain a lot."

"What are you going to do?" she asked him.

Damian opened his mouth to reply but she cut him off. "Can we please do joint custody?" She found the courage to ask.

Damian's eyebrows shot up and he leaned forward in his seat. "Joint custody? Why? Where are you going?"

His questions came in rapid succession and his intense reaction surprised her.

"Didn't you come here to ask me for a divorce?" And to take Claire away from her?

A pained expression filled his eyes. "You want a divorce? I guess I deserve that, after my behavior of the past two weeks."

Did that mean he didn't want to divorce her? "I'm confused."

"I am too but maybe this will help. Please hear me out until the end." He stood from the sofa and sat on the coffee table, right in front of her. "I came to apologize, Gabriela, to ask for your forgiveness. I've been a complete idiot, a total fool, in my actions, in my lack of words and explanations, and just about in everything else. I should never have left from Highland Park the way I did."

He wanted to apologize?

"The truth is, I've been falling in love with you little by little, more and more each day."

Gabriela's cheeks flamed at his confession and she brought her hands over her chest.

"It scared me, thinking of the contract we'd signed and how much I grew to love you. How was I going to ask you to reconsider the deadline and separation we'd agreed to when I didn't know how you felt about me? Was there a chance you could love me too?"

She shifted forward. He didn't know.

"But after that night—that one perfect, amazing night—I realized there was a strong possibility you loved me too. And that scared me even more." He sat up straighter. "I'm sorry I left like a coward. Nothing happened in L.A., not with Sabine Chamberlain or anyone else. We sat at the same table and discussed what she wanted in her contract. One of the photographers took a picture of that and spun it into something else with a speculative headline. And again, like an idiot, I didn't call you, I didn't come home immediately. I've made a lot of mistakes in my life, but my biggest was leaving to figure this out on my own. I should have talked to you, showed you the letter after I read it, I should have turned to you for counsel and comfort. By the time I realized how wrong I was, I came home but you and Claire were already gone."

Damian took both her hands and brought them to his lips. "I should have gone straight to you. I promise I will from now on, with anything and everything, because that's what husbands and wives do."

For a moment, she didn't say anything, but stared at Damian, who still held her hands.

"I do love you," she finally managed to say.

Relief filled his eyes and he went down on one knee in front of her. "Gabriela, will you please stay married to me? Will you help me raise Claire, the two of us together? And maybe give her a sibling or two?"

At his words, she dropped her hands from his and covered her face, overcome with a roil of nausea. She swallowed, then got up and moved away from Damian.

Before she lost her courage, she blurted, "I can't have children."

He stood and frowned. "What do you mean?"

She had to tell him everything. "I came to Hydrangea Manor in May to recover from an emergency hysterectomy. I'll never be able to get pregnant."

He stared at her.

"I had a cyst that exploded and caused a hemorrhage. There wasn't much they could do. Physically, I was getting better, but mentally and emotionally I was in a very dark place when I arrived, trying to come to grips with the fact I'd never have my own baby." She could still remember the black cloud hanging over her. "And then you came to me with that crazy proposition to marry you and be Claire's mother, and that gave me hope where none had been there before. I couldn't pass it up."

"Why didn't you say anything?" Damian asked quietly.

"Because I didn't think we'd be married more than a year. Call it insecurity, fear, lack of courage to confess the truth. I had them all. I can't—we can't—I'm sorry I didn't tell you." She turned her back on him and cried, unable to hold the emotion in.

After a moment, Damian's arms came around her and hugged her from behind. She turned and lay her face on his chest, her own arms around his middle.

He didn't say anything. Just held her until her sobs subsided, until the fabric of his T-shirt absorbed her tears, until his embrace lent her the comfort she needed.

"Do you understand now why I can't stay—"

Damian took her face in his hands and kissed her. Oh, she had missed this too.

All thoughts left her mind, her doubts dissolved.

There were only his lips on hers, his skin soft and hot, burning and branding her, with the confidence and claim of a declaration she would never doubt.

When at last he eased away, Damian led them to the sofa, where they sat together with Gabriela tucked closely to his side, his arm firmly around her, and his free hand gripping hers.

Gabriela looked at him and he kissed her again.

"I'm sorry you had to go through that," he said, "but it doesn't change how I love you and it doesn't stop me from wanting to be with you."

"How can it not? I'm not whole—"

He fixed his eyes on her. "It doesn't change what I feel for you. You are whole to me, and beautiful, and I love you so much."

"Where does this leave the status of our marriage?" She had to know without any doubts.

"It's a real marriage, Gabriela. I want to tear up that contract and forget it ever existed."

As Gabriela opened her mouth to reply, a wail sounded from the bedroom.

They chuckled.

"That's our girl, doing what she does best," Damian said in a teasing tone.

"Ask for food and interrupt us," she said with a smile.

He stood and held his hand out to her. "Let's go get her. Together."

Together.

EPILOGUE

Gabriela woke up with Damian's left arm over her hip, the weight of it so familiar to her by now. A lazy smile bloomed on her lips.

Today marked the one-year anniversary of their wedding. To celebrate, they had invited their families and closest friends to an informal party taking place in the early evening, with good food, an anniversary cake, and lots of music and dancing.

Most of their guests would arrive this morning and throughout the day, and spend the night at Hydrangea Manor, which Damian had made available for the occasion.

Gabriela was looking forward to spending some time with her family. She hadn't seen some of her cousins in a while and appreciated the effort they made to attend.

Jacinta and Knox were coming, along with their one-year old boy, Carlos.

Matias and Vanessa had already arrived, and she was resting. At seven months pregnant, she had to take it easy.

Catarina and Afonso had arrived with Carlota and her little sister Mariana.

Luciana and Jack hadn't been able to travel from New York, as she was due any day with a baby boy.

Filipe and Celeste had arrived two days ago with Lucas and six-month old Marcos.

Gabriela's brother Alexandre had promised to come, and her sister Juliana had arrived with her parents the day before.

As glad as she was to see them all, celebrating their first year together as husband and wife was the event that brought Gabriela the most happiness and gratitude—she and Damian together.

Damian turned on his side and cuddled up to her.

"You're awake too?" she asked him.

"Getting there," he replied, his voice deep and hoarse.

Morning had barely started, slow-coming and awash with pink skies. It would be a busy day but, for now, she wanted to linger in bed with Damian.

"I never told you, but I dreamed about this," she said softly, not wanting to break the spell of their early-morning cocoon.

"About what?"

"You spooning me in bed, kissing me behind the ear."

He got closer, lifted her hair from her neck, and kissed her in the exact spot. A trail of goosebumps broke on the surface of her skin. She trembled.

"You dreamed about this, huh?"

"More like daydreamed."

"I hope the reality is better."

"So much better."

She turned to Damian and rested her head on his chest and he adjusted to bring his arms around her.

"I need to go check on Claire. She's too quiet."

Damian's arms tightened around her, holding her in place.

"That's because I asked Juliana to watch her and I moved Claire to her bedroom when she woke up at night."

"How did I not notice that? Any reason in particular or is it so we can spend more time in bed?" She couldn't hide the smile from her voice.

"That too, but I have a surprise. Just for you and me."

"What is it?"

Damian kicked the blankets off and jumped out of bed though Gabriela tried to hold on to his arm.

He leaned over her and kissed her. Just as the kiss turned hotter and deeper, he grabbed her along with him. "Come on. let's go before anyone else is up."

"What do I wear?"

"Anything you want. Just bring a sweater and good walking shoes."

Ten minutes later, Damian took Gabriela's hand and led her out the French glass doors to the patio and back garden.

What had he planned? Her curiosity lent a string of ideas, but he hadn't given her any clues.

They walked to the center of the private garden in the back. Damian took both her hands and stood facing her.

"I remember the first time I saw you at Filipe's wedding. You brought Lucas in and when you looked up, our eyes met. You have the most amazing brown eyes and that blue dress looked stunning on you."

Gabriela smiled. "I remember seeing you too, hoping I'd see you later after the ceremony."

"It wasn't meant to happen at that time."

"We met here instead," she said.

"I bet you were very impressed with a mad baby and a guy who couldn't calm her down."

Gabriela chuckled. "Very much so."

Damian kissed her, skillfully, taking his time until the heat rose between them again.

"Let's go back inside." she suggested.

"Not yet."

They walked around the house and the manor, picking up the hiking trail until they reached the hills. With the sun cresting, the pale light glinting off the surface of the water, a flock of clouds chasing the seagulls—with Damian's arms around her—this was a perfect moment to hold in her heart and memory.

A wave of happiness filled Gabriela's chest and she sighed.

"This is the spot where you told me you'd marry me," Damian said.

"I thought I was doing the craziest thing," she confessed.

"Not any more than I did. Luke has had a lot of off-the-wall ideas, but this one—"

"Was inspired," she finished.

"Hands down, his best idea ever." He brushed a kiss on the side of her forehead, then turned to face her like before, lacing his fingers through hers.

"A year ago today, when you married me, I promised you respect, appreciation, and friendship. Love wasn't part of it at the time, but in the year since then, my love for you has grown." He paused and took a breath. "Gabriela Romano Vaughn, I promise to love you every day, to remember the love we have for each other, and not let other things get in the way of that love."

New vows. He'd brought her to the same place where it all had started. A new dawn, a new beginning for the both of them.

"Damian Vaughn, I promise to love all my life, and to remember this love and hold on to it, especially when we need it most."

Damian reached into his pocket and took out a half-sheet of paper. He unfolded it and showed her the small typing, from top to bottom and side to side. "This is a copy of our contract. I think it's about time we tear it into pieces."

"I couldn't agree more," Gabriela said.

He ripped it in half first, then each piece into smaller and smaller bits that fell into Gabriela's cupped hands. As she caught the last little scrap, the morning breeze blew them like flower petals in the wind, and they flew away down the hill and into the ocean below.

Damian wrapped his arms around her. "I love you. I'm so happy to celebrate today a year of being together in our journey."

"I love you too," she said. "We did everything backwards, and I'd do it all over again to be here with you today."

He chuckled lightly. "I got the baby and then we got married."

"And then we fell in love."

With the glorious colors of the dawn shining around them, Damian took her face into his hands and gently kissed Gabriela, sealing their love with a promise of all that was to come in their future together.

DEAR READER,

Thank you so much for reading Damian and Gabriela's story, Marry Me At Dawn. I hope you've enjoyed reading it as much as I enjoyed writing it. You may learn more about them and their story on Pinterest.

Please consider leaving a review on Amazon and Goodreads. This is the best way to support me as an author.

For news of upcoming books and promotions, join my readers club.

I love to hear from readers! You can email me at lucinda@lucindawhitney.com.

Thank you!

ACKNOWLEDGMENTS

$\mathscr{I}$ can't believe the Romano Family is coming to an end with book 6, Gabriela and Damian's story.

I started writing Matias Romano's story in the late Fall of 2016. That's right, Matias' story was the first one to be written. In the Spring of 2017, a few weeks before publishing Meet Me At Sunrise, the idea came to write a series about cousins who grew up together. Hold Me At Twilight came to be book one, and the Romano Family tree was born.

And here I am, almost two and a half years later, with the last book in the series, having mixed feelings about it—I'm ready to move on to a different series, but I'll miss the Romanos a lot. The good news is, this is not the last time you'll read about the Romano cousins. I like them too much to let go of them, and I think my readers do too.

How can I begin to thank everyone who's helped me with this book? My writing group, Laura and

Lindzee, who are always ready to brainstorm; Michele Paige Holmes, my amazing content editor, who always has the best suggestions to turn my ideas into better stories; Julie Carpenter, who helped copy edit this book and catch all the little things I missed; Lori Parker, for the beautiful paperback interiors in the whole series; April W., who came up with the perfect quote to use as an epigraph for Damian and Gabriela's story.

And thank you, dear reader, for loving the Romano family as much as I do!

THE AUTHOR

$\mathcal{L}$ucinda Whitney was born and raised in Portugal, where she received a Master's degree from the University of Minho in Braga, in Portuguese/English teaching.

She lives in northern Utah with her husband and four children. When she's not reading and writing, she can be found with a pair of knitting needles, or tending her herb garden.

She's the author of *Romano Family* series, of which *Marry Me At Dawn* is the sixth book. She's also a co-author of the Royal Secrets series with Lindzee Armstrong and Laura D. Bastian.

Please visit her website at lucindawhitney.com for more information and news